THEY ARE THE HUNTERS

FAITH GARDNER

MIRROR
HOUSE
·PRESS·

Be the first to learn about Faith Gardner's upcoming releases by joining her newsletter!

For my newsletter subscribers,
who voted for me to write this book.

If you hate it,
you have only yourselves to blame.
cackles in villain

History may not repeat itself,
but it often rhymes.

—Mark Twain, or so they say

AUGUST

THE HUNTERS

At ten past midnight, on a silent cul-de-sac, a picture-perfect house bursts into flames.

Flames melting the thick carpet. Flames leaping across the drapes. Flames creeping up the grand piano legs and crawling over the floral sofa. They hurry up the wallpaper and blacken the popcorn ceiling. They curl up the photos pinned to the refrigerator with fruit-shaped magnets and turn the grinning family's faces to ash. The boy's chess trophies to plastic puddles. The girl's closet full of sparkling leotards and dance shoes to rubble. The man's tennis rackets and true crime paperbacks swallowed by the blaze. The woman's plant-filled office spun into a mountain of cinders, her wall of accomplishments and degrees that took years to earn erased from this world in a matter of seconds.

It's a very particular flavor of devastation to lose a home, to lose everything you have in an hour's time.

Some things are irreplaceable, like baby teeth, childhood drawings, a pageant crown, yearbooks signed with a rainbow of penmanship. But laptops with evidence, a notebook under the bed titled *Notes From a Psychopath*— those are irreplaceable too.

Some might consider themselves lucky to have lost such things.

Police arrive at the scene after the inferno has been extinguished. The firefighters' uniforms are charcoal-streaked, their faces exhausted. One is coughing so hard he's leaning over and puking on the sidewalk. A deputy is currently unrolling the yellow tape around the premises and politely asking the crowd of neighbors to step back. A few are still in slippers and robes. One neighbor, hair in a towel turban, is cradling her Scottish terrier like a baby and crying. The house is skeletal now, windows blown out, roof obliterated, chimney collapsed. The smoke is gone but the stench of it is pollutant. Everyone has a hand over their face to try to hide from it.

The dawn sun is out and the weather already balmy. Despite the morbid circumstances, the birds keep singing. As the firefighters take leave, applauded by the audience of onlookers, police and arson investigators cross the cheerful emerald rectangle of manicured lawn and swarm the house with gas masks and cameras. Within the first hour, the cadaver dog begins barking. It barks and barks and doesn't stop. Curiously, it's not when the dog is inside, sniffing the charred debris in the living room and bedrooms. It's in the backyard, near the fence, a place the flames never touched.

Fifteen minutes and a lot of digging later, the investigators gather around. They crouch to peer in the hole, a hush expanding between them as they understand what they're looking at.

A human head is buried in the rose garden.

JULY

ELIZA

Angela Hunter waters her blooming roses, steeped in deep thought. Look at her there through the criss-cross frame of the back window. What a picture. Specifically, a catalog picture. You know the lady who still comes with the frame when you buy it? The model who's supposed to not look like a model?

Well, that's what Eliza's mom looks like.

Her orange sandals match her maxi dress patterned with citrus slices, which matches her gardening hat, which matches the band on her smartwatch, which matches her lipstick, which matches her fingernails. Her mouth, usually cemented with a joyous smile, is down-turned. Her brow is furrowed.

This is the Angela Hunter who thinks no one's watching. She's wrong.

"I hope I look that good when I'm your mom's age," says Eliza's best friend, Olivia, who stands next to her at the kitchen window and munches an apple. "How is she so perfect?"

"Who knows," Eliza says.

The real mystery is how a woman this perfect gave birth to Eliza, who never feels right in her own skin.

"All of you Hunters are beautiful," Olivia says softly, as if their thoughts are in sync. She gives Eliza's arm a loving squeeze.

Both girls still wear pairs of Eliza's pajamas. Traces of last night's makeover are still smudged under their eyes and around their lips. Eliza plucks a box from the cupboard and shoves honey-nut cereal straight into her mouth. Through the window, her mom still waters the roses.

"I don't even know if we're related sometimes," Eliza says.

"Of course you are," Olivia says. "It's the eyes. So blue. Your brother has them too—heartbreaker eyes."

Eliza takes another handful of cereal. Like she's ever broken any hearts. She catches her own reflection in a silver mirror that hangs above the dining room table. Dyed black hair with an inch of light brown roots, a round face, skin pale as a doll—nothing like her blond, freckled mother. It's not just looks, either. Eliza is stamped with a darkness and disorganization that are all her own.

"I look nothing like my dad," Olivia says, so softly it's almost to herself.

"You really don't," Eliza assures her.

Olivia's dad is a weird slob, and that's putting it

lightly. Eliza has only met him once, when they stopped in to grab something, and he ended up yelling at Olivia for a half hour about not rinsing her dishes properly.

"Wassup, shorties?" a voice says, startling them.

Eliza's dad Carson stands at the sink, filling up his water bottle. His dark, wavy hair is mussed, his Run DMC shirt has sweat stains in the armpits. No glasses—he must be wearing his contacts today. His tennis racket and duffel bag are leaning against a cupboard beside him. He offers a conspiring grin. "Spying on your mom?"

"We're totally creeping," Olivia says, laughing at herself.

"Hey Dad," Eliza says.

Eliza's dad stands next to the girls, gulping his water down. As if the sight of him is a magnet, Eliza's mom turns her head from across the yard for the first time. Her face lights up and she waves.

Her face never lights up like that for Eliza.

"Swear to God, she gets more beautiful every day," Carson says, waving back. "Aging like a fine merlot."

As Carson smiles at Angela through the window, Eliza watches as Olivia's eyes linger on him extra-long, unblinkingly, unflinchingly, as if their happy marriage is a curiosity. Eliza sees the way her friend ogles her parents sometimes—like their love is such a shock or a wonder she's staring at naked people. Maybe it's growing up without a mom and a dad who's off the deep end.

"Hey," Eliza says, pulling Olivia's sleeve. "Want to try that contouring video again? Or we could watch *The Shining*."

"Sure! But the book's way better," Olivia says.

"You always say that."

"I know, right? I should put it on my tombstone. 'The book's way better.'"

When Eliza first met Olivia, she thought she was lying about how much she read. Every book ever mentioned, Olivia piped up saying she'd read it. But as they got closer, Eliza found out it was true. Olivia's backpack is always heavy with library paperbacks and anytime she has a spare moment, she's not on her phone. She has her nose in a book. Despite Olivia's natural beauty, her radiant sunshiney charm, she's a nerd at heart.

"Tell your brother he needs to take out the trash," Carson calls after them as they thump up the stairs.

OLIVIA

"**K**nock knock," sings Eliza, pushing Ezra's door open.

Ezra's room is painted a deep blue, and even though his childhood obsession with marine life long ago passed, there are still outlines from the fish stickers like finned ghosts on his walls. There's a dark mirror of television next to a case filled with chess club trophies that collects dust next to sci-fi and fantasy paperbacks. It's yet to be determined if his curtains have ever been opened or if his window has ever been cracked—there's a musty permanent smell in his room like chips and dirty laundry.

Olivia hasn't spent much time in boys' bedrooms. In cars? Under bleachers? In a library bathroom stall once? For sure. But a boy's bedroom might as well be Mars.

Ezra plunges a book under his pillow. "What the hell's the point of saying 'knock knock' and then walking right in?"

"Oooh, what are you hiding under there?" Olivia asks

with a thrill, waltzing in and bouncing to a seat on the edge of his unmade bed. "Porn? Hope it's kinky."

Eliza wears a look of disgust as she eyes her brother from the doorway. "I don't even want to know. Dad says you have to take out the trash."

"Why don't you take it out?" he shoots back.

"That's kinda sexist, trying to get a woman to do your dirty work for you," Olivia jokes.

"Get. *Out*," Ezra says.

Eliza obeys, the look of disgust still frozen on her face.

Olivia, however, lingers. She studies Ezra's freckled face and his shaggy, dark hair. He's wearing his glasses. Usually he's not. There's something about the boy that makes her want to dig into him, pry and find out what's inside of him. He's prickly and secretive. And he's hot in a special way—like he grew from an awkward, gangly teen to tall, dark, and handsome so fast even he isn't aware of it yet.

"Tell me what's under there, Ez, I swear I won't tell." Olivia circles her fingers around Ezra's wrist, which is still plunged under his pillow. The feel of his skin is electric. She creeps her fingers up to the book he holds. "Your diary? 'Dear diary—'"

He pushes her hand away. "How could my sister have possibly found a friend more annoying than she is?" he asks, getting up.

Ezra's lanky, with slouched posture like he wants to disappear into himself, but when he aims to intimidate, he straightens up and claims all his six feet three inches.

Olivia stands and peers up at him from her five feet two, hands on her hips.

"You write about me in your diary?" she asks, cocking her chin.

She loves teasing him. He must enjoy it too because he shoots it right back at her every time, sharp and quick as a snap. Their dialogue is like something out of an old Raymond Chandler novel. Olivia doesn't know what lives inside of Ezra, but she's determined to someday find out. And she catches the way his gaze passes over her breasts before landing back on her face.

"Hate to break it to you, but you're nowhere near as important as you think you are," he says.

"But I will be someday," she says, pointing a finger at him. "Just you watch, Ezra Hunter."

He pushes her out of his room, closes the door, and locks it with a *snick*. Eliza stands in the hallway with her arms crossed over her chest.

"Are we contouring or not?" she asks Olivia.

"We are," Olivia says. "Though hopefully this time I won't look like a battery victim."

Glancing back at Ezra's room, Olivia gives the shut door a secret smile. Sometimes there's a force that surrounds people. She feels it, pulling her like a magnet.

OLIVIA

Olivia West has no siblings. Since childhood, she's happily entertained an elaborate fantasy that she's an orphan. She likes to imagine herself as an anomaly that somehow spawned from asexual reproduction, like a sea star or a jellyfish. Anything to forget about the hulking, muttering, beer-soaked shadow that is her father.

She lives in a trailer on the edge of Riverwood where the small town's sprawl dissipates into oak-darkened flatlands. She never calls it a trailer aloud, though. Her father takes pains to remind her that it's a "mobile home park" and that it's "just a house without a foundation"—a description haunted with a secondary meaning. Whatever it is, a mobile home, a trailer, or a house without a foundation, the double wide at the back of Paradise Springs never feels like a home. Which is one reason why every time Olivia heads back to it after a sleepover at the Hunters', her stomach sinks like it's filled with sand.

The ride from Eliza's only takes ten minutes, but those ten minutes are full of a mounting dread. It begins as soon as they leave Riverwood's foothills, the older and wealthier houses with generous front yards and old-fashioned street lamps and towering maples lining the lanes. Soon they pass through the sprawl of open land where developers are erecting cookie-cutter houses, skeletons with wood-plank bones. Then there's the downtown strip, the boutiques and brick apartment buildings still adorned with painted advertisements from the last century. After that, a scenic despair creeps in with every mile. The industrial buildings, the houses on the outskirts with sagging chain link fences and rusted vehicles and garbage dumped on the side of the road. As Olivia stares out the window, she has a hard time keeping her fingernails out of her mouth.

"Excited about the Strawberry Festival?" Carson asks, finally breaking the stifling silence.

Olivia's attention snaps to the present and puts her hands back in her lap. "I don't know. When is it?"

"End of the month. July 31." Carson flips on the stereo, a hip-hop song coming on full blast. It's a man rapping about a woman suckin' on dicks and lickin' up nuts and Carson clears his throat loudly with an *Ahem* and shuts it off right away. Olivia bites her lip to not laugh out loud. "We're trying to convince Eliza to enter the Miss Riverwood competition. Think we'll have any luck?"

"What's Miss Riverwood?"

"That's right, you just moved here. You know, just

one of those fun titles. Angela won it back in the old days. Comes with a rhinestone crown and a thousand bucks and a special spot in the summer parade. And *prestige*, of course." He says this last bit with a dorky British accent and glances at Olivia. "Just thought it might be something to help coax Eliza out of her shell."

Olivia's eyes widen. "I didn't know ... Eliza never mentioned it."

Really? Imagining Eliza chasing a crown and a banal title like Miss Riverwood is straight-up bizarre. Seems like something Eliza would never do in a million years.

Then again, Eliza's full of surprises. When Olivia first spotted Eliza at school in her black clothes and dyed black hair, she assumed she listened to bands like Black Sabbath. Turns out she's a closet Swiftie. Olivia thought she was a rebel who wouldn't mind blowing off classes and causing some trouble now and then—but instead, Eliza's a straight-A student and a ballerina. In Eliza's bedroom, Olivia spotted pink paint underneath the fresh black coat on her walls.

"What does Miss Riverwood do?" Olivia asks.

Carson unrolls his window and the hot summer wind blows in. He slows the car as they creep down Oak Creek Drive, minding the potholes. "Normal pageantry stuff. Look pretty, do a speech, and then impress in the talent show."

"What was Dr. Hunter's talent?" Olivia asks, trying to imagine Angela with a sash across her middle, doing a queenly wave. It seems too silly, too beneath a woman who's now grown up with her own psychiatric practice.

"She could solve a Rubik's cube in under thirty seconds," Carson says. "Swear to God, that's when I fell for her. It was the sexiest thing I've ever seen."

Olivia shifts in her seat at the word *sexiest*, giggling.

"You thinking of entering?" he asks. "What would your talent be?"

"I don't know," Olivia says. "I hadn't thought about it. Probably reading? I once won first place in a summer reading program when we lived in Colorado. But that's not exactly a pageant-worthy talent."

"Girl after my own heart." The SUV rolls to a stop in front of the driveway for Paradise Springs, where a drab complex of mailboxes waits like a mausoleum. "You sure you don't want me to drive you on up to your house?"

"No, this is fine," Olivia says, grabbing her backpack. "Thanks for the ride, Carson."

She says his first name, not Mr. Hunter, almost to test the boundary between them. To see if it bothers him. To see what it feels like. She likes that name, Carson, the way it curls in her mouth and rolls off her tongue. She lingers an extra-long moment in the car before opening the door. She's not sure why—maybe to enjoy his calming presence and the easy air of the car that still smells like brand-new leather. Maybe to avoid the inevitable.

"You take care, Olivia." His kind eyes are so light brown they're almost gold. "If you need anything, anything at all, I mean it, you just say the word."

Olivia nods, hopping out of the car, feeling the warmth of his stare as she walks into the park and away from him. He always says that to her when he drops her off and waits until she's out of sight before leaving. By the time she reaches the crooked steps of her front porch, the magic wears off. She's Cinderella after midnight again.

Wait, though. What's that there under the side of the stairs?

Stepping back, Olivia stoops to investigate the dark blob that lurks there. When she recognizes it, it spooks her deliciously: it's yet another black widow spider.

"Hi little lady," Olivia whispers, blowing gently to see it move. Shiny, spindly legged, with a fat round body and the telltale red hourglass on its belly.

Is it a sign? Surely it must be a sign.

She runs inside to fetch another little jar and, with a rush of adrenaline and a quick swoop, she scoops the spider up and twists the lid on tight. As the spider thrashes, turning to hopelessly search for an exit, Olivia puts her lips to the glass and kisses it.

When she gets inside, she puts the jar next to the other two on her dresser next to her music box with a twirling ballerina. Three jars. Three black widows, all found around the outside of her house. *Tap, tap, tap.* Some might think it's a curse, but Olivia considers it a good luck sign. It's exhilarating to have them a foot away from her bed—her poisonous little pets.

Although they moved here in March, and now it's only early July, Olivia never gets used to this place. In fact, the more time she spends away, the more she sees it for what it is. Low ceilings and doorways that her father has to duck to avoid. The shady windows, barely big enough to fit your face up to and made of plastic that even a weakling could punch out in one go. The suicidal moths that fling themselves against the flickering bulbs in the kitchen lights, the fake wood paneling, the moldy smell that hangs in her room no matter how much incense she lights.

Olivia keeps her room clean, her bed made. She tapes quotes from her favorite books on the wall: Sylvia Plath, Toni Morrison, Mary Shelley. She tapes them next to printed-out pictures of Eliza and a couple other come-and-gone friends she left behind in the many cities where she lived. Other than those slips of paper, her walls are blank and even though she adores reading, she owns only a modest stack of books of her own.

Her whole life has to fit right there, in the storage trunk at the foot of her bed. The same trunk she dragged from Pittsburgh to Cleveland to Houston to Denver to Naperville to Kansas City to Riverwood.

The same trunk that once belonged to her mother, who's now serving twenty to fifty years at Louisiana State Penitentiary for attempted homicide.

ANGELA

Angela Hunter sits in her egg chair, rubbing her ruby teardrop necklace between her fingertips and contemplating the ash tree out the window.

These precious ten minutes between sessions are supposed to be about her. "Allow yourself just a sliver of *stillness* for decompression, can you do that, Ange?" is what Patrick, her therapist, asked. But when Angela sits still and lets inertia take over, it's agony. It doesn't feel still at all. She can feel the earth moving under her feet, the sky shifting, the motion of the world. And it's dizzying. Every worry she compartmentalized throughout the day comes marching through her in a horrid parade—Carson's agent dropping him, the foundation work that needs to be done, the search history she glimpsed on Ezra's tablet. These worries have enough velocity that they could crush her.

Angela grew up in a house some people might have

called a mansion with a copper gate that required a
punch code. She got a slick black convertible when she
turned sixteen. She was soprano in choir, champion
mathlete, school vice president, and she even modeled
once for a local department store's back-to-school
campaign. Straight As and a name on the homecoming
ballot.

On paper, her life provoked envy but behind the
façade, there was rot.

She fantasized about killing her parents. She stole her
mom's vodka and spiked her water bottle before heading
to school. Once, she witnessed her dad knock two of her
mom's teeth out and blitz her into a concussion and then
the whole family had to silently pile into the family
minivan to perform to the ER together. Their father
coached Angela and her three younger siblings to collectively agree to tell lies to exonerate him. That night,
Angela came home so numb that she wasn't sure if she
existed anymore. The next day, she won the Miss Riverwood title. Her life was a nightmare pretending to be a
dream.

When Angela went away to college for the first time,
a university a state away, it wasn't just the distance
between herself and her dysfunctional family that put
her identity into focus, nor was it the freedom of her
newfound adulthood. It was the sudden access to an
explanation for what she long survived and tolerated that
never made any sense. Why would her mother stay with
her father? Why would her father act the way he did?

Why would the family go along with it? Why was she always the favorite and yet she felt pained sick about it? Why was she so empty inside, despite all the opportunity afforded her?

After her first month of Psychology 101, she was stunned to discover that her family was, quite literally, a textbook case.

There wasn't even anything that unique about it. It was as simple as knowing her hair was honey blond and she loved dark chocolate—her father suffered from narcissistic personality disorder, her mother was codependent, her older brother was the scapegoat. This new knowledge changed everything. It became the glasses she saw the world through, the way to make sense of chaos. The sick feeling in her stomach when she sees pictures of her mother and the heart palpitations she gets when she sees movies where people punch one another is PTSD. The man yelling on the street corner about Satan simply has untreated psychosis.

The world suddenly feels manageable when you put it into boxes like that. What's wrong with being put in a box? Why does everyone say it like it's a bad thing? Boxes keep things organized, keep things contained. Angela's a woman who loves boxes. She loves colored tabs, well-kept file cabinets, and matching outfits. She loves her label maker. And she loves a diagnosis.

She breaks her gaze with the tree branch and gets up, opens her computer and reviews notes prepped for her next session. When her pulse doesn't slow down, she reaches inside her desk and pulls out an orange canister. She looks inside, a bit surprised at how few are left, and fishes a pill out with her finger. By the time Jaycee Sandoval pops on the screen, Angela spreads a pageant queen smile on her face like butter on bread.

"Jaycee!" she says. "So good to see you."

"Hey Ms. Hunter," Jaycee says.

Ms. Hunter. Like she's a high school teacher. Angela keeps smiling and pulls out a pen and her notebook, where she still takes notes the old-fashioned way. The date, Jaycee's full name, and her basic info: dual diagnosis of bipolar disorder, borderline personality disorder; 250 mg Depakote and 50 mg of Zoloft twice daily and Ambien as needed for sleep.

"How are you, Jaycee?" she asks, putting her pen down and trying not to think too hard about how long it will take the pill to kick in and calm her racing mind. "How was summer camp?"

Jaycee has the bad habit of getting so close to her camera that nothing is visible except her forehead—or maybe it's purposeful, a statement? Teenagers are always testing limits with her on these virtual calls by keeping their cameras off, their music on, putting themselves on mute and not answering.

"Well, I got kicked out," Jaycee answers after a long pause.

"Oh no," Angela says in surprise. "What happened?"

"I was messing around with one of the senior counselors. They made such a big thing out of it."

"Jaycee," Angela says, in a warning tone that she restrains enough to hopefully sound welcoming, playful. "Define 'messing around.'"

"You really want to hear about me sucking dicks, man?" Jaycee says, her pitch rising.

"Um—okay. We don't need graphic details, I was just ..."

Angela hears a hissing sound coming through her heating vent suddenly. Alarmed, she turns and glares at it. It's old-fashioned with a rose-patterned grill. These are the minor accents that made her fall in love with the house when they bought it fifteen years ago and they are now threatening to unravel her. First the roof, now the foundation, and what next? Their heating system?

Her face stings as she stares at the vent and she asks herself, with the steely detachment of her inner voice, are you really going to cry right now, Angela? On a call with a student who is likely telling you she had relations with someone in a manic episode and/or BPD episode? Who it may not have been entirely consensual with, knowing this poor girl's age? Jaycee Sandoval isn't even sixteen and already dealt with date rape, foster care, and a drug overdose. And here you are about to burst into water-works because your furnace might need work?

No one is meaner to Angela Hunter than Angela Hunter. But hey, it works. Angela swivels back, sits up straighter, and snaps to attention. She swears she could feel the first kiss of her GABA transmitter rising as the pill performs its magic.

"Okay, let's take a step back," she says, facing the

computer screen and checking her expression in the dollar-sized window at the top. Yes, it's the correct amount of concern on her face. "And take a deep breath in and out." She demonstrates, blowing the air through her teeth. "And once we're centered, let's shift the conversation to how your medication's working."

Ezra

Summers in Riverwood are glimmering and endless, lazy and sticky, where the aroma of barbecues lasts for months and evenings swell with the symphony of frogs and crickets. Every year, the Riverwood Art Association hosts a chalk-drawing festival in the downtown plaza. The cement is divided into dozens of colorful paintings that fade throughout the season and then get washed away by the first spell of autumn rain.

Riverwood's downtown street Dickinson Avenue, known by most snickering teenagers as simply "The Dick," is lined with pastel-painted storefronts. A road separates the shops from the plaza and a stretch of lawn separates the plaza from the river. There's a wrought iron fence that lines the river's edge with a silver plaque that reads:

> Water is taught by thirst;
> Land, by the oceans past

Ezra has no idea what the hell that means. Poetry seems as pointless as the careful chalk paintings on cement, a heartfelt waste of time born to be forgotten.

He's spent a lot of time here at the river's edge. It's mesmerizing. Thanks to algae that blooms in cheerful weather, the Full Moon River takes on an almost neon shade of green every June. His summer job last year was right around the corner at Nice to Meat You, a butcher shop that declined to rehire him again because they're a bunch of fascists. And this is also where the permanent chess tables live, massive and made of cement with chess boards etched onto the round table tops.

When the weather is cooperative and Ezra has free time, he's often found in the spot where he is today: slouched in thought over the board, contemplating his next move.

He has his eye on the knight right now, which is, in his opinion, the most underrated chessman of the set. It devastates a game when it dominates the center of the board. Most players argue with him in favor of bishops, but Ezra considers it the literal dark horse of the game. And right now, with Izzy's king forced to the side of the board, Ezra's knight makes a swift checkmate.

"Come on, Ez," Izzy says. "You kidding me?"

Ezra fist pumps. He loves pissing Izzy off. He beats her again and again and she keeps coming back. Izzy works at her mom's new age shop up the street. She has a permanently hoarse voice, dark intense eyebrows, a buzzed head, and dresses exclusively in overalls and combat boots. She's been Ezra's best friend since the

Espinozas moved here freshman year and they have three passions in common that glue them together: riding bikes, board games, and misanthropy.

Everyone at school thinks there's some kind of romance sewing them together. Even his family seems to think so. The truth is, in the past few months, Ezra *has* started having secret feelings for Izzy ... but they aren't romantic. Sometimes he stares at her head and wants to know what her skull looks like under there.

"I've gotta go," Izzy says, getting up and grabbing her skateboard. "Call you when my shift is done. What are you gonna do today anyway, you lazy ass?"

"I don't know. Go to the library."

"The *li*brary? Bitch, come to the shop."

"The shop" mainly stocks metaphysical books, candles, and crystals. It doesn't have what Ezra's looking for. Plus every time he goes in there he stinks like nag champa until his next shower.

"Maybe," he says vaguely.

Izzy gives him a long look. "You okay?" she finally asks.

"Is anyone?" he asks.

She rolls her eyes, hops on her board, and rides across the chalk-painted plaza. His heart beats wildly as he watches her. He doesn't know how he feels about her anymore. He doesn't know anything.

It's dizzying.

Ezra knows society wants him to get a job again. He's seventeen, almost an official adult. Society wants all sorts of things from him that Ezra feels stingy about giving: his time. His respect. The older he gets, the stupider the rules seem.

He watches the people-river on the sidewalks on Dickinson, hurrying to run errands and buy nonsense to distract from the loom of existential dread.

A little dollhouse world, isn't it? A world full of plastic people and their silly accessories.

How exciting it would be to watch it all burn.

The licks of story-high flames and wails of emergency vehicles, the orchestras of sniffling citizens.

God, what the fuck is wrong with him?

Ezra walks his bike to the library two blocks away. It's a neoclassical stone building with pillars out front and a creepy concrete owl atop the steps. He locks his bike up and exchanges a dead-eyed look with the statue before descending the short flight of stairs to the library's front doors, which open automatically with a *swish*.

Inside, the air conditioning is gloriously chilly. Ezra knows exactly where he's headed. Years ago, it would have been upstairs in the sci-fi/fantasy section of the teen room. But these days he always heads to the adult section, non-fiction. Biographies. Sometimes criminology, psychology. His worst nightmare is turning a corner and seeing his mom there doing some kind of research, but that would never happen because his mom lives almost her entire life on her computer.

Ezra squats so he can survey today's most alluring shelf. There's a book with yellowed pages just called

Serial Killers he's never read before. Well, that's going in today's stack. Ezra turns a corner to another favorite section, delighted to see someone finally returned the book on diagnosing psychopathy. He grabs that, too.

As he passes the paperback section toward the front of the library, he stops to gaze at a shocking red cover with a demented painting of a man on it. *American Psycho*. Seems like a sign, doesn't it? He grabs it and adds it to his stack.

And then, near his battered black sneakers on the linoleum tiles, Ezra notices something. A fat leather wallet. He looks around the visible part of the room he's stepped into—an empty carpeted reading area with an unlit fireplace. Stuffed chairs and Victorian furniture, but no people.

It's as if the universe is testing him, isn't it?

The universe seems to be testing him an awful lot lately.

Ezra picks the wallet up, runs a finger along its smooth brown surface. He can feel his body leaning one way, his so-called conscience pulling him toward the front counter where he should do the right thing, the good thing, and turn the wallet in. But lately he's started wondering if that isn't his conscience. If it isn't this innate thing inside him, but just some learned rules that he's been blindly following all his life. Just an inner urge to people-please. If underneath it all, there's nothing.

Ezra zips the wallet into his backpack and waits for the guilt, but none comes. Inside him, only the hum of silence. He walks to the front counter with his books and smiles at the librarian, noting to himself that his smile too is nothing but a learned twitch. There's no joy in greeting the frazzled librarian who beeps his books and eyes him over the rims of her reading glasses. There's no reason to really, truly smile. So after a moment of politeness, as if trying on a piece of clothing he doesn't like and then returning it to the rack, Ezra stops smiling and takes his books without a thank you and goes outside to where his bike's parked.

"Hey creep," a voice says.

Ezra glances up from his bike lock, spotting a pair of shapely tan legs just a few feet away from him. The next thing he notices are the shoes—clunky, beat-up Mary Janes that he's seen strewn on his front porch. His gaze rises past the flower-printed sundress to Olivia's face, which is screwed into a playful little smirk.

He can't tell who he's more annoyed with: Olivia, or himself for the strange attraction he feels whenever he sees her. Her olive skin and waist-length brown hair which always looks like it needs brushing. And then there's the fact she's over a year younger than him and a full foot shorter and yet somehow he always feels smaller.

"What do you want?" Ezra says, standing up.

Olivia glances at the library books in his hands and raises an eyebrow. "Got a thing for psychos, huh?"

He doesn't answer her, zipping them into his backpack and then yanking his bike from the rack.

"You think those dudes are brutal, you should read

about Elizabeth Bathory," Olivia says. "She killed over six hundred women in Hungary back in the sixteenth century or something."

Olivia's probably pulling facts out of her ass. "Sure she did."

"Don't believe me? Google it. Then there was Giulia Tafora—she poisoned over six hundred men."

"Uh-huh. And how do you know this shit?"

"Because I'm a morbid weirdo, like you."

Ezra wants to call her out on her lies, so he takes his phone out and quickly searches the name "Elizabeth Bathory." To his shock, Olivia's right. He scans the article.

"Bathory bathed in her victims' blood to look younger," he says.

"*Told* you." Olivia frames her face with her hands and bats her eyes at him. "There's a big brain underneath this beautiful face, okay?"

"Let's not get ahead of ourselves here."

"Take me to your house," she says. "Let me ride on the handlebars."

Ezra scoffs at her audacity, ordering him around like he's her court jester. "Hell no."

"Come on. It'll be fun."

"Eliza isn't even home. She's at Tutu Camp all week."

Ezra walks his bike up the sidewalk. He can hear Olivia's shoes clicking on the pavement behind him. "Okay. How about you and me hang out and talk about serial killers then?"

"I'm busy."

"Doing what?" she asks as she catches up with him. "Reading books about psychopaths?"

"Yeah."

"Why are you so into psychopaths? Are you one?"

"Keep bugging me and you'll find out."

She shoots him a smile. "Why are you so mean to me, Ezra?"

He can't tell if she's being serious, whether the hurt in her face is genuine. He's tempted by her, intrigued by her, but he doesn't trust her. She has an air about her like she shares a secret with the universe, her hazel eyes dancing with something akin to mockery.

Ezra isn't good at reading girls, but Olivia is another case entirely. He gets the feeling she's used to getting what she wants, that she knows how to crack into people, skating on her charm and beauty and, apparently, her big brain—and that makes him want to give her nothing at all.

They're stopped now at the corner of Dickinson and First as they wait for the walk signal. In the plaza, there's a juggler and a few people gawk and applaud. But Olivia isn't looking at the juggler; she's looking darkly at the man across the street who speaks into his megaphone.

"Fear not, I am the first and the last, and the living one!" the man shouts to the passing people who ignore him entirely. He holds a cardboard sign that says *Satan is coming*. Ezra studies him. What kind of damage has to be inflicted upon a person to get them to such a sorry state? Doesn't seem like such a chasm that separates him from that man. "I died, and behold I am alive forevermore, and I have the keys of Death and Hades!"

When Ezra turns to Olivia again, she's gone—vanishing on quick feet up the avenue as if she's been spooked.

CARSON

Carson whistles with Snoop Dogg on the stereo as he peels his SUV into the Lavender Meadows Retirement Chalet lot and parks in a space in the visitor's section which is, tellingly and sadly, empty.

He grabs his courier bag. As the car stays on, the chorus of "Gin and Juice" is too much to resist—Carson sings along with gusto until he notices a janitor glaring at him as he sweeps the sidewalk outside. Carson clears his throat, rolls up his window, and pulls his keys from the ignition.

"Hey, how are you?" Carson asks as he steps out of the car. "Gorgeous weather today."

The janitor grunts and kicks up a cloud of dust with his push broom. Carson gives him a wave as he walks toward the front entrance. It's fine. It's not anything he did. That man is probably having a bad day. As a former reporter and now a true crime writer, Carson is ever-aware of the fact that you never know what struggles people carry around with them.

Inside the lobby, it smells like farts and antiseptic, a warm wind blowing through the vents. No AC. Carson notes these things not just because he's a trained journalist and he can't help but fixate on the details, but because he recently put his own Pop into a retirement home and went through a period scoping out these places. Pop is a senile grouch, but Carson would never consider sending him to a place like this. To his right, in what looks like a living room, three women in wheelchairs are in front of a window with its curtains closed, sitting still as corpses. Jesus, this is depressing. At Pop's place they have bingo and music piped through the speakers and everything is painted cheerful colors instead of this watered-down-piss shade of yellow.

"Can I help you?" a woman asks him, in some kind of eastern European accent.

He turns and sees a lady at the counter who has lovely wavy red hair and the bored, doomed look of a government employee on her face.

"Yes!" he says. "My name is Carson Hunter—the writer? I called in earlier. Was it you I spoke to?"

"I have no idea who you are, sir," she says.

"Sure. Yeah, I didn't get the name of the person I spoke to. It was yesterday. She said to just come down and sign in during visiting hours. See, I'm looking for a short interview—"

"You're looking to be visiting someone."

"Yes. Emilia Rodriguez." He whips out his wallet and holds out his driver's license. "I—"

"Sign in on the sheet," she says, uninterested in his license and pointing to a clipboard. Security here. Yikes. If this book falls through—knock on wood, he shouldn't even think such a thing—maybe he could pitch a feature about the sad state of these affordable retirement homes.

"Sure. Sure," he says, putting his wallet away. "Thanks."

"She's down the hall, then to the right," the woman says. "Names are on the doors. Please sanitize your hands before visiting time." She points to an enormous dispenser on the countertop.

"Thanks. Yes, got to be careful about germs around here," he says.

She doesn't answer. Carson is determined to get a smile out of her—just one. After signing the sheet, he looks up at her and says, "Your hair color is absolutely beautiful."

The woman breaks into a shy smile, covers her mouth with her hand. "Thank you."

Compliments: the lowest-hanging fruit of friendliness. There's a flex of one part relief, one part triumph in seeing that he can crack her façade like that. He sanitizes his hands and waves goodbye before whistling up the hallway. Then he thinks the better of it and stops—this place is far too clinical and somber for sauntering and whistling. This place is the bardo. It's a place where neither the living nor the dead reside. Carson has pored over gruesome crime scenes. Read police reports until he thought he'd go blind. Visited morgues a handful of times.

This is worse.

At least the dead aren't lonely.

Passing by the open rooms where various elderly people either sleep or sit on their beds with bewildered looks on their faces, he thinks of all those angel of death killers. That nurse in upstate New York murdered,what —seventeen people? Has anyone written a book on her yet? Life's too short for all the story ideas Carson gets even on a single day.

E. RODRIGUEZ. He stops in front of an open doorway where a frail woman in a kimono sits in an armchair, white hair a delicate cloud framing her face. She positively lights up at the sight of him, as if Carson is her long-lost son.

"Hi there, Ms. Rodriguez, my name is Carson Hunter. I'm a writer. You mind if we chat for a bit?"

She claps her hands. "Come, come!"

"I was hoping to talk to you about your husband, Sheriff Renaldo Rodriguez?"

Not a flicker or a flinch. "Well, okay then!"

Wow. He expected more difficulty getting access to her from staff, definitely some pushback from Emilia Rodriguez herself. Reporters chased her for years and she remained tight-lipped about her husband. But that was twenty years ago. Interest in the case has faded and now most of the coverage of it sits in university basements slowly decaying on microfilm. And this old woman dwindles in a nursing home, finally ready to speak.

Sad, isn't it? At the end of a life, people are so desperate for companionship they'll talk about their greatest shame in exchange for a few intimate minutes of conversation with a stranger.

CARSON

After Carson sets up the recorder on a night table, he scoots a footstool to sit near the old woman.

She isn't merely old, she's desiccated. He imagines how he'll write it in the book one day: *Emilia Rodriguez had hollow cheeks, a mouth caved in from lack of teeth, with eyes clouded by cataracts.* She's unrecognizable from the few pictures he's seen during his preliminary research, white hair now instead of black, skin paled by her exile to indoor life. The room is warm and stifling. A dirty diaper smell hangs in the air. Carson clears his throat, uncaps his pen, and begins the interview.

He eases her in with small talk, admiring the pictures of sunsets with Bible verses on her wall, the knit throw blanket on her bed. She nods and smiles as he rattles off his background as a crime reporter and then his book published on the Freezer Man, not mentioning the fact the book has been discredited and is now out of print. Minor detail. Doesn't matter. He thanks her for the honor of sitting with him to answer his questions and makes sure to slow his speech and enunciate. It's anyone's guess how alert she is and how much she understands.

"I know it's a sensitive topic and one you avoided discussing for years, Ms. Rodriguez. I realize, regardless of whether Sheriff Rodriguez was indeed guilty for the murders he was accused of, it caused you a lot of pain."

"I'm fine." She waves a hand and leans in. "What a handsome man you are, Mason."

Carson is thrown off and lets out a laugh. "Thank you, very kind." He glances down at his yellow legal pad. "I wanted to begin with talking about Mary May Summers."

"Sure!"

"She was your neighbor when you resided on Fourth Street with your husband, correct?"

Emilia nods. "Yes."

"And she'd lived next door to you for how long?"

"Hard to remember now," she says. "I couldn't say."

"And do you remember your husband having any interaction with her during your time living there?"

"Hmmm. I couldn't say. I think … I think yes, she did."

"What kinds of interactions? Can you remember?"

"Well," Emilia says, staring off. "Family barbecues, block parties, church services. That sort of thing."

"Church services?" Carson asks. "I didn't realize you attended the same church."

"Oh yes. Every Sunday."

Carson jots a note. "What was the name of the church?"

Emilia rocks in her chair as she considers. "I don't recall."

"Was it in your neighborhood? I might be able to look it up."

"Yes, yes, it was that one. With the steeple and the lawn out front with a bell. My papa installed that bell. It's still there."

Carson scribbles this down: *look @ churches in neighborhood l8er*. There can't be many—Raven's Landing is a small community. "Ms. Rodriguez, did any of the other girls go to your church? Allison Chambers, Melody Jackson, Paige Ostrowski ... even Penny Patterson?"

She smiles. "Yes, nice girls."

Carson repeats the question to make sure he heard her answer right, and she confirms.

He's shocked.

This is an unexpected lead—there has never been a real link between the five girls whose body parts were sprinkled in dumpsters throughout the county. They all resided either in the town of Raven's Landing or the outskirts, down the Full Moon River from Riverwood. But they attended different schools, different jobs. None had any connection to the sheriff's office.

The church, though—now, this is interesting.

"How involved was your husband in the church you attended?"

"Oh, he loved teaching Sunday school. And the Easter egg hunts every year."

Carson's brow wrinkles as he writes this tidbit down. Emilia's milky eyes lift up to gaze at the miniature window with the lace curtains. She looks blissful. The memories she's experiencing appear to be pleasant. She isn't imagining five young women cut up in a grand sum of fifty-six pieces. She's thinking of them alive again, young and smiling, like the missing posters once plastered all over town.

Carson still remembers seeing them as a teenager, stopping to stare at the black-and-white fliers with a morbid fascination. He remembers the frantic stories that blared from Pop's five o'clock news. This story has been stuck in his mind since then. In some ways, his agent Chaz deciding to part ways and nuking his other book idea is just the kick in the pants Carson needs to focus on the case that jumpstarted his love of true crime: The Raven's Landing Dismemberer.

As Carson continues asking Emilia questions, he pushes with a bit more pressure, asking about the sheriff's behavior at home and whether he ever discussed the missing girls or their cases.

"Yes, he liked to talk about the news over dinner," she says. "Are you married, Mason?"

"I'm ... yes," he says, sitting up straighter. "Why?"

"Of course you are," she says with a smile. "Handsome man like that."

He chooses to not react to that one. "And the sheriff." He taps his paper with his pen. "When he discussed the cases, what did he say?"

"About what?"

"The missing girls," Carson says, perhaps too loudly.

"Oh, sure. He was concerned. He cried, of course."

Carson nearly chokes on that one syllable. "*Cried?*"

"Every night."

Carson's mouth hangs open. The sheriff, who his squad dubbed "The Stone Wolf" because of his cold brutality when it came to interrogations. Who, in every dated profile, is described as an abusive, narcissistic tyrant. Then again, the only people willing to be interviewed about the man were those who worked with him. Perhaps the people in his home life—all of whom refused to be interviewed when the case was actively investigated —were acquainted with an entirely different side of him.

As Carson chases the words frantically with his pen to paper, a thrill travels through him like a delightful little electrocution. It's been a long, long time since Carson stumbled upon anything this promising. A true turn in the suspect's character, a connection to the church ... these are directions no one has pursued before.

When he looks up from his legal pad to ask a follow-up question, Emilia has fallen asleep in her chair, head fallen forward.

"Ms. Rodriguez?" he whispers.

She doesn't move. Carson clears his throat, loudly, but that doesn't work either. God, what if the old woman keeled over right now? Wouldn't that be just his luck? Carson whispers her name once more and then puts a hand under her nose to be sure she's still here in the land of the living. Thankfully, he feels the hot wind of her breath.

"Guess that's it for today, huh?" he says, mostly to himself.

He gathers up his things, zips them in his courier bag, and gets up for a nice, long stretch.

"Thanks again, Ms. Rodriguez," he says on the way out.

In the hall, Carson allows himself a still moment to appreciate what just happened. To appreciate the new leads he's been given, a real breakthrough on a case, something promising that could definitely be what he needs to put together this book proposal and get a new agent. And justice! That too. Justice for the families of those five young victims. As he lets out a sigh of relief, the woman from the front counter turns the corner from the end of the hall and startles at the sight of him.

"There you are!" she says. "You found her, yes? I didn't see you in there."

"I did, thank you," he says with a smile. He points to the doorway. "We cut it short because she fell asleep, but it was really helpful. Thanks for letting me see her."

The woman frowns at him. "Her? This is not Emilia Rodriguez."

Carson's smile remains cemented on his face. "What?"

"This is Elsa Rodriguez." The woman points behind her. "This is why I tell you—down the hall, then right."

"Right," he says.

E. RODRIGUEZ, the sign laughs back at him.

Now his smile is downright painful.

"This woman, Elsa, she—" The woman does the circle-around-the-ear motion with her finger.

"Uh-huh."

Carson tries to ignore the pitch in his stomach. The church connection, the new details of the sheriff's character—all nothing but the ramblings of a senile old woman. A spell of déjà vu tinged with self-loathing blows over him. For the love of Christ, why is it always something? Some people swallow their pride. Carson swallows his humiliation and it hurts like a sharp pebble on the way down his dry throat.

"So," he says, trying to recover and still feel some semblance of hope. "Where is Emilia Rodriguez, then?"

"She's in her room, end of hall, to the right," the woman says.

Carson thanks the woman and walks down the hall to the real Emilia Rodriguez. When he knocks on her door and introduces himself, a crabby woman in men's pajamas immediately starts yelling at him and tells him to —and this is a direct quote—"piss himself and die." After thanking her for her time, Carson walks out of the Lavender Meadows Retirement Chalet, feeling like a man on fire, but still smiling all the way until his car is on the road.

And then he drops that smile like the mask it is.

ELIZA

E liza knows it's dumb, but she loves teaching the little squirts at Tutu Camp.

She says she does it for the money—and, no doubt, five hundred bucks a week is a serious chunk of change—but she also does it because kids just make her happy. At sixteen, childhood already feels like so long ago. She's starting to develop nostalgia for the time before the weight of hormones and loads of crap homework bogged her down.

As she packs up her backpack, she watches the little ones get picked up by their parents and wishes them happy weekends and smiles and she isn't even faking it. When they all leave, and the studio is empty (the ballet master Charlotte is in her office, arguing with what sounds like her husband on the phone), Eliza stands alone among the mirrors and doesn't like what she sees. Her smudged charcoal eyeliner. Her bruise-black hair with an inch of brown roots. Her stupid face, round and pale as a sugar cookie.

"Who even are you?" she asks her reflection.

She pulls her backpack over her shoulder, shouts a half-hearted goodbye, and exits the studio through its double doors.

Outside, the sun blazes even though it's nearing dinnertime. As Eliza pulls her phone out to check the bus schedule—ugh, she can't wait to get her license—she feels a tap on her shoulder and startles to see Olivia here, a fat paperback copy of *Practical Magic* in her hand with her finger in it like a bookmark as if she's in the middle of reading.

"Hey Black Swan," Olivia says, smiling. "How's it going?"

Eliza swoops in for a quick hug. "What are you doing here?"

Olivia shrugs. "I was downtown already. Figured you'd be getting out soon so I waited for you. What are you doing tonight?"

Eliza studies her chipped black nails. She'll sound like a baby if she says how she really feels—peopled out. Wiped from a week of little kids in leotards. In fact, Olivia already texted her three times about what she was up to tonight and Eliza hasn't answered yet because the day is a whirlwind and all she's dreamed about is the hug of her bed. So she shrugs. "No plans yet. Headed home."

"Can I come with?" Olivia asks, linking arms.

"Sure," Eliza says.

They head to the bus stop which is, thankfully,

shaded. As they plunk down on the bench, Olivia shows Eliza something she has balled up in her fist. It's an eyeball-sized chunk of shiny black crystal.

"What is that?" Eliza asks, reaching out to touch its sharp edge. It's dark as a raven, shiny as a diamond, with a pointed top and a flat bottom like a cylinder.

"Black obsidian," Olivia says. "It's supposed to absorb negative energy from toxic people and then it sends it right back to them."

Eliza pulls her hair down from its sweaty topknot. "Where'd you get it?"

"Swiped it from that new-age place where your brother's girlfriend works."

"She's not his girlfriend."

"You really think so?"

"Honestly, I don't really care."

"That girl's weird. She always vibes me whenever I'm in there."

"Maybe that's because you're a kleptomaniac."

Olivia points the obsidian at Eliza and grins, exposing her silver molars. "See, I'm sucking up your negative energy and blasting it back at you."

Eliza answers with an eyeroll and a half-smile. She doesn't say it, but whatever powers the crystal has—if crystals *have* powers, which, doubtful—are probably canceled out by the fact Olivia stole it. Talk about bad energy. Eliza feels a twinge of guilt, even though she wasn't the one who shoplifted. She knows that Izzy is kind of a freak. But she's also her brother's best friend.

At the bus stop, the sight of a disgusting enormous

spider whose web they almost stumble into gives Eliza a miniature panic attack. As she catches her breath, Olivia points at the sterling silver spider webs hanging from Eliza's ears.

"Excuse me, but how are you allowed to wear those earrings and be that scared of spiders?" Olivia asks. "Biological appropriation!"

"Because real spiders are gross."

"But ..." Olivia shakes her head, like it isn't even worth arguing about. "You're silly, girl. I love spiders so much I catch black widows in jars."

Is she being serious? Who *does* that? "That's ... very strange."

Olivia reaches out to gently flick one of Eliza's earrings. "Stranger than rocking these if you're an arachnophobe?"

They catch the next bus and Eliza is home in under twenty minutes. Even this late in the day, it's so hot the girls walk across the lawn to enjoy the sprinklers. Eliza does a jeté in the spray.

"I'll bet you and Ezra used to run through the sprinklers when you were kids," Olivia says.

"Of course. Didn't you?"

"I never lived in a house that had them. I always wanted to."

A little soaked, they reach the front door where the wooden hand-carved *The Hunters* sign hangs above the matching hand-carved mailbox. Eliza wrings her long hair out. "You ... never had a yard with sprinklers?"

"I never had a yard."

Eliza punches in her code and the door unlocks. "That's so sad."

"You should appreciate what you have," Olivia says.

They step inside and Eliza tries to ignore the prickly feeling on her neck. She loves Olivia, she does. She's never fallen so hard, so fast into a friendship as she has with Olivia. But it annoys her the way Olivia seems obsessed with this idea that Eliza's family has everything, that they're wealthy, that they have some perfect life. And knowing what she does about Olivia and what a little klepto she is, she can't help but wonder if her friend can be trusted.

It's just a feeling she has sometimes.

ELIZA

As soon as they walk into the house, the smell of curry makes Eliza's nose wrinkle. She kicks off her shoes near the doormat and heads into the kitchen with Olivia trailing behind. Hip-hop blares from a Bluetooth speaker and her dad is rapping along to it like a dork and wearing an apron with sunflowers over it that probably belonged to her mom at some point, but of course her mom never wears it because her mom never cooks.

"Hey," her dad says, waving at them with a wooden spoon. He turns the music down. "Sorry, can't resist singing along with Warren G."

So embarrassing.

"It smells spectacular!" Olivia says. "I'm salivating right now."

"Olivia, what a nice surprise! I didn't know you were coming for dinner," he says.

I didn't know either until she ambushed me at Tutu

Camp and invited herself over, Eliza thinks. That's mean though, right? Olivia's her best friend.

"You staying the night?" her dad asks Olivia.

She turns to Eliza, eyebrows raised. "Um ... I mean, sure, if that's okay?"

And now she's spending the night, too. But what can Eliza say? *No, you can't spend the night, I'm busy doing absolutely nothing by myself.*

"Of course," Eliza says.

Olivia hangs her backpack on a dining room chair. She slides her sandals off and walks barefoot across the Spanish kitchen tiles, doing a poor pirouette and coming to stand with Eliza's dad at the stove.

"What's cooking, Carson?" Olivia asks. "Anything I can help with?"

"Chana masala," he says. "You like chickpeas?"

"I'll eat anything," Olivia says.

He laughs. "Maybe you can give Eliza a few pointers. I've never known a pickier eater."

"Thanks," Eliza says sarcastically. "Where's Mom?"

"With a client. She'll be done soon, though," her dad says. "How was Tutu Camp?"

"Fine. Exhausting." Eliza comes and gives her dad a hug. "I'm so glad it's Friday."

"You and me both," he says.

"Holy crap, Carson, what is this?" asks Olivia. She's a few feet away, leaning over the kitchen counter to gape at his open laptop. "Is this real?"

"Oh ... don't look at that," he says, but it's too late. Now Eliza has to see it, too.

Looking over Olivia's shoulder, she sees pictures of rotting body parts photographed in the dirt—a partially decomposed skull, a foot bone, a finger bone. Crime scene photos. Eliza knows because of the colored flags in each photo and also because her dad looks at disgusting shit like this all the time.

"Dad, learn to shut your laptop." Eliza reaches over Olivia's shoulder to snap it closed. "Nobody needs to see that, especially when we're about to eat."

"Sorry. It's for a case I'm looking into. Might write a book on it," Carson says.

Olivia's eyes are still wide. Unlike Eliza, she's not used to seeing the disturbing research that her dad is always doing.

"What case?" Olivia asks.

"The Raven's Landing Dismemberer." He sprinkles salt over the pan. "Cold case from a couple decades ago."

"So the killer, like, chopped the bodies up?" Olivia hops to sit on the counter. "Why?"

Wonderful. Now Eliza's dad has a captive audience—they'll be hearing about forensics and body parts for hours now.

"No one knows for sure, could be he liked to keep bones as trophies," he says. "Could have been because hacking a body to pieces always makes it easier to transport the victims—more compact. But most likely it was because he thought it would make them harder to identify ..."

Speaking of victims, Eliza is feeling like one herself

right now, forced to listen to this. Without a word, she heads up the stairs that creak under her feet. She expects Olivia to follow her, but nope. Too busy laughing with Eliza's dad about hacking up dead bodies in the kitchen. In her room, Eliza plops on her bed with a sigh and lies down, eyeing the dreamcatcher on her ceiling that never does its job. She still has nightmares.

When Olivia first transferred to Riverwood High a few months ago, Eliza was completely smitten by the new girl in town who seemed to spring from absolutely nowhere and adore Eliza from the first moment they met. Eliza has a hard time feeling like she fits in anywhere— most of her friends ended up in the cheerleading squad this year and drifted away from her. She has so little in common with that group now.

But with Olivia, it was like love at first sight, only with a friend. They share the same sarcastic sense of humor. The same taste for scary movies and thrift stores. They even share the same taste in boys, which caused their only real fight ... but it ended up not mattering in the end because neither of them even got a chance to chase after JJ Silva because he started going out with Marian Zaytseva.

Eliza still adores Olivia, she does, but lately some of the things that Eliza originally loved about Olivia, the things that made Olivia so compelling, have started becoming a little annoying. One example: Olivia is one of the friendliest souls Eliza has ever known. Eliza struggles with small talk, with opening up to people, but Olivia has this quality about her where she can just start chatting with anyone and put them at ease. But sometimes it edges almost on ... Eliza doesn't know what to call it, exactly. Flirtation? She notices it especially when Olivia talks to Carson or Ezra. It's just a little bit *too* friendly. And it's incredibly irritating how sometimes it makes Eliza feel like a ghost in her own house—like Olivia takes so much of the spotlight of conversation that Eliza's family forgets she's even here.

"And what are the symptoms you're talking about?" her mother's voice says.

Eliza watches the vent in her wall. It's a laptop-sized grating almost invisible against the blue-black paint. Standing up, Eliza tiptoes to her bedroom door and closes it almost all the way so she won't be visible. Then she gets on her hands and knees and presses her ear up to the vent.

"Like, the same thing, panic attacks," a voice responds. Friday evening—it's that girl Nadia Peters. She goes to Riverwood High. She has a distinct whiny voice Eliza recognizes. "I feel like I can't breathe."

"I'm sorry to hear that. Can you tell me how often this has happened since we last spoke?" her mom asks.

Such concern in her mom's voice, such attention, Eliza gets a pang. Sometimes she fantasizes about getting in costume and pretending to be a stranger who needs therapy—maybe then her mom would talk to her that way, too.

"Maybe every other day?" Nadia answers. "I ..."

"Um, babes, what are you doing?" Olivia asks.

Freezing, Eliza turns her head to see her friend staring down, hands on hips. How did she sneak up like that? Usually you can hear the creak of every step on the staircase. Eliza's face flushes and her mouth goes dry.

"I was ... I was looking for, um—"

Eliza can't even think of a way to end the sentence. In the pause, Eliza's mom's voice carries up through the vent loud enough that Olivia's attention is visibly piqued. Her mouth turns into a little *o*.

"Are you listening to your mom's session?" Olivia asks.

"Shhh!" Eliza says.

She can't believe she's been caught. God, so humiliating. Her heart thumps. She must look like such a freak right now. But kind of the same way Eliza expected Olivia to be revolted by her dad's talk of dead hacked-up corpses, Olivia's eyes only widen. She squats on the floor next to Eliza.

"Let me listen." Olivia playfully pushes Eliza to the side. "Who's she talking to?"

Eliza puts a finger to her lips to remind her to *shhh*. The vent goes two ways, after all. "Remember that girl Nadia Peters?"

"The one with the—" Olivia makes a giant circle around her head with two hands to pantomime enormous hair, which Nadia has—a strawberry-blond cloud, her only memorable physical feature.

Eliza nods.

"What are they talking about?" Olivia whispers.

"She has panic attacks, apparently," Eliza whispers back.

They both push their ears closer. It's not that exciting. Eliza's mom is recommending upping a dosage of Klonopin as needed and recommending Ambien for sleep.

"Dang, your mom's, like, a drug dealer for rich kids," Olivia whispers.

"I mean, it's her job," Eliza whispers back. "She's a psychiatrist. And they're not all rich. She takes insurance."

"I don't even *have* insurance," Olivia says back.

The session must have ended, because now nothing but silence comes through the vent. As they stand up, there's a sick little pill of guilt in Eliza's stomach. She wishes Olivia hadn't walked in on her doing that. Eliza feels so exposed now that someone knows about her little trick, her creepy eavesdropping habit.

"Are they all that boring?" Olivia asks.

"Most of them. Though last week I heard Jaycee Sandoval trying to tell my mom about the dicks she sucked at summer camp."

Olivia gasps, delighted. "Seriously?"

Eliza snickers. "Yeah."

"That's amazing." Olivia's hazel eyes are so bright, you'd think she's *proud* of Eliza or something. "You must have so much dirt on so many kids in town."

"Kind of," Eliza says. "Hey ... please don't tell anyone."

"Of course!" Olivia squeezes Eliza's arm. She leans in close and adds, in an ear-tickling whisper, "Your secrets are my secrets."

But her assurance doesn't get rid of that pit in Eliza's stomach.

Dinner is way too spicy and all Eliza's parents talk about is the Miss Riverwood competition and how proud they are of Eliza for entering. As if she's actually excited to go up onstage in some ridiculous pageant for any reason other than possibly winning money for her future car fund. Eliza notices how sickly sugar-sweet Olivia is to Eliza's parents the whole time. How she sprinkles their names in constantly, *Oh Carson! Oh Angela!*

After dinner, Eliza is bothered by the weird way Olivia greets Ezra when he comes home, saying in a bordering-on-flirty voice, "Hey psycho!"

And then later that night, Eliza notices that Olivia brought her pajamas and toothbrush in her backpack, almost as if she knew she was going to sleep over before swinging by Tutu Camp earlier.

It's just *weird*. Eliza can't explain it, not even to herself, but she feels a fresh, sharp edge of suspicion. After they watch a dumb movie about killer bees while mostly scrolling on their phones the whole time, the girls turn the lights off and Eliza is glad for the dark and the silence. She can't wait to have her space back to herself.

Then, quietly, she hears Olivia from her air mattress on the floor. "Eliza, your secrets are my secrets. So that means mine are yours, right?"

Eliza opens her eyes. The ceiling is lit up by the

moonlight streaming through her window. A tree branch's shadow shifts there like a spiderweb in a breeze. "Of course."

There's a long silence. It's so long Eliza hears an owl cry, footsteps downstairs, and the shooter sounds of Ezra's video games through the wall. It's so long she begins to drift to sleep, sucked into the undertow of unconsciousness, until Olivia breaks the silence.

"I'm going to murder my dad," she says.

Eliza goes totally still in her bed. She gets a chill, an ice that blooms from the inside out. She's quite literally frozen with fear. She doesn't know how to respond. Is this a joke? She knows Olivia's lighthearted voice and this isn't it.

No, she's dead serious.

Eliza searches desperately through her mind for the proper response but she can't think of any. Instead, she closes her eyes tight, the way she did when she was a child and feared a monster was in the room with her. She doesn't want to have heard that. It makes her even sicker than when Olivia discovered her listening through the vent. Way sicker. Murder? Is this why Olivia seemed so intrigued by the Raven's Landing Dismemberer earlier? Was she getting *inspiration*?

"Eliza?" Olivia asks the darkness.

But Eliza doesn't answer. Instead, she pretends to sleep, faking a snore.

Olivia doesn't say anything else and soon Eliza hears her snoring for real. But Eliza doesn't fall asleep for a long time. She tallies up all the ways Olivia acted today that bugged her. All the oddities stacking up. There's something off about her. And now she's threatening to murder her fucking dad? Yeah, time to put some distance between herself and her friend, starting tomorrow.

Tomorrow can't come soon enough.

OLIVIA

On the car ride home the next morning, Carson whistles along with some oldies rap song and Olivia rolls her window down with the push of a button. The breeze is hot and intense as a hair dryer on her cheeks and she closes her eyes and lets everything turn gold.

For just a moment, she feels free.

When she opens her eyes again, a rush of trees whips by, then a wide-open expanse of farmland. Men and women in hats stoop to tend to the careful rows of lettuces. Her smile falters. Her dad's somewhere out there. Not *there*, exactly. He does seasonal work at a strawberry farm over the hill—on good days. But Olivia's stomach is a nauseating brick of dread, expecting to come home and discover him there instead. It's been happening more and more. He's slipping again. She looks at herself in the side mirror and tilts her head, thinking, there I am.

Olivia West hates her life almost as much as she loves herself.

Swallowing, Olivia turns to Carson and decides, to hell with it. She'll just ask. When she gets nervous, when she has a hard time summoning the nerve to keep going, she has a trick her mind likes to play. It's her Inner Thesaurus. She takes a word and thinks of every synonym she can to calm herself down. Right now the word is *question*. She thinks, *Inquiry. Ask. Request. Query.* And then, when she can't come up with another, she just blurts it out.

"Hey Carson," she says, in an upbeat tone. "What's the easiest way to get away with murder?"

Carson asks, jokingly, "You planning a murder, Olivia?"

She laughs. "Um, no. Just curious. Like, you're the expert, right?"

"I suppose I am."

"I'll bet you've seen tons of crazy stuff."

Carson turns the stereo down. "Why are you asking?"

"Because." Olivia's mind reaches for the right answer. Not the true answer, but the right one—the one that will get her what she wants. "I was thinking I might want to write a book about a murder."

Olivia can tell she's done well because Carson lights up like a candle wick. "Fiction or non?"

"Fiction."

"Like a mystery?"

"Something like that."

"You read mysteries?"

"I read everything."

"You want to know the easiest way to murder someone ... I mean, it's hard to come up with a simple answer for you. It depends on the circumstances and the motive. Is this a crime of passion? Is it premeditated? Tell me more about the story and I can help you brainstorm."

Olivia's stomach is tightening as the car passes the bend with the fruit stand that marks the halfway point home. She wishes the car would get a flat tire. She wishes it would start pouring rain and the road would become undrivable. She wishes she would get home only to find her trailer burned down.

"Well, there's this girl, this lady, and she has this uncle she wants to murder. For like ... revenge, because he's a bad person."

"Ahh, okay. *Revenge*," Carson adjusts his glasses. "See, revenge could be interesting. Because with revenge, the person wouldn't necessarily be looking for the easiest way to murder. They might be wanting to make the person suffer a little bit, too."

Olivia nods. The pressure rises in her as the car's odometer ticks up and they creep closer to her trailer park. She isn't sure what's dread and what's guilt. They're just talking about a fictional story, a story she's writing.

"Yeah, I think ... I think my character would want to see him suffer," she says. "Though I think it's important that she gets away with it."

"She's not going to get caught?"

"I don't know, I haven't figured the end out."

"In most mysteries, the person gets caught."

"The Raven's Landing Dismemberer didn't."

"True." Carson points at her. "But that's real life."

What Olivia doesn't say is this: her mother is also real life, and she's in prison. This is why it's so important to plan this out, to research. She doesn't want to end up in a crime of passion situation where she grabs the nearest butcher knife in the block. Olivia can't count the number of times she's wondered how different her life would be if her mother had twisted the knife in just a little deeper— but she might as well imagine she was a princess in a fairy tale.

Carson taps his wedding ring on the steering wheel as he considers this fictional murder. "Hmmm. Maybe this girl poisons her uncle. Poisoning is very easy and often hard to trace. Rat poison's readily available. If this lady's got any knowledge of plants, maybe she goes with nightshade."

"Oooh," Olivia says.

"Fires are relatively easy. Gas can and a match, kaboom."

Olivia is almost turned on by the thought. "Yeah, true. What about black widows?"

"What about them?"

"Could you kill someone if you let them loose in someone's bedroom?"

He laughs. "Creative, but a bit far fetched. You can't force a spider to bite someone. And black widow bites rarely actually kill people."

How disappointing. She's sworn all those spiders around their house are a sign, like the devil is winking at her and begging her to go through with it.

"Oh," she says. "Okay."

"Are they near water? Because shoving someone off a boat and faking a drowning's a good way to go. Or cutting someone's brakes, you know that's got to be a terrifying death. Sever the brakes just enough that they don't fully snap until the car's on the freeway. Though there are no guarantees there."

She likes that one. The idea of killing the man and the vehicle in one go is tempting.

"Yeah." Olivia's heart beats so fast she puts two fingers to her wrist to feel the flutter of her pulse. In the distance, across a meadow with knee-high grass, the spread of trailers, and then the Paradise Springs sign. *Home.* The word is a heavy stone. "Maybe poison. Could I ... could I email you about it? I mean, as I start writing. Could I run some ideas by you?"

"Of course," he says. "Consult me anytime."

After a couple of minutes, Carson pulls the SUV up to the row of mailboxes at the park entrance and the car rolls to a stop. From the center console between them, he retrieves his wallet. He plucks a card and hands it to Olivia.

Carson Hunter, Crime Writer.

She runs her fingertip along the embossed letters on the card. It's corny with a cartoon fedora hat and a cartoon feather pen printed on it. But he knows who he is and what he loves to do. Olivia wonders if she'll ever be like that. So far, life's just felt like one long fight for survival.

She smiles and holds the card up. "This is cool. Thanks."

"Have a great weekend, Olivia."

Her eyes linger on his. What was he was like when he was younger? Probably like Ezra, except more chipper. To test the boundary between them, Olivia slips her hand on his arm and gives it a squeeze. He doesn't flinch or withdraw. Doesn't react at all.

"You too, Carson."

Reluctantly, she opens the car door and hops out into the stifling heat, which seems to come from two places at once: the blinding, suffocating sunshine and the black asphalt beneath her feet. She can almost feel the soles of her Mary Janes beginning to melt as she trudges to her trailer.

She knows her dad's home because his truck is in the driveway, that rusted piece of shit truck with the embarrassing array of shouty messages he stickered on the back of the cab letter by letter in such a chaotic pattern you can barely make sense of them. HONK IF U ♥ JESUS bleeds into JESUS SAVES bleeds into JESUS IS LORD bleeds into GET BEHIND ME SATAN! which bleeds into THE LORD REBUKE YOU, SATAN!

It's a dizzying, screaming battle between JESUS and SATAN and in some ways, it's like peeking into the horrible inner workings of her dad's tortured soul.

OLIVIA

All it takes is a split second for Olivia to assess which version of her dad she's dealing with on any given day.

On a good day, he'll be showered, shaven, his bright blue eyes clear and sparkling. He'll be at work. Or dressed and cleaning the kitchen, maybe, or watching TV and talking back to it like an old friend. But Olivia can tell the moment she sees him today that it's not a good day. His eyes are bloodshot and he's in his bathrobe sitting at the kitchen table with a beer and a scowl on his face like he's hungry for a fight. Olivia steps inside quietly as she can, murmuring a "Hey Dad," and then turns toward her room.

"Now wait a second," he shouts after her. "You come here, now."

Her hand is on her doorknob and her chest squeezes. Sometimes he lets her go if she steps in quietly and slips into her room and locks the door. But if she ignores him now, it'll turn into a fight. She turns and tiptoes toward the living room, lingering in the mouth of the short hallway.

"Come here, I said." He points to the other chair at the table. "Where the hell've you been?"

She slides into a chair across from him, folding her hands on the tabletop, and speaks to him as slowly and deliberately as someone speaking to a toddler. "I told you I was spending the night at Eliza's."

"Mmm," he says, like he doesn't believe her. "Dressed like that?"

Olivia looks down. This? It's a white dress with red rosebuds printed on it. She bought it for three dollars at the thrift store yesterday and it still smells of someone else's perfume. It's not revealing. It's knee-length and covers her chest. If her dad was in a better mood, he'd tell her how pretty she looks. Instead it's fuel for a fire.

"Dressed like what?"

"Don't lie to my face, Ollie. What trouble've you been up to?"

"Dad, I was seriously sleeping over at Eliza's. You can call her parents and ask."

He studies her, drinking his beer. Behind him, on the countertop, she spies three empties and a nearly full bottle of Wild Turkey. It's going to be a long day.

"Weren't you supposed to work today?" she asks, injecting honey into her tone so he won't think she's being judgmental.

"My work's not your business." He points at her with

the tip of his bottle. "You care so much, why don't you get off your lazy ass and get a job?"

"I've been looking."

It's not a lie. She's been looking. She just doesn't like what she sees.

"When I was your age," he says.

Here we fuckin go, she thinks, careful not to let her face show her feelings.

"I worked six days a week at my daddy's cafe," he says. "Starting when I was thirteen years old. All the money I made went to help buy our family's groceries that week. I didn't expect to flit about town looking pretty and acting like a prince. Look at me when I'm talking to you."

Olivia aims her stare at him, intentionally keeping her face as blank as possible. It's hard to look at her dad when he's like this. He looks mean and pained and old and tired, like a wax museum version of himself that spent a few minutes in the heat. He's sweaty and unshaven. She can't stand when he doesn't shave, when she can smell him. She feels like an animal when he looks at her sometimes, like a rabbit stilling itself to try to make the snake forget it exists.

"I can sense Satan around you," he whispers. "Lingering. Like a black cloud. When there's trouble, you know I can tell, Olivia Wren, because you're a part of me. You're a part of me and I can feel what you feel."

Poison, Olivia thinks.

"You're like your mother." His voice rises. "That way you're watching me right now, that hawk-eyed stare?

Gloria, straight up. And I always knew when Gloria was lying just the same way I know you're lying right now. Because her face went flat as a mannequin. Gave me nothing. She could lie like it was a talent. You're the same."

Pushing him off a boat, Olivia thinks.

"I'm not lying to you about anything, though," Olivia says.

"Don't talk back to me." He sips his beer. "I'm not done. I want to know what it is you're not telling me. And if you're not going to come clean with me, then we're going to sit here and we're going to pray together."

Gun to the temple, Olivia thinks.

"You want to play this game, Little Miss Pokerface? Better yet, how about we go downtown? We'll preach. Repent in public for all we've done wrong. *Offer our bodies as a living sacrifice, holy and pleasing to God.*"

Olivia gets up out of her chair, gently, as gently as she can, careful not to move too fast or drag the chair across the floor and make a sound. She breaks the intensity of his gaze and clears her throat. "Can I make you some food?"

"Don't change the subject. I mean it, girl, we're going preaching." He drains his beer and stands, placing it on the counter next to the other empties.

Olivia's dad is six feet tall, tall enough to cast a shadow. His curly hair is just beginning to bald and gray. When he isn't drinking, he's a big teddy bear. Olivia has happy memories with him during those sober years. But that was before she fully knew what he's capable of. Right now, she can feel the temperature of his anger.

This isn't going to end well.

Living with him is like trying to guess the next plot twist of the worst novel in the world. She has to constantly imagine all the scenes that could be written with her next move. If she says no, will he start screaming at her in a dragged-out fight that could last the rest of the day with him haranguing her about imagined transgressions? If she reminds him he's been drinking and shouldn't drive, will he get even angrier and drag her to the truck to show her she's wrong? If she tries to calm him down, will he begin weeping and pull her in for a smothering hug and not let go?

Rat poison. Nightshade.

In a swift movement, fast as prey, she snatches her backpack and sprints out the door as fast as her legs can carry her. The door smacks shut behind her before she can hear him protest.

The one thing Paradise Springs has going for it is the quiet, the desolation. Once she leaves the trailer park, Olivia can run until she feels like her lungs will explode and still not see another human being. She runs through the wide field of grass which tickles her bare legs and ducks into a thicket of oaks, where she finally stops to catch her breath.

She collapses on the dirt. Making a tiny stack of fallen twigs and dried oak leaves with their sharp edges, she pulls a lighter from her backpack and lights a little fire and watches it burn. It's not until it crackles with flames that she can finally breathe again.

Last fall, she dedicated her whole heart and soul to black magic. She stole locks of his hair and made voodoo dolls, she chanted spells and mixed potions and whispered curses to make her dad fall ill and die. But it didn't work. In her heart, she knew it wouldn't. She knows, like everything else in her life, if she wants something to happen, no one is going to do it for her, not even God, not even the devil.

She's going to have to kill him herself.

ANGELA

Whenever Angela is asked what the secret is to her happy marriage, Angela's automatic reply is "weekly dates."

It's not an exaggeration. Sunday brunch dates with Carson are a special glue that holds them together. Throughout the week when Carson chases police records in another county or chews his cheek as he ogles his laptop screen reading about atrocious crimes, Angela is holed up in her office downstairs with back-to-back appointments. She's a morning person. She gets up at dawn to go for a run and drink her smoothie breakfast. Carson's a night owl. And by the time he goes to bed, he snores like a beast. Angela often casts him out of the bedroom and he mutters to himself in the dark as he trudges upstairs with a pillow to the refinished attic that serves as their guest room.

But Sunday brunch dates, in downtown Riverwood right on the water at their favorite restaurant, Happy

Plate—that's the one place where they can finally stop for a brief couple of hours and focus on each other and remember the people they used to be when it was just the two of them.

They sit on the restaurant's back patio at a table with an umbrella, a balmy breeze tickling Angela's shoulders. Behind them, the river sings and everything is green.

"I'll have an egg white omelet with mushrooms, spinach, and no cheese. And fruit instead of potatoes." Angela shuts the menu and hands it to the waitperson with the loud purple hair. Why does Angela even look at the menu? She gets the same thing every week.

"I'll go for the eggs benedict this time with a side of bacon." Carson hands his menu over and flashes a smile. "Thank you kindly."

Carson never thinks of cholesterol. It's one of his many, many flaws. He thinks playing tennis a couple times a week somehow negates the red meat, the beer, the fast-food stops. The man thinks he's invincible. He read too many comic books as a child. Angela takes a sip of black coffee to stop herself from saying something. She doesn't want to spend their one date per week arguing about his cardiac health.

"How's the book going?" she asks.

"Oh, I don't know," he sighs.

Clearly, the book isn't going well. Angela isn't shocked. She's also a little relieved, because chasing the Raven's Landing Dismemberer story is a risky idea and part of her wishes he would give up and move on. But she wants to support him. And they need the money.

"What happened?" she asks.

"I chased a lead I thought I had—the main suspect's wife ... talked to this woman for a good hour, she had all these crumbs to follow. I got so excited, Ange, I thought I had a breakthrough. But then—get this, you're going to think it's hilarious—turned out I wasn't even talking to the right woman. She was this ... senile old woman, I guess, who was just saying nonsense to me." He chuckles and shakes his head. "I don't know, you've got to laugh."

"What? How—"

He waves a hand. "Not worth going into. Anyway, I've been chasing paper trails all week instead, immersing myself in a forum."

"Another forum? Carson, the forum was the reason you followed bunk information with the Freezer Man—"

"I'm not joining the forum. Don't worry. I'm just scanning them to get up to date on what the amateurs think these days. You *know* there are nuggets in there."

"Have you considered another project, maybe?"

He gives her a look.

"Just asking!" she says.

"No, *dear*, I haven't."

"What sort of timeline are we thinking here for this book? Are you ready to pitch it to agents yet?"

"Not quite yet." He takes a sip of his giant mug with whipped cream on it. "God, this mocha's hitting the spot."

"May I make a suggestion?" she asks. "I think you should reach out to Chaz again."

He groans.

"You worked with Chaz for years, Carson, you know him. He knows you."

"Burned that bridge down already."

"Well, build it back up!"

He shakes his head but admits, "I've considered it. I don't know."

"When are you going to be ready to pitch?"

"I'm feeling some pressure from you." He rakes his fingers through his hair. "Am I right in reading that?"

"Not 'pressure.' Just concern about our budget."

"Look, I told you it was going to take time."

"I understand that. There's just so much work we have to do on the house. The heater's been making noises. I'm worried there are rodents in there."

"I'll get some traps, rat poison."

"We have to get a new roof by September or we're going to have to deal with leaks again."

Carson reaches a hand across the table to grab hers. "Relax. We've got this."

Angela breathes in, counting to eight, focusing past Carson and on the river. The river where her father drowned. The beautiful river.

"Let's not talk about money on our weekly date, okay?" He takes his hand back again. "The whole point is we get away from everything."

He smiles and she mirrors back a smile and then she feels it in her eyes. She loves that about him. He lights her up. After nearly twenty years, he still knows how to flip the switch in her that sometimes even she can't find.

"You're right." She leans an elbow on the table. "Carson, I have to confess something to you."

"Uh-oh. What?"

"I picked up Ezra's tablet the other day. It was lying on the couch in the living room—"

"Oh no."

"—and ... I'm aware that this is terrible, but I used his password and unlocked it."

"Ange!" Carson's eyes widen behind his glasses. "That's such an invasion of privacy."

"I know it is. I feel incredibly guilty."

"How did you know his password?"

"I've seen him unlock it." She rolls her eyes. "It's 6-9-6-9."

Carson gives a knowing and approving nod. "Classic."

"Look, I know what I did was wrong. I don't even know why I did it, curiosity got the best of me. He's so withdrawn lately, have you noticed? It's been hard for me to get through to him. I've wondered if he has major depressive disorder." She straightens her silverware. "Not an excuse, I know my behavior is inexcusable. I should trust my children enough to not go through their search histories."

"So what did you see on there?" he asks in a quieter voice. "Porn?"

"No. Porn I can deal with, porn is normal. This was not normal."

"What was it?"

"He was looking up 'flaying.' It's a method of execution when you skin someone alive—"

"I know what flaying is."

"Well, he was looking at ..." Angela remembers, nauseated. "... at pictures."

"Okay." Carson folds his arms. "And?"

"And he was looking at photos of executions and mass graves in the Holocaust and ... and this was all in the span of like an hour's time, Carson. Some of the ugliest things you could imagine. He's just staring at these pictures, I guess, I don't know."

Carson appears to be contemplating this deeply. He takes another sip of his mocha, leaving a little whipped cream mustache that Angela points to and he then wipes off with a napkin. "I disagree. Seems like normal teenage stuff to me. And I mean, some people just have dark minds, you know? You ever look through my search history?"

Angela shivers. She hates glimpsing crime scene photos when she passes by his laptop. "I don't want to."

"Maybe the kid has a future in true crime. Following in his dad's footsteps."

"Maybe," she says. "But ... it made me think about last summer."

Carson blinks, expressionless. He apparently has no idea what she's referring to.

"When Ezra got fired from the butcher shop," she reminds him, in a whisper. There's a white-haired couple now seated next to them, dressed up as if they just came from church. "For masturbating in the meat locker."

"Oh, okay, *that*." He holds up a hand as if he doesn't want her to say any more. Which is fine. Angela doesn't want to say any more, either. "Again, normal teenage boy stuff."

"Masturbation I get. Masturbation in a room filled with butchered animals?"

"Sometimes the urge just comes over you, babe. Like you and me in that taco restaurant bathroom."

Angela clears her throat and looks away, fighting the flush coming into her cheeks.

"It's all normal." Carson stretches his arms behind his head. "Or it's not, I don't know, but who cares? Who cares what's normal. So he's masturbating in meat lockers and he's looking up pictures of torture. Does that hurt anyone?"

The woman at the next table over gives them a steely look.

"Shhh." Angela kicks Carson under the table.

But he's undone something in her, in a wonderful way. This must be what it feels like when a corset gets loosened. She breathes in and out, feeling suddenly like her lungs have expanded after her confession. It seemed like such a big deal, so horrifying that Ezra searched out such morbid, gruesome things for no apparent reason. He was her little boy not even that long ago, playing with plastic dinosaurs, building cities out of blocks for hours on the floor. But Carson's right. It's not that big of a deal. What a relief to say it out loud.

"Oh! On the topic of morbid teenagers." Carson

snaps his fingers. "Yesterday I'm taking Olivia home and guess what she tells me?"

"What?"

"She's writing a murder mystery. She's looking for my help in brainstorming."

"I had no idea she wrote."

"Neither did I."

Angela shakes her head. "That poor girl. I wonder if she's working out some of her ... issues."

The shock that zinged through her when she learned Olivia's mother was serving time in prison for attempted homicide and her father is that unhinged alcoholic who yells at people about Satan on the corner of Dickinson and First—her heart goes out to the girl. She tried to pry into Olivia's situation, suspecting abuse. But Olivia is tight-lipped, offering empty, cheerful answers when asked about her home life. Honestly, Angela was the same at her age.

"I'm glad she has an outlet." Angela's eyes drift to the emerald sparkle of the river. "Writing can be therapeutic."

"And I'm glad she has a friend like Eliza," Carson says. "A safe space with us whenever she needs it. I've been sure to let Olivia know that, repeatedly."

"Good," Angela says, the word getting stuck in her throat.

Good. Such a subjective word, isn't it? A little stone that means such different things to people that it means almost nothing much at all. She grew up trying so hard to be good. But when she grew all the way up, she learned the truth: there's no such thing.

CARSON

From: Olivia Wren West
    <missoliviawrenwest@gmail.com>
    To: Carson Hunter
    <authorcarsonhunter@gmail.com>

Subject: murder

hey carson, how are you? thanks again for the ride home saturday. i've been thinking about what we were talking about, that murder idea. you talked about rat poison but quick question: if someone were to buy rat poison to kill someone, would that get flagged by the store/authorities and maybe make that person a suspect? is that a thing?? and then what is the best way to get rid of a body if someone doesn't want to get caught? thanks for your help, i appreciate it.

xoxo

liv

Carson reads the email as he finishes off an IPA in the dining room. It's after dinner, after cleanup, that lull in the evening when the family members each go to their own spaces seeking solitude and the dishwasher hums in the kitchen. He starts to reply to Olivia's email, but then gets stuck in his own head. The door to the back patio is open, a breeze rustling the potted palm in the corner, and through the screen door, the crickets chirp. Carson can never get over the fact that crickets are just yelling because they're horny out of their minds. Good for you, little buddies. Go get it.

Once upon a time, he too wanted to be a mystery writer. In high school, Carson was the founder of the Literary Salon (that apparently disbanded immediately after his graduation, but hey, he tried). He self-published a trilogy about a crime-solving vampire under a pseudonym, Grimm Fang, that didn't sell many copies nor did it receive rave reviews. It was such a shame because it was brilliant—genre-blurring and clever. Should he share it with Olivia? Maybe it would inspire her.

When he first met Angela, she was just about Olivia's age. She was a lot like Olivia: intelligent, curious. They met at a graduation party on the river. The trees were decorated with Christmas lights, kegs aplenty, the reggae was turned to eleven, some brave skinnydippers were hooting in the water. And there was Angela—Miss

Riverwood—a girl he saw getting crowned onstage at the county fair. Her hair was in two braids and she wore a flowy dress to her ankles and sat all alone on a picnic bench. Carson seized that moment as an opportunity that would likely pass within seconds and he swooped right in with a red cup before anyone else had the chance to.

"Anyone sitting here?" he asked, pointing to the bench next to her.

"No, go ahead."

He plopped next to her and held out the red cup. "Brought you something."

She laughed and cocked her head. "Um ... who are you?"

"I'm your date tonight."

"I don't even know you."

"That's why we're on a date. To get to know each other."

She continued to look at him like she thought he was odd, but took the cup, smelling but not tasting it. "I have a boyfriend."

"Yeah? Where is he?"

"Bible study."

Carson raised his eyebrows. "Sounds like a fun guy."

"Who *are* you?"

"Carson Hunter."

He held out his hand. She examined it and finally shook it, reluctantly and limply, then pulled her hand back and shoved it into her puffy jacket pocket.

"Angela Atkins," she said.

"You went to Bishop, right? I went to Riverwood High."

"How'd you know what school I went to?"

"You've got that private school vibe. Gucci boots. Ralph Lauren jacket."

"I see you pay attention to the details."

"Every. Single. One."

She smiled, as if she couldn't help it. She put her cup to her lips and then seemed to think the better of it, putting it on the table and pushing it his way. "I shouldn't take drinks from strangers."

"We're not strangers," he reminded her. "We just introduced ourselves."

"I can't tell if I'm creeped out by you or amused," she said, really studying him for the first time. When she saw his face, something visibly softened in her. A chemistry spread between them and they shared a smile.

"You're special, Miss Riverwood." He traced a little happy face on the table. "I saw how fast you spun that Rubik's cube."

"Ha." She gave him a soft push, a shock, a warmth blooming.

They spent the whole night talking, drinking, and huddling near the bonfire. At first glance, Angela was a glowing, polished beauty queen. But that wasn't what attracted Carson to her. He liked the sarcastic edge in her voice, the wry half-smile on her lips, her dry wit. Just like what made him zero in on her at that silly pageant at the county fair. Yes, she could be in a magazine. But it was the Rubik's cube that gave her an air of mystery.

"Tell me about your family," he said at one point.

Carson noticed the flicker in her face, like someone turned a light switch off for a split second before turning it back on. He noticed the way her eyes dulled, just barely, as she stared at the fire.

"What is there to say?" Angela asked. "We're just a normal family."

She changed the subject then, a sharp left turn into how she really felt about reggae music. But Carson made a mental note in his head that there was something deeper there that made her evade the question. And he was determined to someday know what it was. In fact, Angela made his mind deeply hungry. He wanted to know everything about her. He wanted to see childhood pictures of her and to know what her bedroom looked like and how her hair smelled.

A few times throughout the night, Carson pinched his leg to make sure this was real. There was an instant magic between the two of them—the way she kept touching his arm and her eyes sparkled when he made her laugh. All night, every word he uttered, every move he made, he was so careful to read her reaction and make sure he was playing it right. He didn't piss in the woods even though his bladder felt like it would burst, for fear she was going to get swept up into conversation with someone else.

When the party wound down and the fire was nothing but embers and smoke, Angela gave him a kiss before heading back to her car. It was the softest, slowest, juiciest kiss Carson had ever experienced. It was like a drug, the way it weakened his knees and blurred his vision. She pulled back and smiled at him, ran a finger along his jawline.

"What about that boyfriend?" Carson murmured. "You seemed to have forgotten about him."

"I made him up," she whispered. "He didn't exist."

A grin spread on Carson's face. "I see."

"But don't get any ideas," she said. "I'm leaving next week for college."

She might as well have pushed him in a ditch. "What?" he finally managed.

"Yeah. Going to Arizona."

The word *Arizona* pulsed through his mind like a four-syllable heartbeat. *Arizona. Arizona.* It was an exquisite word, like the name of some kind of warrior princess. And all at once, he saw himself there, in a ruddy desert landscape, Mars on Earth.

"I'll come with you," he said.

She shoved her hands in her pockets and took a step back, pine needles crunching under her boots. "You're crazy."

He shrugged. "I know."

Something shifted in Angela's expression. She chewed her cheek.

"Only took me about three minutes to know I'd chase you anywhere," he said.

It *was* crazy. Carson knew he was like that—he saw something he wanted, and he would go after it with a relentless hyperfocus. It freaked some people out, like that literary agent who blocked him online when he kept sending unsolicited partial manuscripts, or the girl junior year who threatened a restraining order when he wouldn't stop leaving love letters in her mailbox. Which wasn't his fault, by the way, very blown out of proportion, but he moved on. Anyway, Carson was dogged and you either loved it about him or you loathed it and that was that. What would it be, he wondered? Did he just repulse Miss Riverwood forever or was she as crazy as he was?

She stepped forward, laughing a little, put her arms around him, and gave him a second kiss. Then she pulled back and wiped her lipstick off the edges of his mouth.

"Goodbye, Carson," she said. "Maybe in another life."

He watched her go, gravel crunching beneath her boots as she headed toward her convertible with the top pulled up. Its headlights blinked as she beeped it to unlock it. She didn't even look back at him before driving away in a cloud of dust. He vomited in a pile of pine needles, more from the unexpected heartbreak than the shitty beer. He'd fallen stupid in love and had then been dumped like a sack of human compost in the cruel course of one evening.

And that just made him want her more.

CARSON

"Dad," Eliza says, startling Carson from his reverie.

Man, the human brain is an amazing time machine, isn't it? For a few minutes, Carson transported himself back to that riverside party where he met the love of his life, and now here he is at the kitchen table, over two decades later, beholding the beautiful young woman they made. Sure, that beautiful young woman is scowling at him like he's a spider in the shower. Still.

Carson breathes in deeply, appreciating this precious life. "What's up, Lize?"

She points to his computer. "I'm sorry, but is that an email from *Olivia?*"

"It is!" He turns to his screen, where the email is still open. "You looking over my shoulder again?"

Eliza's lip is curled in disgust. "But ... why are you emailing with Olivia?"

"She wants advice on a book she's writing."

The twist of her face—it's like he just sputtered gibberish. "What?"

"She's writing a murder mystery."

Eliza crosses her arms. "Dad, don't email Olivia. Seriously. That's weird."

"What? I'm a writer, I write about crime, why would this be weird?"

"Because it's just ..."

Is she jealous? Carson's trying to read Eliza's face. He can't. His teenage daughter's expressions have become a language he's no longer fluent in.

"You know, when I was in high school," he says, "I wanted to be a writer, too, and I had no one to lean on—no experts, no supporters. My teachers thought my stories were bizarre and tried to get me to walk a straight line, go to college, be a reporter. And man, how I wish I'd had someone there at that time to cheer on my creative side instead. You know?"

Eliza just stares at him. "You don't understand."

"Actually, I do. I very much do." He shuts his computer and pauses as he considers how to get through to Eliza. *She's* the one who doesn't understand. Which is fine, she's only sixteen, but she needs to learn a little empathy. "Olivia's home life seems rough. Her dad—I don't know about that guy. She needs all the support she can get from us."

"Dad, she ..."

Carson waits, folding his hands on his lap. "Yes?"

"She's—I don't know how to tell you."

Alarms go off in Carson's head. Abuse. Eliza knows

of some kind of abuse Olivia is experiencing. Is that the uncomfortable look on her face? "Tell me what? You can tell me anything, kiddo, don't you know that?"

Eliza pales and swallows. "It's nothing," she says. "Just—I would appreciate it if you wouldn't email her anymore. It's *weird*. She's my friend. You're my dad. You know?"

"Okay," he says, hands up.

With that, Eliza crosses to the dark kitchen, fills a water glass, and tiptoes back upstairs with the silent elegance of the ballerina she is. Carson considers what just happened, trying to untangle Eliza's peculiar reaction. It's hard to tell where her moodiness ends and actual issues begin. It's ridiculous that she's jealous. There's nothing weird about Olivia asking for advice from a professional writer.

So he opens his computer and he writes her back.

Ezra

Meanwhile, Ezra's in his room with his headphones on, synthwave music thumping his eardrums.

His phone keeps lighting up on his desk but he ignores it. It's Izzy either wanting to talk about her birthday party or jump online and play Terror Army but he's not in the mood for either. He's been pulling back from her, feeling weird about her, and it's like she detects it and it makes her even more pushy. Lying on his bed belly-down, propped up on his elbows, he studies his red notebook with the words *Notes From a Psychopath* scratched into the cover with black pen.

He opens it and flips the pages, entries written in tiny neat black handwriting, filled all the way to the margins, with some artwork in there as well—sketches of a severed head, a bleeding eyeball, a black-mouthed clown. He finds a fresh page and smooths it out.

Instances Where I Felt Nothing Where I Should Have Felt Something, he writes as a title.

It's important that Ezra documents these things. It's allowing him to extract the worm from his brain that most bothers him, the thing he wrestles with constantly. It's the lurking beast that stands behind him everywhere he goes, the monster under his bed, the ghost that haunts his insides.

Ezra Hunter needs to solve the riddle of whether he's a psychopath.

Stealing, he writes as a bullet point, then lists off the items like a shopping list: *my mom's tranks, cash from dad, the wallet on the floor of the library, Izzy's retainer.*

A little delicious flash of nausea as he imagines how her retainer felt in his mouth, tight on his palate, not quite fitting his teeth, tasting like pennies. He glances at his bedside drawer, where it's hidden in a sock.

Watching True Terrors of Death, he writes as a second bullet point. He watched the entire three-hour compilation of documentary footage of the worst deaths imaginable—people being disemboweled, drawn and quartered, their organs being eaten by vultures, one woman buried alive and screaming. He watched it all without getting up from his bed once. Yes, when it first started, his stomach turned. But he didn't look away. And after a few minutes, he numbed out the way he usually does.

Reading splatterpunk, he writes. Dozens of books with the most disgusting gore and body horror imaginable —nothing.

Izzy, he writes. He doesn't elaborate. The thought makes him shudder.

His pen hovers as he debates whether he dare write down the next bullet point. There's a snake writhing under his skin as he considers it, his pulse racing. Quickly, he jots the word *Bludgeoning* when there's a knock on his door. He pulls his headphones so they hang around his neck.

"Knockity knock," his dad sings.

"Fuck," Ezra whispers, suddenly flooded with guilt. Is it guilt, though? Or just a physical reaction, a learned tic? He shoves his notebook under the mattress and clears his throat.

"Uh, come in," he says, sitting up on his bed.

"Hey, son," his dad says, stepping inside. "How goes it?"

Son. Great. Ezra knows when some kind of probe or pep talk's coming, and that's how it always starts.

Carson points to the chair at Ezra's desk. "Mind if I ...?"

"Yeah. I mean, no. Go ahead."

His dad plops in the chair with an exaggerated sigh, as if the day is so tiring. As if his life of sitting at his laptop dreaming about murder is that exhausting.

"How about you pick up that racket again and come whack some balls with me this week?" Carson asks.

"Dad," Ezra says. "I told you, I'm over tennis."

"Go for a run or something then?"

"What are you, my personal trainer?"

"I'm just trying to find a mutual interest. I'm trying to connect with you."

He sounds like an automaton. What, did his dad look that up online? *Fabulous Tips for Connecting With Your Progeny*: find a mutual interest! Ezra almost feels sorry for him, he's so bad at this.

"Maybe you're, I don't know, interested in true crime." His dad crosses his legs. "Maybe you could come with me when I'm out doing research."

"Maybe," Ezra says, just to put an end to this awkward conversation. What is his dad doing? Did his mom put him up to this? Why is his dad forcing a connection with him right now out of the blue?

"You like true crime?" his dad asks, swiveling a full circle in his chair.

"Um ... I guess?"

His dad points his chin toward the stack of books on Ezra's bedside table. "Got some books on serial killers there."

"Oh, yeah." Ezra glances at them. He flipped through them and read some gruesome parts, but none of them held his attention long enough for him to read them straight through. They seemed juicy but they were pretty dense. *American Psycho* was okay but he felt like it was trying too hard to be funny. "I guess I'm kind of interested."

"The darker side of humanity's fascinating, isn't it?" his dad asks.

"Sure."

"You know, there's nothing wrong with being drawn

to it. And I'm here if you ever want to talk about anything. You know that, right?"

"Dad, I'm sorry, but what the hell is this really about?"

"Nothing." His dad looks at Ezra like he just stuck him with a pin. "Just ... trying to hang out with my kid."

There it is again, that flood of guilt. Though like before, Ezra can't tell how *real* the guilt is. Maybe it's just a reflex from being told repeatedly throughout his life that he should want to be nice to his parents. A learned thing, one that could be ignored or unlearned under different circumstances. He wants to play with that. Play with seeing if guilt is something he can remove from himself like a sick and useless organ. He imagines telling his dad to fuck off and then having to live with the hurt he inflicts. Turns out that Ezra might have had the guts to bludgeon an innocent creature, but he doesn't have the guts to talk shit to his father.

Ezra gives his dad a smile. "Fine. Want to play chess?"

"Sure! I'd love to."

The delight on his dad's face from being invited to play a game is so earnest it's borderline heartbreaking. Ezra gets up and takes his wooden chess set out of his closet.

He beats his dad in eight moves. It takes four and a half minutes. And when his dad leaves the room, Ezra adds *Beating my dad's ass at chess* to the list he started, right under the word *Bludgeoning*.

Eliza

"Oh God," Eliza moans to herself as she peeks through the window and sees Olivia waiting for her outside of the Tutu Camp building, nose in a book.

It's Friday. For some reason, Eliza had a premonition that this was going to happen—that Olivia was going to be waiting for her again, same as last week.

Ever since Olivia spent the night last weekend, Eliza has been avoiding her. Six texts, three voicemail messages. After the whole *I want to murder my dad* confession and then those emails to her dad for murder ideas (seriously, what?!), Eliza is wary of her. All week, she thought herself into such circles about everything that happened, it turned her feelings about their friendship upside down. Is it crazy to not want to be friends with someone because of one thing they said? But it isn't just that. It's also that Olivia caught Eliza being a creeper and an eavesdropper.

Ugh, Eliza wants to throw up. The thought of having to have a conversation with Olivia about any of this, of having to say out loud that she isn't sure she wants to be friends anymore—honestly, Eliza would rather swim with sharks.

"Why the lingering?" ballet master Charlotte asks Eliza, coming up behind her and jiggling her keys. She has a beautiful French accent and the hoarse voice of a smoker. "You need a ride?"

"No, I'm going," Eliza says. "Just spacing out for a second."

"This hair of yours, it needs to decide what color." Charlotte reaches out to touch Eliza's bun. "Looks like a bruise."

This is good. Maybe if Eliza procrastinates by chatting with Charlotte, Olivia will get bored and go away and then Eliza won't have to deal with anything. The problem will solve itself.

"I know," Eliza agrees. "I dyed it black but it wasn't permanent. I'm still trying to decide."

"Black is sophisticated." Charlotte touches her own blue-black hair that she clearly dyes—the woman's pushing seventy. "If I do say so myself."

"Totally. Though I've wondered if I looked better—"

Charlotte gestures toward the door. "Ready to go, my love?"

So much for plan B.

"Yeah, definitely," Eliza says.

She's about to break a nervous sweat as she pushes

the door open and steps out onto the sidewalk, where the late afternoon sun gives the scene an orange tint. She waves goodbye to Charlotte and Olivia comes up with a wide grin, hair in pigtails. She wears new earrings shaped like perfume bottles, which she probably stole from somewhere.

"Hey gorgeous," Olivia says playfully. "Did you drop your phone in a toilet or something? I've been texting and calling all week."

"Oh, yeah, sorry. I've been busy."

The smile fades on Olivia's face. "Are you okay? What's going on?"

"It's just, like, I have a lot going on," Eliza says, the words feeling clumsy, her mouth going dry. "You know. With the Miss Riverwood thing in a few weeks and everything."

Olivia narrows her eyes. "You're saying you didn't call me because of some ... county fair competition?"

"Well, and Tutu Camp's taken up my time."

"Uh huh." Olivia combs through a pigtail with her long, unpainted fingernails. "Okay."

"What? You don't know what it's like—I'm basically working a full-time job. It's a lot."

"Yeah, I'm sure it *is* a lot," Olivia says. "Plus you're probably exhausted from all the time you spend on all fours in your room, listening to your mom's sessions."

Eliza swallows. "Ha ha," she says, hoping it's a joke.

"Well, I was going to see if you wanted to hang out," Olivia says slowly. "But ... I'm guessing the answer is no."

"I'm sorry," Eliza says, a little relieved at it being out there.

"What about this weekend?"

"Izzy's having this party by the river for her birthday. I was going with Ezra."

"Right, heard about that. I figured you'd take me with."

"Aren't you afraid of the water?" Eliza asks. "You can't swim."

"But I *can* sit next to a river and drink beer."

Eliza bites the side of her tongue so hard it makes her eyes water. "I don't know. I might not even go. If I do go, I'll call you though. Okay?"

"Okay." Olivia steps forward and puts her arms around Eliza, hugging her tightly. "I love you, even if you're a moody wench."

Eliza forces a little laugh and then pats her friend's back in a halfhearted hug. "We'll talk soon."

They exchange goodbyes. As Eliza walks up the street toward the bus stop, she looks back at Olivia there, backlit in the sun. It's hard to see the details of her face, but her hair has a gold halo around it. She's holding her backpack straps, frozen in the middle of the sidewalk like she has no idea where to go.

Olivia was planning to hitch herself to Eliza, wasn't she? Just pack her backpack and come on over and spend the night. How annoying. The audacity of inviting yourself places is beyond Eliza's comprehension.

But once she gets on the bus and slips into her seat

and stares out the window, the green river stretching parallel to the highway like a road made of water, Eliza thinks of what her dad said, about Olivia's home life being awful. Eliza knows it's true. Olivia doesn't talk about her dad much except to say he's a drunk and he embarrasses her. That's probably why she wants to stay over all the time. And maybe why she wants to kill him.

Eliza thought about telling her parents about what Olivia said. But the last time she confided in her parents, it was a disaster.

Last year, her friend Amanda Hart said something about her mom slapping her and it bothered Eliza so much she told her mom. Then, to Eliza's horror, her mom called CPS. Amanda got put in foster care and moved upstate. Eliza never saw her again, but Amanda called her once in tears to tell Eliza she ruined her life.

It still haunts Eliza.

After that phone call, she stomped downstairs and interrupted her mom mid-session to yell at her, using the same words that Amanda used on her.

"You ruined my life!" Eliza yelled, not caring that her makeup was probably smeared and that she was in her mini robe and that her mom's client could see her.

"Um, if you can—if you can excuse me, I have a bit of a personal emergency on my hands. I'll reach out soon to reschedule," Angela said in her irritatingly soothing, proper therapist voice, and then shut her computer and sprang up from her ergonomic chair. Her nostrils flared and her voice resumed its normal pitch. "What the *hell* is wrong with you?"

"Amanda is in foster care now!" Eliza said. "Because of you! Because you called fucking CPS—"

"Eliza, I am a *mandated reporter*," her mom said. "I'm obligated by law—"

"For your clients, Mom, not for, like, your daughter telling you things in *private*."

Her mom put her hands on her hips. Her cheeks were reddening, a sign that she was fuming and trying very hard to keep herself under control. "I consider it a responsibility as a human being to report when I hear children are being abused."

"Amanda says it was one time. And it was, like, funny. She slapped her mom first. And now her entire family's split apart and Amanda is miserable and living in a foster home and it's all your fault."

"Lize," her mom said. Or maybe she said, "Lies." Didn't matter. Who cares what her mom said—bullshit, all of it.

"I'm never telling you anything ever again," Eliza said.

She spun on her heel and left.

Eliza is a girl of her word. She's never trusted her mom since. Her mom's loyalty will always be to her private practice, not to her own daughter. Eliza doesn't trust her dad, either, because her dad tells her mom everything. Two obnoxious peas in one obnoxious pod.

Nope, Eliza thinks, peering out the window as the bus chugs to the bottom of her hill, where sidewalks are pebbled and the streetlamps are old-fashioned and the proud houses have lawns that stretch out like parks. She pulls the string for the next stop. She's just going to have to pretend she never heard what she heard and slowly vibe Olivia away. Eliza will stay busy. She'll start hanging out with some of her old crew again.

Eventually, Olivia will get the message.

OLIVIA

When Olivia doesn't have anyone to take her anywhere, which is often, she simply walks home from downtown.

It's a two-and-a-half mile walk that takes an hour. The first part of it sucks, because she has to walk along the highway. There's no walking path, so she uses the narrow bike lane. It's loud, muddy in the spring, and dusty in the summer. It smells like manure because it runs alongside a long row of lettuce farms. It's also embarrassing because it's the one road that goes in and out of town and no one in their right mind walks it. She gets honked at and hooted at sometimes. But then the trees thicken and the river path opens up and she can cut into the woods, the hairpin trail decorated with clover and purple wildflowers. Instead of hearing the rush of cars, she hears the rush of the river. She can take the whole path home and it gives her time to think.

Sometimes things take time to percolate. Today, Friday evening after her run-in with Eliza downtown, Olivia's brow furrows as she contemplates what happened. When she first starts the walk, she feels almost sorry for her friend. Eliza looked so miserable—tired, haggard, her eyeliner a smudgy mess. And she's right. She's worked a full-time job all summer, which should be illegal. The whole upside of being a teenager and having zero power is that you don't owe the world anything. Olivia would lose her mind having to corral a bunch of rich brats in tutus around a dance studio all summer.

But by the time she gets to the river path, Olivia's thoughts take a turn.

It starts with a seed of bitterness, a whisper in her head. Eliza's a bit of a privileged weakling. Isn't she? The volume of the bitter voice turns up. *Oh, woe is me! Life's so hard because I have a cush summer job to save up for my car that we all know Mommy and Daddy are going to buy for me anyway! Oh, poor me, I have to practice for some numbskull Podunk competition I pretend I don't really want to be in because I'm a foolish little mouse who doesn't know what I want or how I feel!* It's satisfying when that voice takes over. Olivia kicks a rock and watches it dive into the brook, a wave of delight washing over her. *My name is Eliza Hunter and I think Halloween is a whole personality!*

On Olivia's first day at Riverwood High, she spotted Eliza across the noisy English classroom first period before the bell rang and thought, *I pick her. That's my new best friend.* This is how Olivia is. When she sees something she likes, she goes and grabs it, because no one is going to give it to her.

Most of the other students in the classroom had ensemble energy. These were extras and not leading players. This was her fifth high school in three years, she'd seen this movie before. Dudes who wear sports jerseys even though they don't play anything. Girls sucking in their cheeks and taking selfies. Pale nerds trying to vanish into thin air. Everyone talking over each other.

But then there was Eliza, a girl with an air of mystery about her. You know how in true crime shows, the cliché description of every dead girl is that she "lit up a room"? Well, Eliza was the opposite. She darkened the room like a black light. Her long hair was glossy and dyed black, her eyeliner too heavy, her jean jacket covered in pins. She wore fishnets and combat boots. Though Olivia didn't lean goth or whatever style this was that Eliza was going for, Olivia instantly felt a kinship with the sad-looking girl in the corner.

"Hey." Olivia slid into the seat next to Eliza's. She flashed a smile and pointed to one of the pins on Eliza's jacket, some band she'd never heard of. "Nice. Love those guys."

"Yeah, they're pretty cool."

"I'm digging your entire vibe right now," Olivia said, gesturing to Eliza's general existence.

Eliza's lips perked up into a half-smile. "Thanks."

Though Eliza's tone was deadpan, Olivia could tell she had hooked Eliza in, that she had piqued her curiosity. Making friends was a little bit like reeling in a big fish. Just watch. By April, they'd be inseparable.

"I'm Olivia."

"Eliza." Eliza sat up a little straighter in her chair. "Are you new or something?"

"Yeah. Just moved here from Michigan. Before that it was Ohio, Florida, SoCal, New Mexico."

"Whoa. You move a lot."

"Dad was a trucker for years."

Their conversation was interrupted by an asshole cliché in a football uniform who bumped between them in the aisle and barked, "Out of the way, Morticia Addams." Olivia noticed the way Eliza flinched when he said it. She looked tough, but she was a softie.

"Is that supposed to be an insult?" Olivia asked, turning around to the asshole cliché who was taking a seat behind her. "Morticia Addams is a total fox. You look like a human ham."

A few people overheard and laughed and someone said, "*Day*-um. She clocked you, bro!"

Olivia didn't care that the class had quieted and attention had shifted to her, or that the human ham glared at her like he wanted to pound her face in. All she cared about was that Eliza had lit up, a gorgeous smile spreading, and Olivia knew that she'd won her over in record time. Olivia can read people like it's nobody's business. She loves the challenge of getting what she wants out of them. Sometimes it really feels like the world is Olivia's puppet show.

But today, as Olivia walks along the river replaying the memory, it doesn't feel like her puppet show anymore. Something shifted. This isn't how things are supposed to go. When did it shift? This week? What happened? Is it that Olivia caught Eliza snooping like a creeper on her mom's sessions?

Or is it that Olivia said she was going to kill her dad and Eliza's now wary of her like a little wimp?

Olivia's not going to let her friend go that easily.

She turns through the trees and crosses the highway again, that familiar vise tightening as the trailer park comes into view. She spots her dad's truck like a distant red flag. Which Dad is she in for today? Who knows. She hasn't seen him in two days, which could be a good or bad sign. He's either been working hard or drinking hard. He wasn't mortifying himself on his soapbox outside the church today, she knows that.

By the time she walks through the front door, the invisible vise is so tight Olivia feels a little sick. *Sick*, she thinks. *Ill. Unwell. Ailing. Queasy.* But the kitchen's clean, there are no beer bottles, and her dad's sitting on the living room couch in front of the television. His hair's wet, a recent shower. His face sunburnt—that means he worked today. He mutes the pastor on the screen talking about eternal life.

"Hey Ollie," he says.

"Hey Dad," she says, relief washing over her.

"How was your day?"

"Boring. Just hanging out downtown."

"You walk home?"

"I did."

"If I'd have known, I'd have picked you up."

"That's okay."

He watches her like he wants to say more. Olivia knows he wants to apologize. She can smell remorse the same way she smelled alcohol the last time she walked into the trailer. But her dad will never apologize. He'll act nice. He'll bring her something he thinks she likes—a chocolate brownie, a cheap bracelet. He'll cook dinner and play the role of Dad With His Shit Together until next time. But it's too late.

It doesn't matter that he's this version of her dad today, the one she once thought she loved.

She's going to kill him.

In fact, she wants to kill him even more when he has this hangdog look in his blue eyes.

"I have homework to do," she says, turning into the hall.

"On a Friday night?" he calls after her. "I was hoping we could watch a movie."

But she's already shut the door and locked it. She plops on her bed and glances up at the black widows in jars. Over the past week she found two more on the side of the house near the trash bins. She's collected five of them now, all patiently waiting in their little glass rooms. According to the internet, she can keep them for months without feeding them. She comes closer and gazes at them, whispering hello and *tap-tap-tapp*ing the glass.

Olivia's bedroom window looks straight onto the carport at her dad's truck, which is why she usually keeps her blinds closed. That embarrassing truck. That truck where fights happened. The time he grabbed her hair so hard and then—she doesn't want to think about it. Ever, ever, ever. With a shaking hand, she takes out her phone and opens an incognito window and searches *how to cut someone's brakes*. Apparently all she needs are bolt cutters.

There's a small set of bolt cutters in her dad's toolbox.

Olivia gets a rush that's almost sexual in the way it pours over her and perks her up. She's inspired. Let's get it over with, why wait? She doesn't need to buy rat poison or learn how to pick nightshade. She doesn't need a partner in crime. She can wait until he falls asleep, snip his brake line, and her dad will get up early in the morning to work his Saturday morning shift where the farm is. He'll drive up the hill and then down into the valley and then when he tries to pump the brakes and slow down, his foot will reach the floor.

Lying on her bed, hands behind her head, Olivia eyes the pictures on her wall. From the outside, she would maybe look like a girl daydreaming about movie stars or crushes. But no.

Olivia is dreaming of murder.

She dreams of the satisfying *snap* of his brake line as she severs them. She dreams of her father screaming with his hands on the wheel, his truck hurtling off the road and rolling, *bam-bam-bam*, metal crunching, windows shattering, his neck snapping like a wishbone, the car exploding into flames. She knows how wrong it is. She knows once it's done, it's a horror she'll have to learn to live with. She doesn't care. Because guess what? The man deserves it. He's never cared about how wrong his actions are. So why should she?

After all, she's her father's daughter.

EZRA

zra isn't into parties. They bring out the idiocy in people. The only way to tolerate the experience is to get loaded enough that he becomes an idiot, too. He's working on doing just that, sitting on the picnic bench next to the river and gulping a beer down as Izzy and Eliza lay out a few picnic blankets and set up some snacks on another picnic table.

"Thanks for all your help, dick," Izzy says as she passes him, panting and lugging a cooler.

"Whatever," Ezra says. "I loaded everything into your truck. Only fair you two unload it."

"It's my birthday," Izzy says.

"No, it was your birthday on Thursday," he yells after her. "Stop milking it."

Ezra finishes that first beer and wipes his lip. A part of him starts feeling guilty for not helping, but he squashes it down. He deserves to rest. He isn't some lazy ass, he really did work hard helping Izzy with all this party bullshit today. They went to Costco and shopped like a married couple. He grabbed a ton of beach chairs from his family's garage. He did the ice run. He doesn't even want to be here and honestly doesn't even know why Izzy is so into parties when she generally dislikes most of humankind.

The sky's getting dark, the last gasp of sunset up there, and the river gleams and whispers. It doesn't look as green here as it does downtown. It's clear enough to see the colorful stones and darting silver fish and shallow enough that you can roll up your pants and walk across it. Even so, just watch—in a few hours people will be parked there in floaties that don't move. By the end of the night, someone will skinnydip in six inches of water.

This, here, is tradition. This is the Riverwood party spot. It's been here for decades and it will be here for decades more. Hundreds of birthdays, graduations, and excuses for getting collectively wasted have happened here. During the day it's family parties and at night it's teenage ragers. Weird to think that once upon a time, his parents met here. He can't imagine his mom even being in a place like this—she thinks alcohol "clouds the mind." When she celebrates anything, she passes on the champagne and pours kombucha into her flute.

When the truck's unloaded, Izzy goes to find a tree to piss behind and Eliza comes and stands next to Ezra.

"Why are you pouting and being a weirdo?" Eliza asks.

"I'm not. I'm just not that excited to be here."

"So what? It's your best friend's birthday."

Ezra rolls his eyes. Perfect Eliza. Eliza who can do no wrong. She might look tough to other people because she wears all black and has knife earrings dangling from her ears but the clothes are from Target and her earrings are plastic and fake. Behind it all, Ezra sees the real Eliza, the brown-haired Eliza who's spent her life getting straight As and playing piano or dancing around in a tutu. She's utterly normal under that costume.

"What is up with you lately?" Eliza asks, sitting next to him. "You've been acting weird. Even Izzy said so."

"I'm just tired," he lies.

The thought of Izzy talking to his sister about him makes Ezra want to pick up a rock and smash Izzy's skull with it. There it is, that ugly thought again. He doesn't know why. Sometimes ugly thoughts just get stuck in his head like a catchy song. Last summer it started at the butcher shop. It started with the thought of what it would feel like to fuck a piece of meat. He couldn't shake it until he went through with it. Then it finally stopped bothering him. No, he won't smash Izzy's skull, but he's tired of thinking about it. He's so sick of himself.

"Oh shit," Eliza whisper-moans, gazing past Ezra.

Ezra turns to see what she's whining about. It's only Olivia walking up the path that leads here. She waves, still far away.

"What?" Ezra asks, confused.

"I just—I don't want to hang out with her."

"Why?"

"It's—" Eliza shakes her head. She's getting all red in the face. Clearly some girl drama went down.

"Hey!" Olivia comes over and throws her arms around Eliza. "Am I the first to get here?"

"Yep," Eliza says with a tight smile.

Olivia winks at him. "Hey psycho."

Ugh, that nickname. That wink. And Ezra resents the fact that Olivia looks that good. He tries not to study her cleavage or the shapes of her legs. He knows that's what she wants. She wants him to want her. He doesn't want to want her, and he certainly doesn't want her to know if he *does* want her. Which, of course, he doesn't.

"I thought you were going to call me," Olivia says, her hand on Eliza's arm.

"Oh I know—the day was super busy. I was helping Izzy get ready."

"Happy birthday!" Olivia says, waving.

Izzy joins them, wiping her hands on her overalls. She raises an eyebrow at Ezra. She's not a fan of Olivia. She thinks Olivia shoplifted a crystal from her mom's store. Jesus, the party hasn't even officially started and Ezra already wants to walk into the river to avoid the drama.

Right then, a bunch of people start arriving all at once. No one brings presents, but they do bring more beer. A lot more. Soon it's dark and a stereo blasts hip-hop and drowns out the sound of the crickets. Ezra mills around, tipping his beer at people and having a few painfully awkward conversations. Of course, Izzy says she didn't invite that many people and still somehow fifty people showed up. Izzy's a weirdo, but a beloved one. Once the bonfire starts, Ezra's on his third beer and feeling pretty good. He smiles and stares at the flames getting higher and higher. He wonders what everyone would do if he jumped into it.

This is life now since he recently decided he's a psychopath. He's still getting used to it. It's a series of going through the motions. Feelings are performative. He's always wondered what's wrong with him, why his thoughts go in such disturbing directions and won't let him go. This isn't him following in his dad's true crime footsteps like he tried to say the other night during that bizarro, failed heart-to-heart. This isn't depression like his mom suggested recently. To be fair, his mom is such a superfan of the DSM-V that she'd diagnose a block of cheese with depression and prescribe it Zoloft if she could. No, this is something much more serious, much more untreatable. His mom would be devastated if she knew that she birthed a psychopath.

"Hey," a voice beside him says.

It's Olivia looking up at him. She hands him a beer. The flames are flickering in the pupils of her eyes. Squeals of joy drift from the river and people sway to the music nearby, but it's just the two of them here by the fire.

"What's up?" he asks, a little friendlier because of the beer. He takes it from her and they cheers.

"I don't think your sister likes me anymore," Olivia says.

Ezra makes a noncommittal sound, already bored by the conversation.

"She's acting weird," Olivia goes on.

"What else is new?"

"Has she said anything about me?"

"This might shock you, but my sister and I don't sit around talking about you."

Olivia does an exaggerated pout. "You still like me though?"

It takes a lot of effort to not look at her boobs.

"I never liked you," he says.

"Because you're a psychopath."

"Because you're annoying."

"What's so annoying about me?" she says. "I'll bet if you got to know me you wouldn't say that."

He rolls his eyes. She beckons him closer to her with her finger, as if she wants to tell him something. He leans his ear in.

"I tried to murder my dad today," she says.

The hot blow of her words, of her breath, releases an electric shiver through him. He leans back and studies her, his vision a little blurry from the alcohol.

"Sure you did."

"Come walk with me," she says, pulling his sleeve.

Seriously? Why is she playing games with him? Reluctantly, Ezra follows Olivia away from the fire, away from the party, down the bank a bit and away from the squealers in the water. Ezra spots his sister shaking her head at him as she sits on a stump drinking from her cup. Who cares what she thinks. Olivia leads Ezra over a giant tree root and pulls him down next to it. Here, they're hidden; the party is invisible, nothing but noise behind them competing with the rush of the river's flow. They face the darkness of the forest. All at once, Ezra gets very turned on realizing they're alone here and he can't help himself from imagining Olivia's lips on his.

"I did," Olivia says quietly. "I tried to murder my dad today."

"I've never known anyone more full of shit than you."

She sighs out her nose.

"Okay, fine. How?" he asks.

"I cut the brake line on his truck."

"Uh-huh."

"It didn't work though." In the moonlit shadows, her eyes shine. "He crashed into a mailbox on the side of the highway."

Ezra eyes her, trying to figure her out. Is this for real? Ezra has a pretty good bullshit detector, which is why he's had the sense to steer clear of Olivia until now. She seems like the kind of person who will tell people anything they want to hear as long as she gets something out of it. But what could she possibly want from him? What would be the motivation for making up a whopper like this?

"You cut your dad's brake line," he repeats. "Prove it."

"I don't have to prove anything to you."

"If you're going to make up a story like that then yeah, ya do."

Olivia shakes her head. There's something about her lack of expression, the way she isn't trying at all, that makes him think that maybe, just maybe, she's telling the truth.

He swigs his beer. "Okay, I'll humor you. Why?"

"Because I hate him."

"You hate your dad."

"Yeah."

Ezra's baffled. Even as an admitted psychopath, he's never planned on murdering his parents. Far more extreme than fantasizing about bashing in your best friend's skull.

"Why? What did he do?" Ezra asks, still not quite believing her.

"You really want to know?" Olivia says. "Like, for reals-reals?"

Ezra nods. She reaches out in the dark and, like a warm spider, her fingers crawl down his arm and then her palm is against his. She squeezes his hand and at first he doesn't know how to feel about this. His heart's a jack-hammer. Finally, he squeezes back.

"I'm not going to give you some sob story about my life," she says softly. "Even if there is one. My mom was an addict and she tried to stab my dad to death when I was still in diapers. She's been in prison my whole life. I don't even remember her."

"Holy shit."

"Oh, I'm just getting started. So my dad raised me. It's always been the two of us. And it wasn't bad. Like we never had money and we were always moving because my dad was in the trucking business until last year, but he was a nice, sober, upstanding guy for basically the first ten years of my life. Then he started drinking again." She clears her throat. "All day. Every day. From dry to drowning in it. And it was like he just changed overnight.

A switch got flipped. I can't explain it. I mean, I'm trying to explain it." Her voice shakes a little and Ezra holds her hand still in his, wanting to know more. "He gets angry when he drinks. Age-old story. Yelling, throwing things, everything. It's why my mom tried to stab him, apparently. I wish she'd succeeded."

"Does he hurt you?"

"Yes, but it's not even just that, Ezra," she says. And the way she says his name, it's like she has a new voice. It's like Olivia's mask fell off and here she is: raw, vulnerable, the pink creature that lives beneath the shell. "Like yes, he's hurt me when he's been drinking. But that's not even what makes me want to kill him. It's—when that switch flipped, I lost him. Even when he doesn't drink, he's not the same person anymore." She leans her head back on the tree, exposing her pale throat, which Ezra suddenly has the deranged urge to kiss. "He's completely changed. This thing happened when I was thirteen. He made me—he—I don't want to get into it. But it was really bad. After that happened, he started going to church and being like *obsessed* with church. Like pathological."

"What happened?" Ezra asks, confused.

She gives him a long blank look, one so far away it's like a lobotomized patient. "Something that I'll never let myself think about again."

Ezra's stomach flops sickly as his mind fills in the horrible blanks with multiple scenarios. Ezra is a psychopath. He doesn't have a heart. But he can feel the ghost of one, the heart society taught him to have, breaking for her.

"He's not the person who raised me." She dabs under her eyes, though she doesn't appear to be crying. "He's just not. I mean, yeah, there are glimpses, but they're gone in a blink. It's like something broke inside him. He's either drinking and he's a complete asshole or he's absolutely one-track-mind obsessed with a tug-of-war between Jesus and Satan. You know that crazy guy who yells outside the church on the Dick?"

Takes a minute for the words *church on the Dick* to make sense. Finally he says, "Yeah?"

"That's my fucking dad, dude."

Ezra lets the shock of that sink in as he downs the last of his beer. "Seriously?"

"Yup," she says bitterly.

Is this for real? Is he dreaming right now? He's sitting under a tree holding hands with Olivia West while she tells him about why she wants to murder her dad. Weirdest night ever.

"That's why I want to kill him," she says. "I snipped his brakes thinking it'd be easier, that I wouldn't even have to see it, but that didn't work. I'm going to have to try something else. Rat poison, maybe."

She chucks her beer bottle and they hear the crunch of glass shattering. Ezra considers giving her shit for littering, but when someone's telling you about plans for patricide, why bother? They lock eyes. No idea why, but his heart's still pounding. Probably a learned response. Or maybe just a biological one.

"Why would you tell me this shit, Olivia?"

"Because I thought you would understand." She puts

a hand to his cheek for just a second, as if she's checking his temperature. "Psycho."

He narrows his eyes. "Because ... you saw me check some books out of the library?"

"No. Because I think you and I are the same."

"You think we're both psychopaths?"

"I don't know if that's what I'd say, exactly, but I do think we could kill someone and move on with our lives and not let it bother us."

It's such a batshit thing to say that Ezra lets out a laugh.

"Come on," she says. "You know it's true."

"I mean, anyone could kill and move on under the right circumstances," he says. "That's what the entire military experience is predicated on, right? The idea that people can be trained to kill if they have the right reason?"

Ezra's considered joining the Marines on more than one occasion for this very reason.

"*Freedom*," Olivia says mockingly.

"Exactly."

"Freedom," she says again, not mockingly this time. "Yeah, anyone can kill for freedom. I guess I'm no different." She puts a hand on his knee. "But you—if you're really a psychopath—you could kill and feel nothing. Or if you're anything like those bad boys in those books you like to read, maybe you could kill and *enjoy* it." She squeezes his knee, making him reflexively jerk because it's so ticklish. She seems to enjoy his reaction, smiling big enough that he sees a dimple in her cheek that he's never noticed until now. "Do you think you could kill my dad for me?"

"Are you seriously asking me to murder your dad?"

"I'm just asking if you think you *could*."

"If I wanted to."

"Have you ever killed anything before?"

Ezra swallows the shame. Shame's a lie. Shame would never exist if it weren't for other people. A little wind blows Olivia's hair and the contrast of moonlight and shadows on her face makes her different, makes her a masterpiece. She stills, waiting for his answer. He's never told anyone this before. He hasn't even had the guts to write it down in his notebook.

"I killed a raccoon once," he says.

When those five words leave his mouth, they feel stupid. Like it isn't the big deal he makes it out to be in his head.

Olivia's face doesn't falter. "Story, please."

"I was riding my bike a few months ago and—you know that path that runs along the river?"

"Know it well."

"You know where the rope swing is?"

She shakes her head.

"Well, I walked my bike down there and there was this ... high-pitched shrieking." Ezra hear it in his mind. It's an audio clip that replays often. "Piercing. It got under my skin and made me want to turn inside out." Ezra remembers the way his hairs stood on end—how at first he thought it was a person and it scared and excited him at the same time. "I followed the sound."

Olivia's eyes widen. "Creepy."

"When I got there," Ezra says, sitting up straighter. "I found this albino raccoon and its leg was stuck in a hunter's trap."

"What the fuck is an albino raccoon?"

"It's exactly what it sounds like, genius."

Olivia punches his arm and Ezra smiles a little as he flinches. Maybe he likes the crap they give each other. Maybe they've been flirting all along.

"And?" she says. "Get to the good part."

"It was a really pretty creature, honestly," he says. "It looked like a little white teddy bear with a puffy tail." Ezra lets a pause build as he approaches the climax. "And I looked it in the eyes and I picked up a rock and I smashed its head in."

Once again, Olivia appears totally unperturbed. She'd kill it at poker. Is she seriously not horrified by his story?

"I smashed it once, then twice, then three times," he says.

Still, nothing flickers in her expression.

"Felt its skull crack like an eggshell," he says.

Olivia blinks.

"There was blood all over my hands," he says.

Finally, Olivia's brows furrow. "A mercy killing."

"What? No it wasn't. Mercy would have been to open the trap and let it go."

"It was already injured."

"Well, shit. Sorry my killing story wasn't good enough for you, princess."

She laughs.

"Have *you* killed anything?" he asks.

She shakes her head. "I did start a wildfire once in Michigan." She leans in closer and whispers, "Burned a barn down."

"Pyromania too," he says. "Man, you have it all. My mom would have a field day with you."

"You'd better not say a fucking word—"

"Come on. Give me a little more credit, I'm not going to tell my mom."

Olivia leans her head on his shoulder and they stay like that awhile. Ezra feels as if the plot of tonight's story is like one of those fat sci-fi paperbacks he used to read. A wormhole to the multiverse opened and in this wacky universe, he's smitten with Olivia West. Distantly, sounds of the party still drift in and out—a swell of laughter, someone playing the guitar, water splashing. None of it matters.

"How would you kill my dad if you were me?" Olivia asks.

Ezra yawns. "Gun?"

"If you didn't have a gun readily available."

"Hit him on the head with a baseball bat. I don't know."

"And hypothetically speaking, what would it take for me to get you to help me?"

"I'm not going to help you murder your dad, Olivia."

"Just watch me change your mind."

Ezra stares at her. This is insanity. And yet he's lit with something—the first something resembling a real feeling he's had in who knows how long. Is desire a feeling? Is need? It's hard to tell what this is. He's incredibly turned on. It isn't just something happening in his pants. His entire being is turned on. Olivia has put him on alert and he can't stop looking at her. And then, as if in slow motion, she stands up on her knees and moves onto his lap, straddling him, and they kiss like two starving animals in the dark. He didn't realize how hungry he was until now.

"See?" she whispers in his ear.

"I won't help you." He slips a hand up the back of her dress. "But I will *support* you."

She dives in for another long, savory kiss. "I've always wanted an accomplice."

He's throbbing. She's beautiful. His sister is thirty feet away from them as they make out against the trunk of the tree. What a goddamn mess they're making. Funny how it takes patience in life to build anything worth having but only a minute to destroy it. His sister will kill him when she finds out what they're doing. Izzy will kill him. Actually, they aren't capable of killing anything—it's Olivia West who's apparently capable of that. That's why this feels so right. Olivia's lips are plump, soft, with a succulent force to them, wet and warm and tasting of candy and blood.

As they continue devouring each other's faces, Ezra pulls Olivia to him as tightly as he can, a squeak escaping her. He's jarred by an unexpected shiver that moves up his spine and the sudden urge to cry. He's made out with girls before; hell, he had sex with Sonia Reynaldo last year. Is he really about to spill tears like a baby because of a makeout session with his sister's friend? He exchanges a look with the scatter of silver stars above their heads and gets that *fuck it* feeling he had when jumping off a bridge into the river. Either it will kill him, it will leave him paralyzed, or it will make him feel more alive than ever before.

Maybe Olivia West is what he's needed all along—the person most like him in the world, hidden in plain view.

CARSON

"Olivia West!"

Carson stands in the *Household Chemicals* aisle of the downtown hardware store. To his surprise, Olivia just came around the corner and now they've found themselves face to face among the mousetraps and bug sprays. In Carson's hand, he holds a package that says "Rat Killer." Olivia seems so stunned to see him she's frozen, her eyes wide, her mouth open.

"What a coincidence!" he says. "Did I scare you?"

"Yeah." She relaxes with a laugh and steps forward. "I didn't—I wasn't expecting to see you."

Something about Olivia is so … antiquated. She's an anachronism. Her long hair parted in the middle, her shift dress and Mary Janes. She could have stepped out of a twentieth-century issue of *Life* magazine. Carson knows it's wrong to impose his opinion about his daughter's fashion choices—Angela and Carson agreed to let them be themselves—but he wishes Eliza would give up the funeral couture and dress with a little more class like Olivia.

"What are you here for?" Olivia says, glancing at the bag he holds as if trying to read it.

"Oh! Rat poison." He pats the bag. "So funny, right? We were just talking about rat poison."

"We were." She turns to the aisle and plucks a pack of mousetraps off the rack. "Just here to pick up a few things for the house."

"How's the book going?"

"Good! I haven't started it yet. I'm still figuring out the plot."

"Well, I'm here if you need to bounce ideas around. You coming over anytime soon?"

"Maybe ... I don't know. I saw Ezra and Eliza last night at Izzy's birthday."

Carson inhales deeply, lovely hazy memories of river parties from years past. "Fun times." He reaches out and places a hand on Olivia's shoulder, bare and warm under his palm. "Have a good day and reach out if you need me."

After paying for the rat killer, Carson heads across the sunny parking lot, saying hello to the people he passes and whistling the gliding synth riff that opens one of his favorite songs, "Big Poppa" by Notorious B.I.G. He gets into the SUV and waits a moment with his hands on the wheel. There's something still spinning inside him even as he sits still. A longing.

Olivia stirs something in him. Is it creepy, how he touched her shoulder back there? Is his genuine interest in her creative endeavors a bit too much? God, he hopes he doesn't come across as some creepy old dude. Carson glances at the rearview. No matter how many times he looks, he's never ready to see the wrinkles forming around his eyes, the occasional silver hairs, the fullness of his cheeks. Every picture someone takes of him is a shock. That's really him? In his mind, in his heart, he still feels twenty years old.

After the night when Carson first met Angela, the river party lived with him for years. The memory of it, after enough replay, took on a sort of mythology. Angela became more than an out-of-his-league girl he'd wooed once. She grew in importance to a human goddess. She might have lived in Arizona, but she still had a full-time residence in his head. Carson skipped college, too boring, he hated sitting still, and interned at the *Riverwood Gazette*. He started in obituaries, moved to sports, and by his third year he was on the crime beat. Didn't pay well but it sure gave him a rush every day to chase stories all over the county and to be known by name at the courthouse. Every girl he dated, he knew he would dump in a heartbeat if Angela ever came back into his life, but she didn't come back into his life—until he was twenty-two and assigned a blotter story about an assault and battery. The perpetrator's name? Angela Atkins.

Carson's phone buzzes. Speak of the devil, it's Angela.

How long can it possibly take to pick one thing up from the hardware store?

"For the love of," Carson says, putting on his seatbelt. "What, Ange, you sitting at home with a timer?"

As Carson heads out of the parking lot, there's Olivia again, walking to the bus stop. He beeps the horn. She looks startled as he rolls to a stop next to her.

"Need a ride?" Carson asks. He points with his chin to her bags. "Looks like you've got a lot to carry."

Olivia appears to consider it as she glances down at her bags, but shakes her head.

"No, you go ahead. Thanks, though." She smiles. "Tell Ezra I say hi."

"Will do," he says, saluting.

Saluting? Carson doesn't know why he did that. He rolls up his window and drives home, putting on "Big Poppa" and rapping passionately along with it. It isn't until the song is over that the thought occurs to him: Wait. Ezra? Did Olivia just ask him to say hi to Ezra and not Eliza?

He must have heard her wrong.

Angela

Sundays are supposed to be when Carson takes care of things.

Angela keeps a running list tacked to the refrigerator along with her collection of fruit magnets. There's the rodent problem, the gutters that need cleaning, the furnace issue, the mildew smell in the garage. She's breathing fine and yet she's drowning. She gets so upset seeing that Carson didn't take out the trash that, after taking it out her freaking self, she goes into her office and punches the throw pillow on her sofa that says *Blessed*. Then she remembers she has a call with Jaycee's mom Elvira, who alluded to some kind of emergency, and Angela gets up and goes to the mirror to smooth her hair. She sits at her desk and pops a pill. As she opens her laptop, she can hear Carson's footsteps thundering down the basement stairs.

"Hey gorgeous," he says, opening her door.

He's in one of his "moods," bounding down the stairs

and buttering her up in hopes of a couch quickie. So transparent.

"What the heck took you so long?" she asks.

Carson comes behind her and massages her shoulders. "Oh, come on, I wasn't gone for more than thirty minutes."

"Not now."

"Not now what?" he asks innocently, bending down to kiss her neck.

Angela melts at the touch of his lips but pushes him away. "I have a call."

"Tell them you're running late. I won't take long."

"No," she says a bit more sharply.

He stands up and sighs in defeat, squeezing her shoulders and taking a few steps back. He pretends to be interested in her bookshelf for a few seconds, touching the spines, before he turns back around.

"It's been what—three weeks?"

"Have you been living in a hole?" she says. "Sometimes I feel like I carry the entire weight of this family on my shoulders and you can't even be bothered to take out the trash when I ask you to."

"Oh, okay, so that's why you don't want to have sex anymore—because I didn't take out the trash. Thanks for clarifying."

She wants to take off her Croc and throw it at his head when he talks to her like that.

"Did I do something to offend you?" he asks.

"Carson, I would tell you if you did."

"I mean, today you canceled our date because you want me to poison some rats. Really? It couldn't wait?"

"I've been hearing them in that wall!" Angela nearly yells, pointing behind her. "They're—" She closes her eyes. "I'm sorry. I love you. I'm stressed. PMS symptoms. I need to take this call."

"Okay," Carson says, hands up. "Good luck. I'll be massacring rodents if you need me."

He heads upstairs, his footsteps in a much more subdued rhythm this time. Angela massages her temples. Raising her voice at him and acting so uptight—she doesn't want to be like this. She really doesn't. She wants to want sex. It's hard, though. When every damn thing in her life feels like an obligation, pleasure becomes one, too.

She tries to channel those old feelings she had for Carson. The allure and adventure of him—the man who convinced her to jump into the river on the rope swing, who asked her to marry him on a hot air balloon ride, her savior, the only person in the world who shares her darkest secrets. He's handsome and disheveled and goofy and the best dad her kids could ever ask for. And yet she has to wonder at times what it all adds up to if the thrill is gone.

"Hello Ms. Sandoval," Angela says, peering into the screen and checking her face to make sure she looks concerned and not annoyed. "Tell me what's going on."

ELIZA

Eliza heard it all through the vent.

She isn't trying this time, she swears—she quit the bad habit ever since Olivia caught her. Eliza is innocently seated at her desk, working on her stupid speech for the stupid Miss Riverwood competition. Sometimes the sounds drift up whether she likes it or not.

She isn't sure what's worse: the sound of her parents having sex, or the sound of her parents arguing about *not* having sex. Either way, pass the barf bag. Then there's the whole depressing conversation with Jaycee Sandoval's mom tearing Eliza's mom a new one for "pilling" Jaycee out and "zombifying" her "baby." Eliza wanted to run downstairs and interrupt in her mom's defense—*Dr. Hunter is a psychiatrist, idiot!* That's what psychiatrists do, they give your disorder a name and kill it with pills. Also Eliza actually knows Jaycee Sandoval from school. She's seen her rip a freshman's earring out for looking at her funny. If anyone needs zombifying, that's your girl right there.

Meanwhile, Ezra's been laughing in his room and blabbing on and on to someone for almost an hour at this point. He's usually sullen and quiet in there while he blows people's heads off in his imaginary world. But today the rise and fall of his baritone is distracting. He also sounds weirdly playful. To repeat: her brother. *Playful.* She puts in her earbuds and turns up *1989* (*Taylor's version*) and scrawls in her notebook.

> *Stupid Pageant Speech*
>
> *Good evening,* ~~ladies and gentlemen~~ *humans! My name is Eliza Hunter. Welcome to the best-kept secret in the country: Riverwood, California. I'm not going to lie to you all. Growing up, I dreamt of* ~~leaving this place~~ *being a big-city girl. You know, living in a land where you could hear the rush of traffic and the honking of horns, glowing with city lights and bursting with opportunity.* ~~While small-town life might seem boring~~ *But now that I'm older and wiser I've realized* ~~it's not so bad~~ *that everything I wanted was right here all along. Who needs the rush of traffic when you've got the rush of the Full Moon River? Who needs the honking of horns when you have the honks of geese? The glow of city lights could never compare to the glow of the stars in our night skies. Once I wanted the Big Apple. Now*

I'm content with a lifetime supply of straw-
berries.

That time she sprained her ankle was less painful
than this. Writing this speech is like kissing an entire
town's ass. She'd better fucking win. Staring into space,
Eliza lets herself imagine it, really imagine it—an audience applauding for her, a rhinestone crown on her head.
Her mom in the front row, glowing with pride, seeing her
with new eyes. Eliza taps her pen on her paper until she
hears her dad yelling "Dinner!" Grateful for the break,
suddenly realizing how starving she is, she takes the notebook with her and heads to the kitchen.

Sunday night dinners are a whole thing in her house.
Tablecloth, jazz music, battery-operated fake candles.
Her mom usually clips fresh roses or flowers from the
yard and puts them in a jam jar but tonight they're
noticeably absent. Probably Jaycee Sandoval's mom's
fault. Her mom's tired expression is probably her fault,
too. The table is set with cloth napkins and napkin rings
with their names monogrammed on them, a colorful salad
in the center of the table. Her dad waves at her with a
knife he's using to cut the chicken.

"Hey Lize," Angela says as Eliza sits next to her.
"What've you been doing up there?"

"Working on my intro speech for Miss Riverwood."
Eliza pushes the notebook for her mom to see. Nervous,
she asks, "What do you think?"

Angela pulls her reading glasses down from the top of
her head. "Let me give it a read."

"Hey kiddo, can you run upstairs and tell your brother that dinner's ready?" Carson asks as he heaps meat on a serving plate. "He must have his headphones on."

"He's on the phone with someone," Eliza says, standing up.

"Yeah, it sounds like he's talking to a girl," her mom says as she squints at the page.

"A *girl*?" say Eliza and her dad in unison.

Someone might as well have said he's talking to Bigfoot.

"What do you mean?" her dad asks, putting the knife down as if he's trying to focus, to not to get too excited.

"Like a *girl* girl?" Eliza asks, not able to picture it. "Or, like, Izzy?"

"Didn't sound like Izzy," Angela says as she reads. She doesn't seem at all perturbed by this. "He sounded ... different."

"What, Angela—were you eavesdropping?" Carson asks.

"No! Of course not." She shoots Carson a look over her glasses. "I can hear the lilt of your *deep male voices*—" She does her best imitation of a *deep male voice*. "— through the walls."

"Well, good for him." Carson picks up the knife and resumes cutting the chicken into pieces.

The Riverwood Dismemberer, Eliza thinks as she heads up the stairs.

There's a screw turning in her gut as she mounts the landing and slowly walks past her own room. The idea of

Ezra talking to a girl on the phone is weird enough. First off, he never talks on the phone, period. Second, she's wondered if her brother is asexual or something, he seems so disinterested in romance. But what really bugs her is the memory of him and Olivia going off in the bushes for however long last night. He said nothing happened, they were just "talking," but come on. The timing of this chatty call with a mystery girl makes last night's dubious rendezvous even more dubious.

She lingers outside Ezra's door. All she hears is a long silence and then Ezra saying, "John Wayne Gacy!" excitedly. Maybe he's not talking to a girl after all. But then he breaks in with, "You're cute," and Eliza is even more confused. Though she's dying to eavesdrop, she resists the urge and pounds on the door with her fist.

"Dinner!" she yells.

"Jesus Christ," he yells back.

Eliza heads down the stairs. She doesn't even want to know. She really doesn't. She slips back into her seat at the table, the steaming platter of meat in front of her. Her dad sits next to her and points to the chicken.

"It's a mess, I know," he says. "It's usually your brother's job to carve the meat since he's a retired butcher, but I guess he's too busy up there flirting."

"Ew, don't say that," Eliza says, reaching for the salad.

"What? Don't you want him to be happy?"

No comment.

Angela pushes the notebook back to Eliza and takes off her reading glasses. "This speech has potential."

Potential. People always say that word with a

promising flourish, but Eliza's old enough and wise enough to know it's just an insult in disguise.

"So you didn't like it," Eliza says.

"I was just looking for more of a why. You know? It's cute and all. We get it, you used to want to move to New York City but now you see the beauty in your own home-town. But why? What happened? What provoked that change?"

Eliza knows what a popped balloon feels like. Great. She has to slave over that dumb speech some more. This is how it always is with her mom. Everything needs improvement. Nothing she does is impressive.

"Wait, you don't want to move to New York anymore?" Carson asks as he stabs a chicken thigh with his fork and migrates it to his plate with a *plop*.

"I do," Eliza says. "I mean, I definitely want to apply to schools there. NYU's on my list."

Angela fills her plate with salad, no dressing, and a single bite of chicken breast. She's all about body posi-tivity when she gives Eliza pep talks, but when it comes to herself, she eats like a runway model. Do as she says and not as she does and all that.

"You have a list already and your brother up there's about to head into his senior year and doesn't even know if he wants to go to college yet," Angela murmurs, salting her salad.

"Excusé moi, college isn't for everyone," Carson says through a mouthful. "And Ange, with everything else going on, might be nice to save some Benjamins, if you know what I'm saying."

Eliza loves her dad but *Benjamins?* Cringe.

Her brother bounds down the stairs in his socks, a suspicious amount of pep in his step. Eliza raises an eyebrow as he slides into his spot at the table.

"Look what a mess I made of the chicken without you here to carve it," Carson says, pointing to the mountain of flesh with his fork.

"Yikes," Ezra says. "Looks like roadkill."

"So who were you talking to?" Eliza asks.

"No one," Ezra answers, laying his napkin in his lap.

Eliza and her parents collectively stare at Ezra, waiting for his lie to turn into the truth as thcy chew their meal.

"So you're in there laughing and talking to yourself?" Carson asks.

Ezra puts an insane amount of pepper on his meat. Eliza wants to sneeze just looking at it. "You are all incredibly nosy," he says, not looking up but clearly feeling the heat of the family's gaze. Finally, he meets Eliza's eyes, fighting a smile. "It was Olivia, okay?"

"What?" she says, as if she's shocked.

But she's not.

Somehow, without actually thinking the words aloud, she already knows this. She knew when she watched Ezra and Olivia peeling off from the party last night and she knew from the way they came back together with a secretive glow between them. The idea of her brother stealing her friend is a spider that crawls under her skin and now it's laying eggs. It's making her itch and she wants to get up and stomp away but she knows that's childish, that's dumb, why is she fighting tears because her brother talked to her best friend on the phone? Especially when Eliza decided she isn't that into Olivia anyway. Maybe that's what bothers her—the idea of Eliza trying to distance herself from Olivia and being unable to get away from her.

"Well, that's a plot twist," Carson says, reaching out and clapping Ezra on the back as if he's proud of him.

Dude behavior is so bizarre.

Angela just says, "Interesting. I didn't know you two were close."

Ezra shrugs. "I like her."

If anyone else uttered those three words, it would seem like a nothing-statement, a boring admission. But Ezra? Scowling Ezra who locks himself in his room not out of shyness, but because he seems to think he's too good for everyone and everything?

Eliza shakes her head and tries to ignore the sinking feeling because even though her brother is an obnoxious know-it-all, he's her brother. She can still see the little boy in him, the one in the family photographs with the wide smile and bowl cut who came into her room and played dolls with her, who raced bikes with her around the neighborhood during blazing, eternal summers, and who held her hair when she came home drunk after the homecoming dance and vomited in their bathroom. He's the co-star of her childhood. She really doesn't want to see him get hurt. And she has a gut feeling that Olivia's going to hurt him.

"How do you feel about this, future Miss River-wood?" Carson asks. "Ezra and Olivia. Can you see it?"

"Yes, I'm curious about your thoughts," Angela says.

Everyone at the table stops and waits for Eliza to answer. After swallowing a mouthful, Eliza just answers, "I think it's cute!"

Hear how smooth that lie was, how convincing the smile?

Maybe Eliza will make a good Miss Riverwood after all.

OLIVIA

Cutting her dad's brakes on a whim was a bust, obviously.

Olivia cut them too deeply. According to a Reddit discussion, she should have cut juuuust enough that they'd bust farther from home when the truck amped up to a higher speed. Carson said the same thing to her when he was giving her ideas, but Olivia got impatient and sloppy.

She won't be impatient and sloppy next time.

But even the failed attempt comes with a perk. As Olivia gives her plans more thought, she realizes that the easiest place to kill her dad would be at home. And if she kills her dad at home, his truck would still be parked in the carport. And that might make Olivia more likely to be seen as a suspect when he goes missing. But with his truck in the shop now because of the brakes and the minor accident, it makes things easier.

The truck in the shop means her dad has been home

now for days, drunk and muttering and slamming things around. Olivia locks herself in her bedroom when he's conscious and, like a mouse hiding in the shadows, darts out now and then for food and water when he's passed out in his room.

Since the party Saturday night, Olivia's been walking on sunshine. She went there to stalk Eliza but ended up making out with Ezra instead. She's still dizzy with surprise at how it all played out. And here's the weirdest part: Olivia is truly smitten with Ezra. She's not faking it. She's always had a thing for him. And that night was pure magic. She's never been able to just show someone the monster she is underneath her girl costume. Everyone else runs away when she flashes them a glimpse—like that little creampuff of a sister of his. But not Ezra. Ezra saw it and was turned on. And under the moonlight, next to the river, Olivia got the most delicious shivers all over her when she realized that Ezra is just like her. He, too, has an inner monster he keeps hidden from the world.

Olivia's monster hasn't always been there. Her monster was made, not born. It started that night that she will never let herself fully remember. It started because she saw the monster that lives inside her father. Maybe monsters are contagious. As her father grabbed her hair and pulled her inside the house, as he dragged her kicking and screaming into his dark room and talked to her like she was a woman and not a girl, a whore and not his daughter, Olivia's lights went out. That's it—they went out. She was so scared, the world seemed to have ripped right open and she was falling, and then she just went into a place inside herself that was quiet and deep enough that no one could hurt her, not even the man who was pinning her to his bed with his hand to her throat. In that quiet, deep place within, she imagined it was like the inside of her music box. The plastic ballerina folded into herself and it was warm and velvet in there and she was alone.

After that horrible night was all over, Olivia went into her room. Everything hurt in her body, but her mind was oddly clear. She just thought, I'm never going to think about that again. That wasn't real. It was a bad dream. She took the experience and she locked it in a room in her mind and she ate the key. She and her dad never speak of it. Her dad talks about repenting for his sins a lot though and cries sometimes when he's drunk asking for her forgiveness, though he never says for what. And she doesn't want him to. On the surface of her mind, it never happened, it was never there.

On the surface.

That was when she was thirteen, over three years ago. Three years, when you're a teenager, is enough time to change into a different person. It's enough time for fear to turn into rage and enough time for a monster to mature. When the thought first occurred to her a year or so ago that she wanted to kill her father, she didn't let herself dwell on it. It seemed crazy. It was a terrifying thought to have—killing the man who raised her, the man she thought she loved. But the more the thought returned, the more she realized that she doesn't love him. She loves the person she thought he was. That man died when she was thirteen. And she isn't terrified of killing him. She's only terrified of not getting away with it.

It's easy to think about doing it now. It's the easiest thing in the world. Because he's pounding on her door and won't leave her alone.

"Olivia Wren, I'm gonna bust this door down if you keep ignoring me. This is *my* house, you understand? I will not tolerate disre*spect!*"

It's Tuesday afternoon and he's been yelling through the door on and off for an hour now. She had a wonderful two days of silence when her dad disappeared. She lived a whole fantasy imagining he'd never return, just vanish into thin air, one of those alien abduction stories she's seen on TV. But then he came home disheveled, in a cab, cursing and smelling like BO and still wearing the dirt-streaked clothes he wore when he went to work on Saturday. Sadly, he's still very much alive. Angry at nobody. Now knocking and yelling at her.

Olivia stares at the flimsy door, the way it seems to bend as he smashes it with his fist. And the wheel of dread, it turns.

"Still hear him?" Olivia asks Ezra, who she's Face-Timing with while he plays video games. They've been on the phone for three hours. They spent most of yesterday the same way. "He's off his rocker. This is what he's like sometimes. Believe me now?"

"I believed you when you told me, Liv."

The pounding on her door stops. He gave up. This is the pattern: come harass her, experience the dead silence she gives him in return, and then retreat to his room muttering and kicking things. She breathes a little deeper.

Olivia touches the screen with her finger, right on Ezra's lips, which are shockingly good at kissing her. They have a gravity to them that she can't wait to lose herself to again. She thinks about him constantly since the kissing happened. She isn't usually like this. She doesn't let herself want boys or get too attached to them, because she has a protective shell and she doesn't stay anywhere for long anyway.

"I wish I could be with you right now," Olivia says softly.

"Just come over to my house. Crash in our guest room up in the attic."

"Your sister would love that. You know she hasn't returned a text to me in like two weeks?"

"I don't know what's up with her," Ezra says. "She's been moody."

"When is she not?"

"Forget Eliza, she's on her own trip," he says. "If you stayed in our attic, then you can sneak into my room at night."

It sounds like a dream. She's seen the refinished attic before: a long, bright room with cream carpets, slanted ceilings, a turret, built-in bookshelves. A queen sleigh bed no one sleeps in. Can you imagine? Having a beautiful room like that, for no one?

"Tempting," Olivia says. "What would your mom think about us getting it on in your room?"

"Right. She'd notice. She's too busy living in her office."

Olivia thinks about Eliza's ear pressed to the vent, listening to her mom's sessions. She wonders what Ezra would say if he knew about his sister's dirty little habit— but no, Olivia won't tell him. It's good to hold onto secrets you know about people sometimes, in case you need to use them later. Which reminds her of something.

"Funny story," Olivia says. "Oh my God, Ez, you're going to think this is hilarious. How could I have forgotten to tell you this?"

"Mmm," he says, his mind on his video games. There's something about how little Ezra seems to need her that makes Olivia need him badly.

"You know how I told you I bought that rat poison?" she says, dipping down to peek under her bed and make sure the plastic bag's still there. And it is—shiny, promising, dangerous.

"Yeah, you told me."

She swings back up and lies on her bed. "Well, guess who I saw in the store buying rat poison at the exact same time?"

"Just tell me. I hate guessing games."

"Your fucking *dad*, dude."

"Huh."

Is he even listening? If he were here with her, she would run her hand up his thigh to make him pay attention. One of the black widows is dancing around in its jar still hopelessly looking for a way out. Poor baby. She'll let it go soon. It's just such a turn on, being in this tiny room with so much danger.

"I pretended like I was just there for mousetraps," she says. "I don't know. I didn't want anyone seeing me buying it."

"Probably smart of you."

"Wait ... shhh."

Olivia hears a creaking sound. She ignores it at first. It's probably the trailer's funky noises, the way the wind blows through crevices and whistles and the walls adjust during temperature changes with wooden clicky noises. But the creaking gets louder and louder. It's as if someone is delicately scratching on a piece of metal. When she listens harder, cocking her ear, it's coming from the door. She gets up and presses her ear to it right under a poem by Anne Sexton she taped up. She inhales sharply. What she's hearing is somebody messing with her door hinges. And she knows exactly who that somebody is.

Her stomach turns and a nightmare flashes through her.

Despite everything with her dad—the ups and downs, the drinking and not, the outbursts and fits and the Thing Never to Be Fully Remembered—an unspoken rule has long been upheld. That rule is that Olivia's room is her sanctuary. No matter what city or state they live in, trailer, apartment, or cheap house, her room is *hers*.

"Hold up," she tells Ezra, tossing her phone on the bed. "Dad?" she asks the door. "What are you doing?"

He doesn't answer her. The sound continues, getting

louder, a *scritch-scritch* that makes her blood pressure rise.

"Dad," she yells.

"Now she talks," her dad's muffled voice says from behind the door. "Privacy's a privilege. You ignore me? You disrespect me like this in my own home? *Mua.* Kiss it goodbye."

"Oh my God, he's taking my door," Olivia says aloud to the phone. "He's taking my door off its hinges."

"What?" Ezra says.

"I can't live like this," Olivia whispers, a cold sweat breaking over her. She pounds on the door from her side. "Daddy, please, don't, okay? I'll come out. Don't take my door. Please don't take my door from me."

Olivia detests the way her voice shakes, how she sounds like a fucking baby. In one swift move, she unlocks the door and opens it. It's halfway off its hinges and hangs crookedly.

Her dad stares back at her. She can't meet his eyes, there's too much emptiness there, so she focuses on his bushy eyebrows instead. A metallic smell wafts off him, a funk of sweat and toxins from days of doing nothing but drinking beer. He breathes heavily and his nostrils flare. She wants to look away, run away, the urge to just flee like a rabbit is irresistible when her dad is like this. There are levels to him. Some days he turns it around and goes to a meeting and pretends to be normal. Some days he drinks too much but he clings to functionality. Others, like today, he's lost. All gone, all monster.

"Now you open the door," he says hoarsely. "Now you listen."

Olivia chooses her words carefully. It's important to defuse the situation—arguing or showing anger will only ignite him. She offers a tight smile. "I'm sorry," she tries in a calming tone. "I was on the phone, I couldn't hear you. Can I make you some food?"

"Useless," he says. "Completely useless. Sitting in here all day gabbing away. Summer's almost halfway over, did you ever even look for a job?"

Olivia says nothing, retreating into that space inside herself, that quiet room. She could remind him that he's the grown up in the house, he's the dad. He's a drunk slob who barely makes it to work himself. But what's the point? It's like arguing with an ape.

"Let me make you some food," she says again.

He smacks the door frame as if frustrated and walks away. He starts quoting the Book of Revelations, his favorite loop-de-loop. *And he said to me, it is done! I am the Alpha and the Omega, the beginning and the end.* The words have a sonic power, echoing in her eardrums like poetry, their meaning ripe. The beginning. The end. She can hear he's in the living room now.

"Be right out," she says faintly, in a cheerful tone that feels like someone else's voice.

Olivia stares at the blank wall of the hallway. At the Hunters' house, every hallway is filled with professional family photos, so colorful and smiling it makes her ache. But in this house, there are no memories to boast of. Of course there have been fun times—fishing on a lake dock, camping under redwoods, Christmas mornings with a miniature tree and a stocking bloated with candy. No pictures exist to prove it, though. And after everything slipped, those memories took on a new hue in her mind. Black-and-white, prologue. That was the before-times.

She shuts the crooked door.

"Ezra?" Olivia whispers, picking up her phone off the bed. "Did you hear all that?"

"Yeah. Your dad's a fucking ogre."

Olivia stoops and peeks under her bed at the package of rat poison. Her heart feels like it might leap out of her chest.

"Should I kill him?" she whispers, wanting someone to validate what she's about to do. "I'm going to make food for him. Should I put rat poison in it?"

He considers her question. "What are you going to do with his body?"

"I don't know. Dump it in the river?"

"How?"

"You could help me, right? You have a car?"

"I mean, my parents' car."

"You could help me."

He makes a doubtful noise.

"There's a tarp in the back of the trailer," she whispers. "Believe me, I've thought it out. I'll wrap him in that. We would drive to the river's edge and dump him in. By the time his body was discovered, he'd be so messed up that they wouldn't be able to tell how he died."

He pauses before answering. "Olivia?"

She likes the way he says her name. There's music in it the way he says it.

"Yeah?"

"Maybe sleep on it."

She nods. "Sure. Okay."

The boy's so sweet with her, she honestly questions if he's a psychopath. Olivia kisses the screen and whispers that she'll call him back later. But she already knows.

Olivia isn't going to sleep on it.

While yes, she heard Ezra say that, while she agreed verbally, in her mind all she's focusing on is the promise he made her—he will help her get rid of the body.

She's shaking with anticipation. It's like a dream. It's not real. She floats out to the kitchen and smiles at her dad, who slouches on the couch watching the TV on mute and guzzling a beer. An ogre—that's a good way to describe him. Her Inner Thesaurus fires away: *ogre, monster, villain, menace.* It's a shame that she has to do this, but sometimes the price of freedom is murder. She's considered running away many times. There's nowhere to run in a world where he still exists.

"Daddy," she says. "I'm going to make you your favorite: tomato soup."

He looks up with surprise, his face soft, as if he forgot she's there. As if he isn't the same man who tried to steal her bedroom door five minutes ago.

"Thanks, Ollie," he says. "My sweet girl."

EZRA

It's one in the morning and Ezra's just dozed off when he wakes up to his phone buzzing on his desktop. Sitting up in bed, he sees the green glow of his screen. A little sick knot twists in his gut when he puts his glasses on and picks the phone up. Olivia's name, six missed video calls one minute apart.

"Hey," he says.

He's dark in the screen, but she's lit up with a jaundiced glow. She looks like she's in a bathroom, mirrors behind her.

"Ezra, you need to come over," she says.

Her hair is pulled back in a ponytail and her face is tear-streaked, but deadpan.

"This is bad," she goes on. "I—I don't know what to do."

"What happened?"

"I—I fed him some of those pellets," she says.

"Crushed them up and put them in his soup. He's really sick right now. I don't know what to do."

"What the fuck?" Ezra whispers. "Didn't you say you were going to sleep on it?"

"Yeah, I was, and then ... I don't know! I changed my mind."

Jesus, she's legitimately crying. Seriously? Did Olivia seriously feed her dad rat poison? Yes, she talks about it. A lot. But some small part of him never believed she would go through with it. Ezra has to pinch his arm to make it real.

"What do you mean he's sick?" Ezra says.

"He's bleeding out of his nose, he's throwing up blood, he's making these horrible noises."

Olivia must have put the phone down, because suddenly he's staring at a vent in a ceiling and listening to her sob. It's a horrible noise, a wet, sniveling, animal noise. She picks the phone back up, her face slick with new tears.

"Please come, Ezra, please please *please*."

Ezra's stomach turns. Listening to her resort to begging is worse than listening to her sob. He wants to wrap his arms around her and quiet her. Ezra runs a hand through his hair and sighs, getting up to grab his keys.

"What's your address?" he asks.

EZRA

On the drive over, Ezra is in a state of shock, gripping the wheel so hard his hands cramp up. That sick knot inside grows and grows like a blown balloon. He rolls the window down so the chill of the night air on his face can remind him he's alive.

"What the fuck am I getting myself into," he mutters.

It shouldn't matter. It shouldn't make him sick. Pull it apart, logically—there's nothing sad about Olivia feeding her dad rat poison. Her dad is a bona fide piece of shit. The only problem here is that this is messy. This is messy and Ezra has no idea what's coming and how it will end.

Ezra pulls his parents' SUV into the carport of Olivia's house. He thinks about parking it up the street and walking, but that almost seems more suspicious. There are no lights on in any of the other trailers—only Olivia's. Olivia's waiting for him in the doorway in a short flower-printed nightgown, jittery bare legs, grinding her teeth.

"I don't know what to do," she whispers.

He gives her a giant hug, dreading what he's going to find when he walks inside.

"It's bad, Ez," she says. "I didn't think it was going to be like this."

He kisses her forehead. He's a psychopath. None of this matters. *What Would Patrick Bateman Do?* he asks himself half-jokingly. He follows her inside.

A moaning corpse lies in the middle of the dining room floor. Ezra stands over it, hands on his hips, to take in the sight.

It's not as bad as many things Ezra has seen online, but it's definitely different to behold a bloody, dying person in real life. He can feel his instinct to look away, his stomach full of snakes, but forces himself to study what he's looking at.

Olivia's dying dad is a lumbering giant of a man. He probably weighs at least two-fifty and here he is, lying on his back in the middle of the linoleum floor, eyes bulging, rivers of blood running out of his nose. A thin orange-red substance streaked with green is splattered all over his once-white T-shirt. The substance is all over the floor in an explosive ring around him. A disgusting smell thickens the air, stale beer and vomit and pennies.

"Okay," Ezra says, working hard to breathe through his mouth. "What the fuck am I looking at?"

"He's sick," she says. "He collapsed like an hour ago in here and threw up all over himself and—see his nose?"

"Is he dying?"

The man moans, closing his eyes.

"I can't look at him, I don't know." Olivia dabs her eyes. "I didn't think it would be like this. I thought he'd just, like, pass out and not wake up."

Olivia's poor decision-making is aggravating. First she cut his brakes and messed that up, now this impulsive attempt with the rat poison. If Ezra was going to murder someone, he would have extensively researched. You know how some people do halfhearted suicide attempts as a cry for help? A shallow wrist cut or a dozen aspirin? This almost feels like the homicidal equivalent of that.

Ezra shakes his head. "You should have waited."

"Look, I know I screwed up, okay?" Olivia says. "I got that part, Ezra, I hear you loud and clear. But what now?" She gestures to her dad, who makes a gurgling noise that Ezra works hard to ignore. "What the *fuck* do I do now?"

"You could just leave for a while and hope the poison does him in."

"What if it doesn't, though?" she says. "What if he survives?"

Ezra puts his hands on his face. He should have ignored her calls. He should have just kept sleeping. He could be peacefully in bed right now.

Olivia comes to him and hugs him hard, desperately, like she wishes she could climb inside him and hide.

"You have to help me," she says into his chest.

"How?"

"Do like you did with the albino raccoon."

Ezra lets his gaze soften, the room and everything in it becoming a blur. This entire scene is so surreal. He's in a trailer where he's never been before hugging a deranged girl he's falling for who's asking him to commit half a murder. That's what she's asking him to do, isn't it? She started it and he'd finish it. It's crazy. It's a crazy thing to ask of someone.

"With what?" he asks.

"Whatever you think is best. I don't know."

"Why me?"

She pulls back and looks up at him. Her eyes remind him of the Full Moon River—bright green like the water, ringed with brown like the riverbank. "You're a psychopath, right? Prove it."

Ezra considers what she's saying. He casts a steely glance back down at the writhing body on the floor, imagining it means just as much to him as a downed soldier in a video game. He *is* a psychopath. He's sure he is. Olivia's pushy and obnoxious and he has nothing to prove to her —but a part of him wants to prove it to himself. He can absolutely kill a person and dump their body and then forget about it. And he can do it *right*. Smart. Ezra has always known if he were a serial killer, he wouldn't get caught.

"Do you have a baseball bat?" he asks.

"Do I look like I play baseball?"

"Don't sass me when I'm helping you off someone."

That comment seems to relax Olivia just a little. She sputters an unexpected laugh. "Sorry." She meets his eyes and he spies fear in there. It makes her strangely adorable. "I don't have a baseball bat."

"A cast-iron pan?"

Olivia points a finger to a cabinet across the kitchen, over her dying father. "Yeah."

Ezra steps over a pile of blood-streaked vomit and her dad's bare legs, pale and hairy and twitching. He doesn't let himself dwell on it or think too hard about it. As long as you keep your brain moving, nothing can bother you. He opens a cabinet and Olivia says "no, no, not that one, *that* one" and then he finds a cast-iron pan and takes it out with two hands.

It's heavy as a boulder. His heart begins beating so fast in his chest, just a biological response, one that will pass, best to ignore it, none of this ultimately matters. Humans kill other humans every day. It's nature. He clutches the handle of the pan, the feel of it replaying a flashback to his years of Little League—all those games condensed into one simple feeling in the grip of his fists.

He's never seen Olivia's eyes so wide, her hand over her mouth.

"You sure?" he asks Olivia.

She nods. "Just do it."

"Maybe you should leave the room."

"I don't want to. I want to be here with you."

Ezra doesn't think. He swings the pan behind him first to get momentum, then uses every ounce of strength within to bring the pan down onto the skull below with a smatter of blood, spatter of tissue, and a *thwack* that shakes the linoleum floor beneath their feet. At the same time, Olivia lets out a surprised shriek. Ezra stands back, panting, not looking too hard at the mess he's made of a man's head, not thinking too hard about it. He kicks the man's arm with his sneaker. He doesn't move.

"That's it." Olivia clasps Ezra's arm. "That was it."

Ezra drops the pan on the floor with a thud, staring at what he's done. There's no more moaning or twitching. The man's forehead is caved in.

"Daddy." She begins to cry. "Oh my God. Oh my *God*. Hold me, Ez."

She turns into him and he wraps her in his arms, feeling nothing, so numb, a boy made of ice. In his tight embrace, she shakes with sobs—sobs, what the fuck? Isn't she happy, isn't this what she wanted? He stares behind her at the man he killed. He killed a man. It's weird, it doesn't feel real, he doesn't feel different. It's like the first time he had sex. He looked in the mirror afterward and saw the same Ezra. None of this matters, he reminds himself. There's no reason to feel sick to his stomach. He pets Olivia's hair and then notices there's blood flecked on his hands and stops.

"We should clean this up," he whispers, kissing her temple.

"I can't believe—I can't believe—" Olivia pulls back. She shakes her head like she can't keep talking. Tears fall as she stares at the kitchen floor.

"It's okay. It's okay. Don't think about it," he says. "Just go get the tarp. Keep moving."

She nods, wipes her face, and hurries out the door.

Ezra's head throbs as he paces the living room, trying not to look at the dead body in the kitchen. He thinks through his next steps instead. Murder's kind of like chess, isn't it? If you make one move, you have to think through every possibility first. They will wrap the body in a tarp, put it in the SUV, and dump him in the river. Most likely the body will be found downstream, maybe in the next town. Ezra imagines police in Raven's Landing discovering the body, forensics specialists swarming the scene. If the body doesn't make it far, who knows—they might discover the rat poison in the stomach. For sure they would know the man's been bludgeoned. Ezra doesn't like that. Fear strikes like a little electrocution. They *have* to be smart about this. They can't get caught. They have to figure out how to do this and then he has to pretend it never happened, for the rest of his life.

A choking thought.

He chews his cheek and walks to a shelf in the corner that has an eclectic array of books like something you'd see in a little free library. The Bible, a biography on Ike Eisenhower, *The Ultimate Fishing Manual*, *The Velveteen Rabbit*. Ezra's gaze falls on a silver heart-shaped picture frame with a dusty photo, a man with a little girl on his shoulders. A curly-haired man with a bushy beard and a crooked grin, the girl in pigtails.

"I just killed you," Ezra whispers, in disbelief.

A horrible feeling overtakes him, one big enough to make the room feel like it's tipping under his feet. It's as if he's experiencing his own private earthquake. He quickly lays the frame down so he doesn't feel tempted to look at it again. He turns to the kitchen and stares at the scene and calculates his next steps. This is a puzzle. A challenge. They need to succeed—absolutely, positively, no room for error.

The blood spatter, the body, it doesn't bother him. It really doesn't, at all. It's just like the butcher shop. At the butcher shop, they dealt with carcasses all day long with the same aloofness as anyone working an office job. You do something enough times, you become numb to it. The shock of the job—of bone saws and butcher knives and animals hacked to pieces and a floor slippery from a coating of fat—it wore off by the end of his first day. Soon he learned to sop up blood and clean up intestines and empty grind buckets like it was nothing. This body is the same. Treat it the same, Ezra, just a carcass.

Shit. Ezra contemplates whether that might be smarter—to cut the body into pieces. He's seen them do it in mob movies. And think about the Raven's Landing Dismemberer, who killed multiple women and has still never been caught. You cut a body up, you scatter the pieces all over the place, it's hard to put it all together.

Olivia comes carrying a blue tarp that makes crinkly sounds as she drops it on the living room floor in front of Ezra.

"I can't look at him," Olivia says. "Makes me want to throw up."

"Well, you're really going to feel like throwing up when I tell you what I think we should do with him," Ezra says.

"What?" Olivia says with a grimace.

Ezra raises his eyebrows. "How sharp are your butcher knives?"

She just keeps staring at him. He can tell the wheels are turning. This girl in front of him—this exquisite, twisted soul with blood in her hair. They're now bonded in a way that Ezra is certain he'll never be bonded to anyone else as long as he lives. It's more serious than a marriage or a child. It's murder.

"Sharp enough, I hope," she whispers, nodding.

EZRA

Four hours later, the sunrise is a pink smear over the hills, bright morning light filtering through the tall treetops as Ezra grips the wheel of his parents' SUV and drives home alone. He's blank and heavy. He's shaking from hunger and probably shock, too. The last few hours of his life have to be something he never thinks about again. It's the only way to move: forward. The only way to move: on. No looking back.

Never thinking about all the blood, so much blood, a ridiculous amount, filling up the bathtub like a horror film.

Never thinking about the snapping of tendon and bone as he knifed a human being into eight pieces and bagged them up in garbage bags one by one.

Never thinking about the long drive in the dark with Olivia, a solemn drive from place to place—a convenience store parking lot, a construction site, the empty fairgrounds, an apartment complex in Raven's Landing—

where they found random dumpsters to scatter pieces of her father.

As the car seems to drive itself down the highway, Ezra keeps smelling the sleeve of his black sweatshirt. Does it stink like blood? Or is it the car? It can't be. They were careful. Everything wrapped in plastic. Everything sanitized. They scrubbed the trailer with so much bleach his fingertips are white.

Ezra swings by a gas station downtown. While he fills up, he stares out at the shops on Dickinson Avenue, still closed. A shaggy man walks a shaggy dog. A delivery truck with a chicken painted on it pulls in front of a market. The river bubbles along like it's any other day. Ezra eyes it all like it's through a windowpane. He hears the birds in the trees, but they don't matter. He sees the cement tables where he played chess on lazy summer days, but they seem unfamiliar to him. Everything is off.

The gas pump clicks, startling Ezra back to the present. He opens the trunk of the car and casts a long glare at the last garbage bag. *There is a human head in my parents' car. I decapitated a man,* he thinks, as if trying reality on for size. But the thought goes through him like he's a sieve, not resonating, not making sense. He closes the trunk and smells his sleeve again before getting back into the car.

He pulls onto the street, passing a playground where he used to spend long afternoons when he was young, the one with the giant metal turtle. Every kid who grew up in Riverwood has a picture of themselves on that turtle somewhere. He climbed that turtle, he swung on those swings, and now he's trying to figure out where to get rid of a human head. He eyes every garbage can he passes. But he knows—mainly from his dad's stories, actually—that the head is the part that puts them most at risk for the body being identified. If they can hide the skull, it doesn't matter as much if an arm or part of a leg is found.

Ezra drives up the hill and nears his neighborhood. He's suddenly so tired. He wants to close his eyes and never open them again. He'll stash the head in the bottom of the deep freezer, the one in the garage filled with emergency food no one ever touches because there's never an emergency. He'll deal with it later. Drive far away and bury it. He pulls up to his house, which strikes him as weird, unreal. A gigantic dollhouse. He opens the garage door and parks the SUV and looks at himself in the rearview mirror, expecting something else. He sniffs his sleeves another time.

He opens the trunk.

A human head is lighter than you'd think. But don't think. He doesn't think about the garbage bag in his hands. He doesn't think about it as anything except another addition to the deep freezer. More meat. He opens the freezer's door on top and moves a bunch of bulk ravioli, chicken breasts, frozen roasts aside. Stashes the garbage bag at the bottom. Covers it back up with bulk bags of fish sticks and frozen fruit. He's so tired. He stares down at it all, the icy fog of the freezer rising up around him like smoke. And in a terrifying flash, he isn't sure how the fuck he's going to live with himself.

Then he pushes the thought down and shuts the freezer.

He walks through the door that leads to the kitchen and sees his mom there, sweaty and in her workout clothes, plunking fruit chunks into the blender and making a smoothie. The clock says it's six-thirty.

It's just an early morning like any other morning. Despite rivers of blood, life hums along.

"Ezra," she says, surprised. "Were you out all night?"

"Yeah."

He doesn't meet her eyes, exactly. He isn't ready for eye contact. Ezra feels like he's been struck with a terrible flu or something. Shaky. Nauseous. All he wants is his bed, is to close his eyes and be nothing for a little while.

"With who?" his mom asks as he heads toward the stairs.

"Olivia."

"*All* night?"

"Yeah."

"Doing what?"

"Hanging out."

"Are you two ... getting serious?"

Ezra holds the banister, feeling like his body is made of bricks. He pulls himself up to the top of the stairs, one by one.

"Yeah," he finally answers. "We are."

There's a long pause as he lingers in the dark of the hallway and studies a family photo from about ten years ago that hangs on the wall. It's as if he's seeing it for the first time. The Hunters wore white shirts and laughed in the grass. Third grade. Ezra just got his glasses, turquoise tortoiseshell, and Eliza cried because she didn't get any. His parents bought her a pair of sunglasses and popped the lenses out and then she wore those for a while, including in the photo. She annoyed Ezra then, but now something about their little smiling bespectacled faces in the picture prickles him with nostalgia, overwhelms him with a desire to wind back the years and be there again.

His eyes are watering, probably from exhaustion. Ezra goes to his room and shuts the door and locks it. He takes off his clothes, shoves them in the garbage, puts on his pajamas, and gets in bed. He sniffs his sleeve six more times before plummeting into the welcome pit of sleep.

AUGUST

The Hunters

At ten past eight, under the screaming morning sun, an SUV pulls into a shady corner of a police station parking lot.

A family of four emerges from the vehicle, all wearing identical stunned expressions. The station is perched atop a steep hill. The view is astounding. Some have said it's the best in all of Riverwood. The family stops for a moment to gaze upon the valley at the lovely town they know like it's a part of themselves. The river is the blood running through their own veins and the forests are their bones and the landmarks are scars that each come with stories. The man is breathing deeply and feeling déjà vu—this view is one he knows well. The woman is following the hairpin curves of the river with her eyes. The girl has spotted her school through tears and is wondering how she will ever manage to go back there again. The boy is gazing flatly out at nothing, at the absolute nothingness that surrounds the beauty. Once again, he dreams of death.

The moment passes without a word. The family shuffles inside like one being. They are greeted solemnly by the clerk, who recognizes them. The clerk puts down his breakfast burrito and stands. He asks if they have seen the wreckage and the family murmurs they have, they drove by it a few minutes ago. The clerk ushers the family into a gray room with a two-way mirror and assures them this is protocol, a quick interview. He gives them all cups of steaming coffee and cocoa and asks if they would like a frozen breakfast burrito or anything to eat. No one is hungry.

A police officer comes in and gives the man a back-clapping hug and whispers an apology. The woman asks tearfully how long it will be until they can go inside their house again, what happens next. The girl is asking if everything is gone in the fire. The boy says nothing. He drinks the hot coffee even though it feels like it's singeing his taste buds. The police officer plops into a squeaky chair, inhales deeply, and informs them there were human remains found buried on the property.

The family exchanges a look of horror, of disbelief.

Human *remains?* the man asks, his jaw still unhinged.

Human remains, the officer confirms, tapping a pen on the table.

Oh my God. Who? the woman asks, putting a hand over her mouth.

We don't know who it is yet, the police officer says.

He leans in and says, to the man, it was a head, Carson. A human head in your rose garden.

Oh my God, the woman repeats.

Does this have something to do with the fire? the girl asks in a confused voice.

We don't know yet, the police officer says. We just don't know.

He reaches across the table and pats the girl's hand. He assures them they're going to be all right. They'll get to the bottom of this. His brother runs the Riverwood Inn, he'll give them a comfy suite for the night at a discount. He's so sorry about what has happened to them, to such a nice family. Tragic. Now if they wouldn't mind answering a few questions?

Inside the SUV, it's hot as an oven. Inside the trunk, it's even hotter.

The sweaty girl locked up in there, curled tightly in the fetal position, is screaming—but no one can hear her.

JULY

ANGELA

Angela has the back of the SUV open, arms crossed, brows furrowed.

The seats are laid flat. There's a bodily fug in the air that wafts out the second she opens the trunk—metallic and sweaty and something else. It makes her stomach turn. She doesn't want to think about her son screwing Olivia West in the back of the family car, but obviously he did. There's no other explanation for him stumbling home in a daze at six in the morning and the car looking this way.

"Why can't you just have sex in a bed like a normal person?" she mutters as she pulls the seats back into place.

She shuts the trunk and opens the doors and sprays Febreze everywhere inside, but as she sniffs, she swears that gross, carnal smell is still there—sex and raw meat. Now it just has a puzzling layer of lavender over it. Angela leaves the doors open for an extra minute and sighs, waving her hand in the air to try to make it go away faster. She shuts each door with a thud. On the garage floor, she notices muddy footprints circling the SUV, trailing all the way to the deep freezer.

"What is this?" she asks, following the footsteps and erasing each one with the toe of her pink sneaker. Why was Ezra tracking mud around the garage at the crack of dawn? She opens the lid of the deep freezer and stares at the contents—bulk frozen shrimp, a few stray frozen burritos, a roast. She peeks underneath some frozen blueberries, sees nothing interesting, and shuts the lid with a gust of icy air.

She stands, shaking her head, steeped in a deep sadness that she doesn't quite understand. What is going on inside her? She suddenly misses her children's childhoods with a smothering grief. She wants her little ones back, the ones she could scoop up and rest on her hips, the ones she could buckle into a stroller and go enjoy a walk together. The ones who crawled onto her lap and thought she was a whole world. Now they're driving her car and having sex in it. Now they're googling disgusting things. Now they come home after parties and mysterious nights out and offer monosyllabic responses. Angela wipes her eyes and holds a deep breath and lets it go. This is normal. This is what time does to people. This is their stage of development and maybe even some of this is simply hormones thanks to perimenopause.

Then she sees what's in the corner about ten feet away from the deep freezer, next to the metal shelving filled with neatly labeled boxes: a cloudlike, black-flecked stain that starts on the floor and seeps up the wall. It's about two by two feet. She knows this sight well. Mold. Dampness. Rot. A house she lived in when she was in college was so infested with it, she was evicted and the place was razed. One of her housemates tried to sue the landlord after developing asthma.

"What?" she whispers. "No, no, *no*."

She squats, examining it from a few feet away. It's wet, all right, and it's definitely defying gravity, crawling upward from the floor. Which means there's probably a piping issue—related, maybe, to the puddle that keeps appearing in the side yard. Meanwhile, she's bracing herself for a possible medical malpractice lawsuit from Jaycee Sandoval's unhinged mother, who claims her daughter has liver damage because of her medication. For a moment, the burdens coming in from all sides converge into a force so gigantic that Angela feels she might implode, like the house itself is a pressure cooker with a roof that might literally cave in, with a foundation askew, with mold creeping in on tiny poisonous feet.

"Ange?" Carson says.

Angela stands up, ripped from her lone pity party. She wipes her eyes.

"You okay, hon?" he asks.

"Mold," she says, the word stuck in her throat. She swallows and tries again. "Mold."

Carson steps closer to her. He's looking more dapper than usual in his sharp blue suit and coiffed hair. She can smell his spicy cologne, the one Eliza gave him six Christmases ago that he still has because that's how seldom he wears it.

"Where?" he asks.

She points. By the way Carson blows out a sigh, she can tell he recognizes what a bad sign it is, too.

"Shit." He rounds to the back of the SUV and opens the trunk to toss his courier bag in. "We'll have to look at it later." He sniffs. "Jesus. Why does it stink like this?"

"You smell it too? I sprayed it with Febreze."

He shuts the trunk. "That's all I can smell, the Febreze. Welp, I'll be driving with the windows down."

"Where are you headed? I was about to take the car to go on a run."

"Downtown. Where were you going to run?"

"Same. Maybe we can head there together?"

"Oooh, a date, me likey." He wiggles his eyebrows at her. Sometimes, at times like these where he isn't taking the situation seriously, she has the urge to hit him. Not hard. Just a little bomp on the chin.

"I don't know how we're going to afford to repair this mold situation," she says.

"Look." He glances at his watch. "I'm off right now to chase an interview with that woman who was Sheriff Rodriguez's secretary for twelve years. I'm *this* close—" He shows her his thumb and forefinger and the tiny space between. "—to getting enough on paper to pitch it."

Angela blinks, a tickle of rage starting in her palms. "You're really still chasing the Raven's Landing Dismemberer story?" It's a question, but the flat way she says it doesn't exactly sound like one.

"We can talk about this another time. Climb in the car, okay? I can't screw this one up."

Angela fetches her backpack from inside and joins Carson in the car as the garage door lifts up with a mechanical groan. It still stinks underneath the fake lavender—coppery, dirty—and she tries very hard not to wonder if she's smelling her son's semen. She clips her seatbelt and checks her face in the mirror, which looks much peppier than she feels. "This is a bad idea."

"What is?" he asks, backing out of the driveway. "God, I can taste the Febreze in my mouth."

"Chasing the Raven's Landing Dismemberer. You know what I'm talking about."

He shakes his head and pulls onto their street, rolling his windows down and waving at every human he passes. *Howdy!* he yells more than once.

"Ange," he says to her in a much graver tone, "as I said, we'll discuss later. It's a double-edged sword. A two-birds, one-stone situation." He squeezes her leg. "I know how you like those."

She focuses on the view, resting her elbow on the open window. The breeze is almost too warm already. Her neighborhood with its overhanging trees and historic houses—it's beautiful, and like most beautiful things, it's a mask.

Counting her breaths. He's right, now isn't the time to discuss his career choices. If he can chase whatever he's chasing and get a pitch in and an agent and a book deal by the end of the year, maybe their problems will be solved. Carson has a magic way of making the biggest problems seem easy to fix. It's partly what made her fall for him in the first place.

"I think our son was screwing Olivia West in this car last night," she murmurs.

He screeches to a stop at a red light and glances at her with his eyebrows up. "Excuse me?"

"He stumbled in after six this morning looking a mess," she says. "He said he was with her. The seats in the car were laid down. And it stank in here like ..."

"Like what?"

"I mean ... *sex*. I don't know how else to say it."

Behind them, a pickup truck honks and they snap to attention, noticing the green light. Carson accelerates and merges onto the highway, where a bright cursive sign from the City of Riverwood promises a Strawberry Festival at the fairgrounds on July 31.

"Well, this is awkward," Carson says.

"I know."

"He's having *sex* with *Olivia*? Christ. I'm supposed to meet her downtown today. How am I supposed to be able to consult for a girl who my son is doing the hanky panky with?"

"I'm sorry, you're meeting Olivia? I thought you were meeting with some sheriff's secretary."

"I'm meeting with Olivia afterward for coffee."

"Why in the—"

"Because she's writing a book, Ange. A murder mystery. Remember?"

She pulls the seatbelt tighter, so tight it steals her air. Oddly, it relieves pressure. "That's ... strange."

"Why?"

She forces herself to loosen it again. "To be meeting with a sixteen-year-old girl? One who's our child's best friend and who's apparently banging our other child?"

He winces. "Yuck, why do you have to say it like that?"

"He had better be using protection."

"Well, obvi. You want me to talk to him about it?"

"Please. He'll listen to you." She swallows, suddenly wanting off time's roller coaster. "I am nowhere near ready to be a grandmother."

A long silence stretches between them. Carson reaches and turns on Dr. Dre and Angela immediately switches it off. She isn't in the mood. If we're being honest? Not now, not ever.

"Alrighty then," he says, giving her a sideways glance. "Where are we dropping you off for your run and what time do you want your chariot to pick you up, mi amor?"

"The Full Moon Bridge." She glances at her watch. "I can come meet you at, say, four?"

"Sure."

Without Dr. Dre there to serenade the ride, Carson whistles the intro to "Nuthin' But a 'G' Thang" on his own over and over again. Angela stares blankly out the window at the tangle of oaks and ache of riverfront green and wonders what her life would be like if she made different choices.

There are so many forks in life's roads, it's dizzying. Who would she have been if she never returned home for that summer after ASU, if she continued on to medical school in New York as she planned instead of doing a virtual program? If she had the wise sense of her brothers, who left Riverwood, scattered over the country like marbles, and never once came back? Who would she have been if she'd never given Carson a chance? She imagines herself married to an academic with a spacious apartment on the Upper West Side, but she might as well imagine herself as the queen of a small European country, it feels so outrageous.

No, this is who she is, and this is who Carson is, and as unlikely as this future is that is now her present, they built the perfect life together. This is the best life. The absolute best.

"Bye, hon," she says as he pulls to a stop near the entrance of the bridge with his hazards on. The sign says WALKING TRAIL: BE SMART! WATCH OUT FOR SNAKES! The sign has been there as long as she can remember, and yet she's never seen a snake. "Is two hours long enough?"

"Should be. Hey." He reaches over and puts a hand on her leg and squeezes like he's testing the ripeness on an avocado. "Ange, don't forget who we are and what we're capable of."

With her hand on the door, she glances back at him, keeping her breath steady. "What do you mean?"

"You know what I mean."

There's a sacred code of silence, one that they long ago agreed to never break. To think he's breaking it now— to think he's referring to *it* after all these years—steals the breath from her, makes her feel like the world is tipping to its side.

"I mean, we've raised two lovely children." He runs his hand up her leg. "We've got a gorgeous house in the best neighborhood in Riverwood. You've built yourself a wonderful career, and so have I. Never letting anything tear us down. Why? Because we're a *team*."

She nods, although her brain is nitpicking, saying, *yes, we do have two lovely children—who are fast becoming ungrateful strangers. And that gorgeous house? It's a money pit falling apart at the seams. And that wonderful career of mine could end if Jaycee Sandoval's mother decides to serve me up a lawsuit that will cost money and energy to fight and your "career," sweet darling, is not much more than a hobby at this point.* But Angela gives him her best Miss Riverwood smile.

"True," she says. "Thanks for recentering me."

She climbs out of the SUV and feels his gaze on her as she starts down the trail. Grabbing her water bottle for a sip, she lingers for a few moments to stare at the water churning—this, here, is the roughest, deepest, rockiest part of the Full Moon River in town. It's where her father's Mercedes crashed and drowned him. She thinks about the sight of it there, upside-down, trapped among the boulders, bobbing with the violent flow of the river. And suddenly she springs into a run, feeling light, free.

After all, life could be so much worse.

CARSON

Carson hardly recognizes Janis Henderson when she answers her door.

He doesn't like thinking it, he understands time's cruelty, but she's much more ... *homely*. With a sinking feeling, he remembers how attractive she used to look—leggy, pouty, always with the searing no-nonsense gaze and the sharp red lipstick. She was ten or fifteen years older than him and when he was a young reporter, he thought Janis was hot stuff. Now here she is, bags under her eyes and cracked, dry lips. She wears a pair of pink sweats and a crusty-eyed cockatoo perched on her shoulder. Thank God Angela takes care of herself better than this woman does. He doesn't want to be superficial! He *isn't* superficial. But only liars say appearances don't matter.

"Hey Janis, you look great!" he says, reaching out to shake her hand.

"Goddammit," the cockatoo says.

"Goddammit," Janis says in the exact same tone, turning to her bird. "Don't embarrass me in front of my guests, Hannibal."

Her voice hasn't changed a bit—still high and soft as a cartoon character. She walks into her house without a word. Carson waits a moment before realizing he isn't going to be formally invited and follows her inside. The house is a wreck bordering on a hoarder situation, with an inexplicable number of hampers filled with clothes on the floor and a large portrait of Jesus Christ wrapped in an American flag on her wall. The air smells strongly of birdseed and some kind of disinfectant.

"Named him Hannibal because he likes biting people so much," she says as she approaches one of many bird-cages stacked against her wall. She opens a cage door. "Get in, ya ass, come on, now."

"Shut up, ya ass," the bird says.

"Oh, these babies are so rude." Janis swings the metal door shut. "Shut your beak now, Hanny." Janis turns to Carson and smiles up at him. "Seat?"

"Truly appreciate you inviting me to your home," Carson says, sitting at a Formica table in the dining room which is, mercifully, clean and uncluttered. He opens his courier bag and takes out his notebook and pen and his phone, lines them up on the table.

"Couldn't pass up *this* little blast from the past," she says. "You're looking sharp, Carson. I hear you write books 'n shit now. That true?"

"It is," he says, proudly.

"I asked my bookstore here to order me one and they said it was out of print."

He clears his throat. "Yes, well ... happens."

There's a twinge of panic as he waits to see if she might say something about the so-called "fabrications" in his book about the Freezer Man. "Fabrications"—the word still makes him itch. Some people don't know a true work of literature if it bites them in the ass. Capote faced practically the same allegations, yet *In Cold Blood* is still revered. Only fools believe you can publish the truth. Every damn non-fiction author under the sun takes liberties. Luckily Janis mentions nothing about it, shooting him a wide smile and offering him tea. He politely declines, wanting to get the interview done as soon as possible. He doesn't want to keep Olivia waiting.

Janis plops into a seat across from him and lets out a sigh as she studies him. Well, many things appear to have changed, but she still has that no-time-for-BS expression of someone who worked with law enforcement for years.

"So you're no longer with the Raven's Landing PD?" he asks.

"Nah, I had to go on disability last year and then by the time I recovered they cut me loose. Twenty-two years I worked there. Can you believe it?"

"Sorry to hear you were ... on disability." Carson opens his notebook to a new page.

"Chlamydia," she says.

Carson looks up at her as if she just hurled a rock at his head. "Come again?"

"Did you know," she says, in a quieter tone, "that you can catch chlamydia from birds?"

The wheels turn in Carson's brain and he kindly asks the wheels to stop. "No, I did not," he says, doodling a question mark on the margin of his paper.

"Not the same kind of chlamydia. Different kind. The bird kind. Damaged my kidneys pretty bad."

"I'm very sorry to hear that."

Janis folds her hands on the table. Despite her graying hair, frown lines, and unkempt bob of hair, her nails are immaculate talons, red and shiny as candy. "You want to know about Sheriff Rodriguez? I remember you coming in trying to flirt with me over my desk to get information about him back when you were chasing the Raven's Landing Dismemberer story. Some things never change, do they?"

"Ha," he says without smiling.

"What's possessed you to chase *this* story again?" she asks. "Lord knows you've got plenty of other atrocities that happened more recently than this."

"Cold cases are kind of my specialty. No one's written a book on it yet. And, you know, the local factor makes it convenient."

"Mmmm," she says, sitting back and eyeing him.

She unnerves him. Most people don't, but there's something about Janis that gives Carson a little shiver and he can't tell if it's the kind of shiver he likes or the kind he doesn't. Often, they feel the same.

"You know, I was very protective of the sheriff for a long, long time," she murmurs. "And if I do recall correctly, which I *do*, you were trying to pin those murders on him. Sniffing out some kind of story, asking about his schedule, asking for records of his shifts. And I wouldn't give you a thing. Want to know why, Carson?" She clicks her fingernails along the table, making a sound like a snake's rattle. "'Cause I'm loyal as hell."

"Goddammit!" a bird yells from its cage.

"Shut up, ya hear?" she yells back. She shakes her head sadly and says, "Don't know where they learn that stuff. Anywho, as I was saying? I was a *very* loyal employee of the RLPD."

She blinks through a hard stare and Carson clears his throat, realizing she's waiting for some kind of response from him.

"Yes, you sure were," he says.

She nods. "But turned out they weren't too loyal to *me*. Gave my job to some dingbat fresh out of high school. I've been taking grief for the sheriff's actions for years and proving myself to be a good lil soldier. Well, when I saw your name pop up I thought, 'Oh, I can't talk to a reporter. Wouldn't be prudent.' Then I doubled back and asked myself, 'Janis, queen, who are you protecting? The sheriff's dead and never did give you a lick of praise for all you did for him. His wife's got one foot in the grave. And the RLPD dumped you like a sack of rancid potatoes the second you caught chlamydia.'" Janis points at him with a red fingernail. "*Bird* chlamydia, remember."

"Yes, I remember."

"So, Carson," she says, sitting back, opening her arms wide. "I'm all yours."

Carson's blood thrums with a rush only a good story can give him. This is fantastic. This is better, in fact, than when he thought he was talking to Emilia Rodriguez, a shameful mistake he'd rather forget. By most accounts Carson dug up over the years, Emilia and Renaldo Rodriguez's marriage was nothing beyond a mutual agreement to live parallel lives. Janis worked with the man. She managed his schedule. She saw his comings and goings. And she's also not a senile elderly woman in a nursing home, which makes her a more credible source.

"May I record this conversation, to be sure I get the facts right?" Carson asks, tapping his phone with a finger.

After what happened with *The Coldest Case: The Freezer Man Cometh*, Carson has to have this absolutely airtight.

"Do whatcha do," Janis says.

Carson starts recording and taking notes as he delves into questioning Janis. Interviews can be difficult, depending on the person and the story. Sometimes they require a certain level of finesse and charm. Cagey or reluctant interviewees take time to work into the meaty, harder questions, easing into it with softballs or even small talk to relax them and build trust. But every once in a while, Carson lands an interview where the person is locked and loaded and ready to fire—and that's what he gets with Janis today. This is a woman uninterested in small talk or delicate handling. She wants to ream the sheriff and the department she dubs the "GOBC"—the "good ol boys club."

Janis lists a litany of ethical trespasses she witnessed

in her time in the department so long and detailed Carson's hand starts cramping up trying to keep notes. She speaks of the excessive force she witnessed in the department office, the rumors she heard about what went on in the interrogation rooms, the inside joke nickname that other officers called Rodriguez—"the chokester," so named for his affection for a certain chokehold Rodriguez loved to use on suspects that he learned from his years of martial arts.

"Chokester," Carson says, stopping his notes to massage the palm of his hand and letting his mind wander over what forensic analysts found. The way the body parts were discovered was scattershot—only one head was ever located, and one of the victims whose torso was found near the train tracks outside of Raven's Landing had yet to be identified. Cause of death was only determined for the first two bodies that were found: strangulation. "Let me think about this. Interesting. Very interesting."

"You want to hear about the hookers?" Janis says in a stage whisper. "Rodriguez liked to pick up streetwalkers and have a little one-on-one time, wink wink nudge nudge, in the back of his cruiser. Everyone knew it. Open secret."

"Did he now," Carson says, not entirely surprised, writing *HOOKERS!* in cursive on his paper. There were murmurs that one of the identified victims was a sex worker, but it was a hard thing to prove. No family member wanted to go on record admitting such a thing. "What about the investigation? Sheriff Rodriguez headed the investigation into the murders, so I'm interested in knowing more about what that looked like from the inside."

"Oh, you know, he oversaw the task force, which he hated. He butted heads with the prosecutor and the Riverwood PD. I just remember him seeming irritated by the whole thing, like it was a pain in his ass. When the media came around, he tap-danced for them but he was ... hard to read. Couldn't tell what went on with him. Those stony eyes."

"And what about after the case went cold?"

"Every year the deputy would open it up again, sniff around for new leads, but Rodriguez didn't want too many resources dedicated to it. He had a hunch the killer had either gotten arrested or moved out of the area, since the murders stopped so abruptly. It was messy, with all the talk of the last victim being a copycat. And to be fair, RLPD's always fighting for resources because of those 'defund the police' clowns and there was that whole fentanyl ring, kids dropping like flies from ODs ... after years without any new info, there wasn't much reason to chase the cold case."

"Mmmm," Carson says.

His phone buzzes on the table. It's Olivia.

I'm here!

She must have arrived at the coffeeshop early. The sight of her name lighting his phone's screen for the first time ever stirs something unnamable in him.

"I really appreciate your time today." Carson stops the recording. "This gives me a lot to chew on. If you don't mind, I'll be following up with you soon to go over a few of these details again."

"Don't mind a bit," she says, standing up. "You're welcome anytime."

CARSON

Carson heads to the coffeeshop, Espresso Yourself.

As he drives and Diddy raps "I'll Be Missing You," Carson recalls the time he drove up to Angela Atkins' family estate and knocked on the door with the lion's head knocker. Their house was impressive. Landscaped to perfection, a fountain with a cherub that appeared to be continuously vomiting water.

The look on Angela's face when she answered the door was something he'll never forget—like she was seeing a phantom standing there on the welcome mat. She looked every bit as ravishing as she looked four years ago when he met her at the riverside party and she gave him goosebumps just the same.

She pointed a finger. "You're—"

"I'm a reporter from the *Riverwood Gazette*," he said.

It took her a second, but her posture slackened and a light bulb went out in her eyes. "Oh."

"I was going to ask you a few questions about the assault and battery I heard about."

Angela's face hardened. "I'm not going to talk about that."

"That's all right," he said with a nod. "I'll tell my boss you said no comment."

"Thank you," she said, starting to shut the door.

He put his foot in the way to stop her. "Now that I've done my journalistic duty—can I take you out to lunch?"

Angela let out a snort.

Carson dropped the smile. "I never forgot about you, Miss Riverwood."

She smiled and it was like the whole world brightened along with her. "Give me five minutes."

They ate drive thru burgers together, sitting in the parking lot for two hours while she filled him in on the four years she'd been away getting her bachelor's degree. She was living at home for the summer studying for the MCAT. He told her about his work at the *Gazette,* how he had plans to write a book one day. The easy roll of their conversation, the way they had so much to say and made each other laugh—it was like they had just been at the party the night before.

As he drove her home, he noticed the way her face dropped and the fire went out in her eyes. He tried to imagine her whacking her father over the head with a fire poker. Carson was dying to know how she could still be living there after that. He could have pussyfooted around the subject. He could have shut his mouth. But Carson has never been good at either. Life's too short, let's get right to it.

"So why'd you assault your pops, anyway?" he asked.

She paused so long he thought he lost her for good. "Because he's a fucking monster."

CARSON

At first glance, Olivia's a picture there in a green plaid dress next to the window. The sunshine lights her brown hair with a golden glow. She has a shapely figure Carson notices against his will. Yes, Ezra probably has a lot of fun with her. Carson clears his throat and asks his thoughts to please center themselves on the task at hand and to remain professional. Unfortunately, his thoughts don't always listen to him.

Up close, as Carson slides into the seat across from Olivia at the wobbly table, he notices her exhaustion. The bags under her eyes. The paleness of her cheeks. Yep, she and Ezra certainly tired themselves out, didn't they?

"Thank you so much for meeting with me on such short notice," Olivia says. She cups a mug of tea with two hands.

"Of course, I told you anytime," Carson says. "I meant it."

The coffeeshop buzzes with conversation, almost

every table filled. Classic rock hums through the speakers along with the noise of coffee-grinding and milk-steaming. There's a faded mural of the Full Moon River on the wall that has been there since this place opened twenty some odd years ago. Carson used to spend mornings here, hammering away at the Freezer Man book. That's a bittersweet memory now. Here he is again, knocked down and still getting back up to fight. He's going to sell this book if it kills him. He glances at his phone to see if his former agent Chaz, who he reached out to again on the way here, responded yet. Things didn't end well with Chaz. Carson is mature enough to now admit he might have overreacted. He's itching to hear back from him, ready to make amends and start over again with this new project.

Carson sips his espresso out of a cute little demitasse. "I was surprised to see you sent an email at—what—seven this morning? I'd have figured you'd be sleeping in." *After having sex with my son in the backseat of our car all night,* he doesn't add.

"Yeah, I'm kind of an early bird," she says. "I wanted to work on my book today. I guess I was just excited."

"I get it." Carson leans in. "When inspiration strikes, you've got to take advantage. So how's the book going?"

Olivia runs her fingernails through her hair. "Well, I wrote the murder part."

"Ah. That must have been fun." He grins. "What did you decide? How does she do it?"

"At first she tries to poison him, but it doesn't work,"

Olivia says. "So she gets her friend to ... finish him off, I guess."

"Oh, interesting. There are *two* killers in your story now."

"Yeah. That was one of my questions, like ... if they ended up getting caught in the end of the book, would they serve the same punishment? I mean, it's the friend who ultimately did it."

"They'd both serve sentences, likely different ones depending on the crime." Carson takes a sip of espresso, but the cup's already empty. Stupid little demitasse. "What did they do with the body?"

"They, um," Olivia tastes her tea and winces as if it burns. "They cut it up. Dismembered."

Carson takes in a deep breath, moved beyond words that his own work served as an inspiration to a budding writer. He savors this moment because he knows it's a rare one.

"Good call," he says with a nod.

"But I ... I wanted to ask if you know more of like ... the psychology of it all."

"What do you mean?"

"Like, how does my main character live with herself after doing something like that?"

Carson opens his mouth. He's caught off guard, the answer stuck in his throat. Finally, the words catch up. "You know, Olivia, I've been in this business a long time. I can't say for sure. There are a lot of theories about the psychology of ordinary people being driven to murder. One expert even coined a term for it, *killology*. In my opinion, what it comes down to in the end is this." Carson selects his words carefully, wanting to be as honest as possible, but also aware that an uncharacteristic anxiety is building in him, a gripping pressure in his chest. "I believe a murderer would have two choices, okay? And they're not necessarily mutually exclusive."

Olivia nods, leaning in.

"They would need to compartmentalize," he says, finger in the air as he lists it off, a finger that quivers just a tiny bit. "Like a police officer or anyone who works a job like that. You can't bring it home with you, right? You have horrific things happen and you put it in a box and you put it aside, otherwise, you can't enjoy your life. And two." Another quivering finger goes up in the air. "You tell yourself a story. You tell yourself you're a hero, you had to do it, you were making the world a better place."

Olivia nods. Her brow is scrunched as she takes this in. "Right."

"It's truly amazing what a person can be convinced of —especially when the person doing the convincing is themself."

Carson's phone buzzes on the table. He can read the text from Chaz. Breathing a deep sigh of relief, Carson holds his phone up.

"Sorry to have to cut this so short, but my agent's texting and I really need to call him." He stands up. "Go ahead and send me any questions you have via email, I'm happy to answer. And ... I'm guessing you'll be coming around the house again soon?"

Olivia smiles, a twinkle in her tired eyes. "I hope so."

"You're a good kid, Olivia West, and I believe in your book." He puts a hand on her shoulder, which is bare and soft and gives him a sweet shiver, then pulls it away like he touched a hot stove. "Have a good one."

Carson jogs out of the coffeeshop, elated to hear from Chaz, to have another chance, to be able to prove to Angela he can pull his weight financially. He turns back just once to catch a last glimpse of Olivia in the window —but she's already gone.

Eliza

Eliza's scalp is on fire.

She's trying to not be a baby about it, but this *hurts*. She's seated in a salon chair at her mom's favorite place called Hair's the Thing. All the downtown shops have dad joke names—Nice to Meat You, Of Quartz (Izzy's mom's store), Prose and Cons (bookstore), Loaf is All You Need (bakery), et cetera. So corny. Eliza tries to ignore the searing, burning pain on her head and concentrate on the view of Dickinson Avenue out the picture window. When she turns to the mirror, she feels ridiculous. She has so many pieces of foil in her hair she looks like she's going for some kind of space-age porcupine look.

"It hurts, Mom," Eliza says.

Angela sits in the next chair over, flipping through a copy of *Psychology Today* under one of those enormous hair dryers that look like half an MRI machine. "Well, maybe you'll think about that next time you make an impulsive decision and dye your hair black."

When Eliza first dyed her hair shoe-polish black, she walked downstairs and expected her mom to flip. "Like it?" she asked.

Her mom barely glanced at her over the screen of her laptop. "What does it matter what I like? It's your hair."

It's disappointing how unflappable her mom is.

Remembering this, Eliza says, "I thought all that mattered was whether I liked it."

Angela shuts the magazine. "Lize, if you want to win Miss Riverwood, you can't go up there looking like you stepped out of a Tim Burton movie."

"Why not?" Eliza says, unable to help herself from arguing. It's like a magnetic pull with her mother some-times. "Aren't I supposed to be my authentic self?"

That's what the Miss Riverwood contest urges its contestants: "Show us your authentic self!"

"Your authentic self has lovely, golden-brown hair," Angela reminds her. "And a big heart. And she's brainy, she's got a dark sense of humor, and she's a spectacular dancer. I get it, you've been experimenting with who you think you are, but ... don't you think you go deeper than all that?" She reaches out and touches Eliza's knee. "You've got a whole life ahead of you. Don't box yourself in."

Eliza sits with this, savoring the rare delicacy that is her mother's full attention. She watches the hairdressers chatting with customers, the quaint downtown scene out the window where a group of girls she recognizes from school walk by. They don't notice her. The Miss River-wood competition is just one week away. The thought of going up there on stage and giving a speech and dancing and smiling in front of her peers makes her stomach ache. She's afraid of looking stupid. At the same time, she really, really wants to please everyone and win the competition. She wants her mom to see herself in her. She wants that cash prize. As usual, her feelings all bleed into each other and don't make any sense.

Last year, she gravitated toward a new look. It started with a studded belt, liquid cat-eye liner, a shirt with a witch on it. She bought some black nail polish and rented some horror movies. She suddenly liked how dark colors contrasted with her porcelain skin and how she didn't feel as much of a need to pretend to be happy when she dressed this way. She liked the nods she got from the stoners and the punks and the curious stares she got from cheerleaders who used to be her friends. Eliza has never known exactly where she stands. She's too weird to be normal and too normal to be weird. With the new dark look, she suddenly felt like she knew who she was. For a while. Then this summer, something happened. It's like the spell wore off and it doesn't work anymore. She gazes in the mirror and sees it for what it is: a costume. But what else is there?

Her "authentic self."

Who the hell is that?

ELIZA

When they leave the salon and head to Angela's car, Eliza catches glimpses of herself in the reflection of store windows. Her head of fresh brown hair feels like an odd homecoming. Like she's been reunited with an old self she didn't realize she missed. She likes the way it glows in the sun and brightens her face. As they round a corner to the parking spot, she hears her name cutting through the peaceful drone of traffic and birdsong.

"Ay! Eliza!" and a whistle.

Eliza scans the sunny avenue and spots Izzy across the street, leaning against her truck.

"Hey Izzy," Eliza calls back.

"Whatcha up to?" Izzy yells.

"Nothing."

"Wanna hang for a bit?"

Eliza looks at her mom, who shrugs as she puts on her aviator sunglasses.

"Can you give me a ride home?" Eliza calls back.

"Sure," Izzy says. "I've got nothing going on."

Angela opens the car door and waves. "Hi Izzy!" She smiles at Eliza. "You girls have fun."

Eliza crosses the street and Izzy gives her a side hug that comes with a little BO. Izzy's the type of girl who doesn't care if she stinks. If only Eliza were that carefree.

"Your hair," Izzy says, reaching out to touch it. "So profesh."

Last weekend, at Izzy's birthday party, they both ended up hanging out for most of the night. It started as a strange commiseration, because Ezra was off in the bushes with Olivia, and Eliza and Izzy needed to gossip about it. But after the shit-talking subsided, they ended up smoking a joint together in the bed of Izzy's truck while the party raged on, lying down to gaze at the stars. Izzy knew all the constellations. She could point out the planets and talk about what life was like on the International Space Station. They giggled and whispered and Eliza was oddly flattered that, while Izzy's theater friends partied near the fire and the river, Izzy spent time there with her. Maybe it was how stoned Eliza was, but it was a magic hour that made her see Izzy in a totally different light—even though it had been entirely in the dark.

"Guess it was time for a change," Eliza says, tucking her hair behind her ear.

Izzy rubs her palm over her own scalp. "I was thinking of growing mine out."

"You should. That'd be cute."

"Hungry? I was thinking of grabbing some tacos."

"Always down for tacos."

Near the river's edge, there's a place—Taco the Town, eyeroll—where you can sit in Adirondack chairs on the shore with your feet in the cool water and eat. It's only a ten-minute walk away. As they make their way along the riverwalk, the sunshine on full blast, they pass the chess tables where Ezra spent most of last summer. He doesn't spend as much time there these days. Izzy must be seeing his ghost there, too, because she turns to Eliza and furrows her thick eyebrows.

"So I guess this Ezra and Olivia thing is ... an actual thing?" she asks.

"Seems like it. He's been spending every day over at her house. I've hardly even seen him."

"Must be weird for you, right?"

Eliza shrugs. "I told you, Olivia and I aren't really hanging out that much anymore. They can do what they want."

"I just don't see it," Izzy says.

This is something Eliza has thought too since last weekend. But despite how much Ezra and Olivia both- ered her at first, the more Eliza thinks about it, the more it seems to make sense. She's noticed a whisper of flirtation between the two of them. And Ezra and Olivia might actually have more in common with each other than they do with her—that's just fact.

"I kind of do," Eliza says. "They're both nerds." Eliza thinks about the dark books she's seen her brother reading lately and Olivia salivating over Carson's true crime stories ... not to mention the weird thing she said about murdering her own father. "They're both morbid."

Eliza doesn't know what's beneath Izzy's pensive expression, hands in her overalls' pockets. Izzy has long been in the background of Eliza's life as Ezra's best friend. The girls passed by one another at school or the hallways of the Hunters' house. But it isn't until right now that Eliza notices how pretty she is—her lips with a striking Cupid's bow. The mole on her left cheek. Is there something going on with Izzy and Ezra? Is Izzy jealous, is that what her preoccupation with the new couple is about?

"He's acting fuckin' weird, man," Izzy says. "Have you noticed that?"

"Yeah, I have," Eliza says. "For the last sixteen years."

That busts Izzy up for a second. She has a laugh like a hyena. "Good one." She goes deadpan again. "But I'm not just talking about Olivia, though I can't wrap my head around that, but whatever. It is what it is. He's just —I don't know. Different."

"Explain."

Izzy shakes her head. "He just seems far away, even when we're right next to each other."

Eliza knows what she means, but she can't pinpoint when it happened. Change is so sneaky.

"Bitch, I'm going to tell you something," Izzy says. "Promise you won't repeat it."

Izzy has never called Eliza "bitch" affectionately before. Apparently an achievement in their newfound friendship has been unlocked.

"Promise," Eliza says with a smile.

Izzy stops, her hand on Eliza's arm. Girl has a grip. And an intense stare. She starts saying something, then stops to look at the river, as if she's lost the words.

"What?" Eliza says, her smile faltering.

Izzy turns back to her, takes a deep breath, and says, "A few weeks ago, Ezra and I were—you know, sometimes we push each other around, just joking and giving each other a hard time. My dad's a boxer, taught me how to fight, so I'm always threatening to kick Ezra's ass. For fun."

"Uh-huh," Eliza says.

Their friendship is ... a freakshow. But she keeps listening.

"So we—we were at my house, playing ping pong. I told him I'd knock him out with one punch. He came up behind me, put his hands around my neck and said that he could kill me with nothing but his two hands any moment he chooses ..."

Eliza's stomach clenches.

"He squeezed me so fucking hard, Eliza." Izzy rubs her throat like it aches. "And he didn't let go for a few seconds. Which wasn't long, really, he said he was kidding, and I know he was, he must have been. But I saw his face in the mirror on the wall. He looked serious as shit when he did it. He said he was sorry. I know it's not a big deal. But he's never done something like that—never put his hands on me in a way that scared me."

Shock blooms within Eliza as she takes in what Izzy just described. She tries to picture it. Her brother. Her dopey, sweet brother who used to help her with her math homework and snuggle up with her while they watched cartoons together on the living room couch. Her brother, with his hands on his best friend's throat.

"I'm so sorry, Izzy," Eliza finally answers. "I can't believe he did that. I'm sure it was a joke."

"Exactly, I know. I know it was." Izzy laughs and pulls Eliza's arm to resume their walk. "Eh, come on—we both know Ezra's too much of a wuss to kill anyone."

OLIVIA

Olivia is in the Hunters' kitchen, locked in Ezra's embrace. His arms are so tight around her she can't get away even if she wants to. Through the dining room window, Angela waters her roses outside. Olivia's own mother is locked up in some faraway prison. Then she has a horrible thought for the first time. Less a thought, more an unspeakable image. What if Olivia gets caught for what she's done and then ends up in the same prison as her own mother? It's enough to unleash a hot flash of panic.

"Squeeze me," she says.

She closes her eyes as his arms crush her.

"Harder," she whispers.

He obliges, making a sound like he's a bodybuilder lifting a barbell. Her back cracks.

Though Olivia is finding it hard to breathe, the panic's still there, flooding her like a bad drug trip. "I said *harder*."

He pulls away and catches his breath. "Any harder and I'm going to break your back."

"It makes me feel better," she says. "New kind of therapy. Squeeze your worries out."

"I'll pitch it to my mom later," Ezra says, stepping back and turning to open a cupboard. He sniffs his sleeve as he gazes blankly inside.

Olivia jumps up to sit on the counter and watches him. She focuses her thoughts on the things she likes about him. There are many. She likes the way his hair curls at the ends and almost touches his shoulders. She likes the exact fit of his jeans—not too tight, not too baggy. She likes the shapes of his forearms. And it's more than physicality. She loves that they spent the afternoon lying on his bed with their legs entwined as they read old Russian novels, that she feels safe with him and the whole world disappears, and that they share a deep, dark secret.

"Peanut butter and honey sandwich?" he asks.

And he makes a mean sandwich, too.

"Sure," she says.

Olivia glances at the window again to make sure that Angela's still there outside. She sure is. Eliza once joked that Angela gives more attention to her flowers than she does her own kids and she's not necessarily wrong.

"Ezra," she says quietly. "I just had the most terrible thought."

He raises his eyebrows as he lines up the honey, bread, and peanut butter on the counter. "Stop it—"

"I know, I know, we're not going to talk about it anymore after this, I swear."

Ezra clenches his jaw. "We said we—"

"Right, I know, we're pretending it never happened. And it *didn't*. Nothing happened." Olivia swallows. "But I had this ... terrible vision in my head just now. It was of me and my mom side by side in orange jumpsuits. I haven't even seen my mom since I was a squirt, but I just imagined her there, saw it plain as day."

Ezra says nothing, taking a plate out. "That's not going to happen."

"But what if it *did*?"

He freezes, gaping at the open cupboard. There's a cast iron pan up there that seems to have caught his attention. He shuts the cupboard again.

"You okay, babes?" she asks gently. "You look kind of ... preoccupied."

"Didn't sleep well again."

"Neither did I." She swallows. "Nightmares?"

He nods.

"Yeah," she says quietly. "Same."

"Regret" is a strong word. Olivia wouldn't say she exactly regrets what they did. There was an instant freedom she was awarded as soon as her dad's last breath sounded, an ugly quiet that she's been dreaming of for so long. Finally, she's truly the orphan she always wished she was. She will never have to worry about being called names, will never have to smell his sour beer breath as he shouts in her face, never be embarrassed of him screaming about Satan on street corners, never have to worry about ... it ... happening again. No, it's not regret she experiences. He deserved to die, plain and simple, the same way she deserves to live.

Long ago, the horrible thing her dad did to Olivia also taught her the skill she needs to get through all this. It lines right up with what Carson told her during their coffeeshop talk. "Compartmentalization"—a fancy word she learned from a self-help book on PTSD she found on a curb one day. She can take something awful that happened, the memory, and will herself to never think of it again. Pretend it never was. Olivia can tell herself a story so many times she starts to believe it, and she has been practicing the art of this lately, whispering to herself, "My dad never came home one day. I have no idea where he is." And when images of him vomiting blood on the kitchen floor flash through her mind, when she cracks an egg and winces as she remembers the sound of his skull shattering, she tells herself it was a horror movie she saw once. It's worked so far, for the most part.

Until sleep comes.

Sleep: the one place she can't control where her mind goes. The nightmares have been relentless this past week, for both herself and Ezra. She wakes drenched in sweat and crying and when she calls out her dad's name and hears nothing, a hollow sound rings deep within her. Still, it's not regret. Most of all, she shudders with a monstrous fear that she'll get caught.

Olivia drums her fingertips on the countertop, wanting to broach the coming subject as gently as she can.

"Ezra," she tries. "We do have to at least talk a *little* about it. It feels like if I don't let someone know he's gone —missing, I would say—it's going to look suspicious—"

At that moment, the front door swings open with the force of a family of bats flapping into the room, spooking Olivia so badly that she jumps off the counter.

"Hello?" Eliza calls from the foyer.

Olivia's blood pressure slowly calms. And she thinks: can you imagine living somewhere with a *foyer*? How fancy does that sound, *I'll hang my pocketbook in the foyer!* Olivia's only read about them in dusty novels before she started hanging out with the Hunters.

"Hey," Ezra calls back, without verve.

Smack-smack. He slaps two pieces of bread on the plate in front of him. He has that grumpy look on his face, the default look that was the only one she knew on him for so long—but Olivia's learning how to melt it off him.

"Hey, so guess who I ran into downtown?" Eliza says, coming around the corner. When she sees Olivia there, she's surprised. "Oh! Hey."

Eliza looks stunning. Just stunning. And nothing like how she looked the last time Olivia saw her.

"Hey," Olivia says back. "Whoa. Your hair!"

"Yeah." Eliza runs her fingers through it. "Time for a change."

She looks just like old pictures Olivia's seen in the hallway—Eliza smiling with her long, brown hair, forgettable and normal. Olivia fell in love with a spooky girl. This, here, is the ordinary creature underneath. More conventionally beautiful, yes, but what a shame.

Ezra squints his sister's way. "You did something to your hair?"

So clueless. So unobservant. Boys are blind.

"Yes, Ezra, I did something to my hair," Eliza says.

An awkward silence thickens the air. Olivia beams at Eliza, who blinks back coolly as a judge. Olivia gets that feeling now every time she's around Eliza—the feeling that Eliza is sizing her up. It's truly baffling how Olivia's best friend flipped on her for no apparent reason. A little fire sparks inside Olivia. Who the fuck does Eliza think she is, looking at her like that?

"Did I interrupt something?" Eliza asks.

"No—" Olivia starts, but Ezra cuts in.

"Olivia's dad hasn't come home in days," he says as he squirts honey on the bread.

Mouth open, Olivia is so thrown by Ezra's remark that she doesn't know what to say.

"Yeah," Olivia finally says. "That."

"Wow, really?" Eliza's expression warms with concern. "Your dad's *missing*? Like you haven't heard anything?"

Olivia shakes her head.

"I'm so sorry," Eliza says. "He's done this before, right?"

"He has," Olivia says, nodding. Which isn't a lie. He's left her alone for days a few times when he went on some especially long benders. "Hopefully he'll be back soon."

"Well ... shit. Let me know if there's anything I can do," Eliza says.

"I will, yeah."

They all endure one more long, awkward silence before Eliza heads up the stairs.

"Really?" Olivia mouths to Ezra.

Dread surmounts within her, hurrying up her pulse. She can't believe Ezra just blurted it out like that without discussing it with her first. He's usually patient and calculating and logical. He's the one who keeps telling her to not be so impulsive.

Ezra slaps two pieces of bread together. "Well, you're right. We should start telling people. You might want to talk to my mom about what to do with your dad missing. Like, shouldn't you make a report? Talk to police, something?"

Olivia breathes in sharply.

"It's been five days now," Ezra says.

Five days feels wrong. It isn't the right length of time, not at all. It either happened five minutes ago or five years ago—not five days. The thought of having to report him missing, of having to lie to uniformed police officers and invite them into her home, is horrifying. She has the sudden urge to flee, to run away and change her name and hair color and never have to face anything about this ever again. Fake her own death and live on a tropical island drinking cocktails with little umbrellas. She could, couldn't she?

As Ezra reaches out to hand her the plate, his expression is so fixed and far away it's as if he's the lone spectator to a movie only he can see. She probably doesn't want to see it anyway. He desperately needs sleep. Look at the dark circles under his eyes—like someone punched him and the bruises are fading. He smells his sleeve again. Why does he keep doing that? It's a tic she never noticed before.

Olivia takes the plate from him, but she doesn't feel hungry anymore.

OLIVIA

Family meetings are real after all.

Olivia's read about the concept in books, a wholesome sofa chat where parents and kids gather 'round to discuss serious issues. Apparently, in the Hunter household, they're taken very seriously.

Angela puts a tablecloth on the coffee table and moves a vase of flowers and a water pitcher with glasses to the living room, adjusts the lighting, and sits down. She and Carson are positioned in white overstuffed chairs that face the white sofa, arms resting on the armrests, posture rigid. They look like king and queen lording over Pottery Barn. Olivia sits on the sofa between Eliza and Ezra. Ezra holds her hand, but Eliza is on the far end of the couch like Olivia has an infectious disease. It makes Olivia want to cut all of Eliza's luxurious hair off while she's sleeping.

The silence in the room is stifling as everyone settles

into what appears will be a long and grave meeting. A cuckoo clock ticks above the fireplace.

"So," Angela says. "Olivia's dad hasn't come home in —what was it you told me?"

"Five days," Olivia says.

Ezra is squeezing Olivia's hand so hard it hurts.

"Five days," Angela says.

"I am so, so sorry to hear that," Carson says, hand on his chin. "I had no idea. I can't believe you didn't mention it earlier."

"He does this sometimes," Olivia says, a little shake in her voice.

She's not faking it—the shake is real. She's covered in goosebumps and she's nervous as hell being in the hot seat. After Ezra told Eliza, they decided to tell Angela, and now within an hour the whole thing has come crashing down with a momentum Olivia is not prepared for.

"Right. But that's not *okay*," Carson says. "It's not okay to up and disappear on your daughter like that."

"A hundred percent," Ezra agrees.

Eliza says nothing, watching it all through narrowed eyes.

Olivia doesn't respond. Her entire face feels like it's itching. She wants this all to be over so badly that she imagines just throwing a lit match in the middle of the carpet and running away to the hills to live out her days like a feral child.

"It's abuse." Angela nods. "Neglect is abuse, Olivia."

"He always comes back," Olivia murmurs.

Angela sits back and eyes her with an impenetrable expression. This is probably what she's like with her patients. "The reason I think we all need to discuss this situation together as a family, family meeting style, is because I think this is going to be something that affects all of us." She gives a grim smile, one of those down-turned sorry smiles that's more like a frown. "I do think that, Olivia, you need to file a missing person report. You can do that online."

"Okay," Olivia says, the scene so surreal that her ears start ringing.

Angela speaks slowly, deliberately. "But once you file that report, emergency child protective services is going to step in."

The words land with a thud, the same way a slammed door can hush a whole house. Olivia's mouth goes dry and Ezra's hand slackens in hers. Then the meaning sinks in and everyone starts back up at once.

"Excuse me?" Olivia says.

"You're fucking kidding me," Ezra says, voice raised.

"Language, buddy," Carson tells him, wagging a finger.

"You mean like Amanda?" Eliza asks, suddenly at attention. "Mom, no."

"Who's Amanda?" Olivia asks, confused.

Olivia's head spins. It's as if she's hanging on for dear life to a psychic carousel. *Emergency child protective services.* She doesn't like the sound of that one bit, and

how did she and Ezra not see it coming when they
discussed all the outcomes? When they thought through
when to file a report? Olivia is sixteen years old. Her dad
has no living family members to speak of and her mom is
in prison. Who even knows what family *she* has. Jesus,
Olivia's going to become a ward of the state. She's going
to end up bumping from foster home to foster home and
who knows what lecherous men lurk there. It could end
up being her nightmare relived over and over again. She
has to work very hard to maintain her breathing. And
this, this is the first glimpse of that myth she's heard about
but has yet to experience herself: regret.

Regret, her Inner Thesaurus says. *Remorse. Sorrow.
Guilt. Shame.*

"I know. It's unfortunate, honey," Angela says. "But
you need to be aware that it's coming."

Maybe it's the heartfelt utterance of the word *honey*,
a word no one's ever called Olivia in her life. Maybe it's
the gravity of her uncertain future. But suddenly Olivia's
eyes are filling with tears—real tears, not fake ones. She
feels small and stupid and even though she's sitting in a
room with a boy's hand in hers and an entire family
beaming their consideration her way, she has never felt
more alone. She always wished she was a jellyfish, an
orphan. Now she finally understands what that means.

"Liv, it's okay." Ezra puts his arm around her. "This
isn't going to happen. We're not going to let it happen."

She only fell for Ezra a week ago, but it's been long
enough to know that denial is a talent of his. Olivia wipes

her face, but more tears come. She can't even manage a word. Eliza watches Olivia with a wince like she's a car accident victim getting put on a stretcher. Pitying her. And that makes Olivia cry even harder because she'd so much rather be hated and judged than pitied.

"Hey, hey, Olivia," Carson says in a soothing voice, getting up and bringing her a box of tissues in a shiny silver holder that seems to have appeared from thin air. "Hang in there. We're going to figure this out."

That's another thing about this wonderful home, they have tissue boxes everywhere. Olivia grew up in houses without foundations where you blew your nose with toilet paper, and not even the two-ply kind. It's soft on her cheeks as she wipes her tears.

"I have a possible solution when you're ready, Olivia," Angela says.

From her white overstuffed throne, Angela eyes her. There's concern in her even stare if you look hard enough for it. This woman sits all day long listening to teenagers sobbing about their problems, so this probably isn't much for her. But there's a softness in Angela as she speaks that Olivia's not used to. She's heard her doctor voice and her mom voice. This, here, is a new voice.

"I'd like to help you file the report and see if I can get emergency guardianship for you," Angela says.

The ache overwhelming Olivia stills for just a moment. "Really?"

Angela nods. "I know the folks in CPS. I've worked with many of them. I'm sure they can help me make it happen."

Crying is a little like vomiting. Olivia does neither very often in her life. At the time, it's the worst feeling in the world. But when it's over, Olivia feels much better. Her face is drying, her cheeks tightening, and her nose isn't running anymore.

Olivia looks around the room with new, clearer eyesight. The fireplace, the carpets lined with neat vacuum tracks, the grand piano that no one ever plays. "You're saying ... I would live here?"

"Well, until your dad comes home and we figure out the long-term solution." Angela nods encouragingly. "But we're happy to have you here, Olivia."

Ezra rubs her arm. "That'd be amazing, right?"

"Thank you so much," Olivia says, mind racing.

Somehow, this week since her dad went missing (that's how she's going to think about it from now on, *shudder*, shove the monster in the closet and shut the door), Olivia hasn't deeply considered what the future will look like. She didn't realize the possibility of being put in a foster home. She imagined she would keep living in the trailer on her own, maybe drop out of school and get a job or something. Olivia lives in the moment, never looking too long at the past or the future. It's a survival mechanism. But it has its disadvantages, too.

"I'll put in a call with my friend Alison over at the CPS office," Angela says. "Get her advice before proceeding with the missing person report."

"Stupid question, but I assume you've been trying to call your dad?" Carson asks.

Olivia nods, though she's thinking, *oh no, I haven't.*

Shit. They disposed of his phone during that horrible night she doesn't want to remember. Will police check her phone and see she hasn't tried? Is it too late now? The image of her mother and her in orange jumpsuits flashes to mind like a jump scare in a horror movie. Olivia breathes and focuses on pushing the thoughts out. It's a lie, a lie her brain is telling, she doesn't even know what her mom looks like anymore. She's going to be fine.

"You can stay in the attic room," Angela says.

"Wow, thank you," Olivia says.

Chills. That room with its vast, comfy bed no one sleeps in and an antique writing desk under the window. This must be what Pip of *Great Expectations* or Mary Lennox from *The Secret Garden* felt like.

"How long will she be staying with us?" Eliza asks her mom, as if Olivia isn't sitting right next to her.

"As long as she needs to," Angela says. "I'm not sure what the timeline here looks like. Even when your dad returns, Olivia, we're going to need to figure something out—I don't know if CPS is going to let you return home."

Olivia nods. She's never going home. Never again.

"How are you feeling about all this?" Angela asks in her doctor voice.

"Okay," Olivia says. "Better."

Everyone in the room watches her like they expect her to explode at any minute. But Olivia hasn't felt this calm in a long time. Know what word Olivia loves most? What's her favorite word in the English language? *Serendipity.* It's a word so unique no true synonyms exist, yet she's never experienced its full meaning until right now.

"Consider this your home, *capisce?*" Carson says. "You're an honorary Hunter."

Olivia Hunter. Has a nice ring to it, doesn't it? She feels so warm suddenly, the way a cat must feel when it curls up in a spot of sunlight.

"Thanks, everyone," she says.

Sometimes Olivia's sure there is a hollow room where her heart should be, but this feels lovely, this means something. Although a cold breeze blows through her when she sees the way Eliza tilts her head and studies her with zero expression. Her friend. She was her best friend weeks ago. She would have been the one sitting next to her, holding her hand. What the fuck is her problem?

Carson offers to give Olivia a ride back to her trailer so she can gather her belongings while Angela stays home and calls her colleague at CPS for advice. Carson bumps Tupac the whole car ride to Paradise Springs, rapping passionately under his breath along with the lyrics and pausing for every swear word. It's cute. She thinks of him as her guardian, as if trying this new relationship out. Olivia knows she's supposed to be sad, her dad's missing, who knows where her dad is and when he'll be home? But it's very hard to contain her smile, which feels like it isn't just her lips. It's her entire body, her entire being.

"Hey, how's the book going? You make any progress since we last talked?" he asks, turning the music down as her trailer park comes into view. Maybe this will be the last she ever sees it. What she wouldn't give.

"Yeah, thanks so much for the advice you gave me," she says. "I think I've got it figured out. I know what's going to happen."

"Glad to be of service," he says, turning the music back up.

Olivia says she'll be just a minute. The trailer's cleaned up, but she's paranoid that Carson might notice something awry with his true crime brain. Olivia enters the house with a stomach bracing itself for some confrontation with her dad, as if her body hasn't yet received the message that he's gone and never coming back. The relief. The sweet lightness she feels when she stands here in the doorway hearing nothing but silence. She glances at the floor, where he—but there's no use going there.

Hurrying through the hallway, she doesn't look at the dark doorway of his room, either. She goes straight into hers, opens the trunk she dragged from state to state and city to city since she was a child. She empties her drawers into there and packs the modest stack of her favorite books she scored in little free libraries over the years: *Misery, Lord of the Flies, The Bell Jar, Crime and Punishment, Beloved, Frankenstein, The Stranger,* poetry anthologies. Her music box fits snugly in a corner. She's going to leave everything else behind. Books and clothes, what else does a girl need? But at the last moment, she sees the six black widows she caught in little jam jars and feels sorry for them.

"My sweet babies," she says, tapping the glass of the fattest one and making it squirm.

She wraps each in a dress and tucks them in, one by one, beside her ballerina box. Then she shuts the trunk's lid with a *thunk* and secures the brass latch. Déjà vu. An intense shiver snakes all the way up her spine.

Once again, here she is—her entire life, her entire being confined in this trunk.

EZRA

Ezra's going to have to get used to the footsteps above his head.

Olivia's a stomper; he never realized it before because he never had to live on the floor beneath her. She's up there unpacking her belongings right now as Ezra sits on his bed with his notebook open on his lap. He has written the words *I killed a man* in neat letters. When those words fail to evoke the kind of emotion he's looking for, he writes it again.

And again.

And again.

And again.

He repeats it in different ways, his handwriting getting messier and messier, the page fuller and fuller. He wonders if it might change the feeling inside him, but it doesn't.

He puts the pen down.

Ezra can't even explain the feeling. He's not exactly

sorry, though there might be regret. He's not exactly scared, but he's full of dread. He doesn't have the words for what he is. It's this heavy feeling, like he's gained a hundred pounds since that night. A dirty feeling, like no matter how many long showers he takes, he can still smell the iron tang of blood. And then there are the nightmares and that eeriness he senses. A sort of haunting.

He smells his sleeve and closes his notebook.

Upstairs, her Mary Janes are clicking across the floor —back and forth, back and forth.

Ezra gets up and goes to the bathroom, washes his hands twice. He avoids eye contact with the mirror. In the hallway, he glances at the narrow wooden stairs that lead up to the attic. He walks up, ignoring the prickly feeling that there's a presence right behind him. There's no presence, he tells himself. There is no God, there is no good and evil, there is no afterlife, there is no such thing as ghosts. None of this ultimately matters. He smells his sleeve again.

Knocking on the closed door, Ezra says, "It's me."

Olivia opens it. "Hiya stranger."

She reaches up, snakes her arms around his neck, and kisses him. He kisses her back, hungry. This is what he needs, his medicine. The antidote. Olivia makes it all disappear. And now she'll be here with him every day, a ravishing distraction with the most magnetic lips he's ever known.

"Mmmm, someone's happy to see me," she says, pulling away and patting his cheek. "Come into my room."

He steps inside and she shuts the door. The skylights on the ceiling fill the space with sunshine. She sits on the bed and bounces on it.

"My room," she repeats. "I can't believe it. This is *my room*."

He observes her trunk at the foot of the bed, the open closet with a rainbow of dresses. Besides these things, it's the same generic attic where he had sleepovers as a kid and where his dad occasionally writes at the desk. He hasn't been up here in a while.

"That's all the stuff you brought?" he asks, gesturing toward the closet. "That's it?"

She points to the dresser. "And a few books up there with my music box."

Ezra crosses to the closet to look at her books. You can tell a lot about a person by the books they keep. He hadn't noticed them when he was in her room this past week. He was too creeped out by the jars of venomous spiders.

"Didn't bring the black widows, huh?"

She pauses. "Nah. Didn't want to freak you all out."

Ezra studies the book spines. There are three short stacks up here and most of them are battered paperbacks. Either they're used copies or she's read them several times. A lot of classics. Adult books. Plath, Dostoevsky, Morrison, a fat poetry anthology. Nothing stupid, like how Izzy still has *Goosebumps* titles on her shelf. He plucks out *Crime and Punishment*.

"You read this one?" he asks.

"Come on, I've read all my books. They're not pretty decorations."

"This one ... it's about a murder, right?" He holds *Crime and Punishment* in the air. "I was supposed to read it last year, but I just looked it up online to write an essay on it."

"Yeah. Dude murders his landlord."

"And then he goes crazy or something?"

"Basically. I'd ... maybe not read that one right now."

He puts it back and picks up *The Stranger* by Albert Camus.

"Or that one either," she says.

"You've got a dark mind," he says, placing it on top of the stack.

"And you love it."

He smiles because she's right. The way she sits there with that alluring sparkle in her brown-green eyes, the simper on her lips, looking like she's won a prize. She isn't haunted. She isn't bothered. For the first time, Ezra considers that he might not be the real psychopath—and the thought makes his stomach pitch.

"Pretty fucking perfect how this all ended up," he says, sitting next to her on the bed.

"I was wondering when you were going to come upstairs and see me."

They start kissing again and he tries to concentrate on how warm and gripping and pleasurable it feels instead of that weird sense that someone is there watching them. He runs a hand up her body and she moves a hand up his leg and starts rubbing around his crotch. Yes, keep going, he thinks. He closes his eyes, but all he sees is a deep red color. He opens his eyes again and, in a flash, in a blink, like a single image inserted into a movie, there's a bloody bearded man—gone again in another blink.

"You're not even hard," Olivia whispers.

"I know, I'm ... I don't know why."

She pulls back with disappointment darkening her face.

The door to the room opens, startling them. Ezra springs to his feet like he's ready to flee a house fire. It's his mom. Awkward. She's doing that thing she does sometimes when a girl's over, even Izzy—sneak mom attack as if she's testing them. She gives Ezra a hard look before walking into the room.

"How are you settling in, Olivia?" she asks.

"Great, fine. Thank you so much."

He can tell Olivia's nervous. She once told him that his mom intimidates her, which ... yeah, no shit. That's kind of her personality.

"We have towels in the linen closet downstairs." Angela crosses her arms. "You can share the bathroom with Ezra and Eliza."

Olivia folds her hands on her lap like a polite pupil. "Sure, of course."

Angela points to the door. "And in this house, when you two are together, the door always remains open. You hear me?"

"Understood. Yes ma'am," Olivia says.

She can be a real kiss ass sometimes. It used to annoy him, but now he thinks it's endearing and clever. She's an expert when it comes to getting what she wants out of people and that isn't a bad thing.

Angela addresses Ezra. "Understood?"

"Yeah, Mom, message received. Door open." When his mom turns around and heads back down the stairs, Ezra rolls his eyes and turns to Olivia. "Sorry about that."

"It's fine. You didn't have a boner anyway," she jokes.

He snickers. "Want to ... go someplace else?"

"To the Dick?" she asks suggestively.

Ezra smiles and reaches out a hand to help her up. They head downstairs and he ignores the feeling like someone's behind him, breathing on his neck. He grabs the car keys and yells that they're going downtown and ignores the metallic smell that seems to permeate the air. In the garage, he passes the deep freezer in the corner, where he imagines he can hear a muffled scream. He sniffs his sleeve and the thoughts quiet for just a second.

In the car, as he's backing out, Olivia turns to the backseat with a frown. He knows what she's thinking about. He sniffs his sleeve again.

"Where did you end up putting the, um ... the ..."

The head. The severed head of her father. She can't bring herself to say it and neither can he. That night, he promised he was going to put it somewhere safe, somewhere no one would ever find it.

"I buried it," he says. "Don't worry about it."

He sniffs his sleeve twice as he closes the garage door.

"Why do you keep doing that?" Olivia asks, looking at him.

"Doing what?"

"Sniffing your sleeve? You've been doing it all week."

"I don't know. To make sure it smells all right."

"You smell fine. Don't worry, I'll tell you if you stink. I'm not one to hold back."

He laughs, but he doesn't feel it.

The whole time he drives, despite the bright day and the lush green scenery, he's aware of the pressure inside him building. The air in the car is stifling even when he rolls the window down. He's sure he smells it again and wants to sniff his sleeve to make sure—not just wants to but *needs* to, like an itch. When Olivia isn't looking, he lets himself just once. He breathes easier for a few minutes. The downtown buildings come into view and he feels even better knowing they'll be out of the car soon. Every time he drives, he can't help but remember that night as he went from place to place, casing parking lots for dumpsters. He can't get out of the driver's seat soon enough.

As they drive over the Full Moon Bridge, he says, "This is where my grandpa drowned."

"What?" Olivia asks, eyes widening. "You never told me that."

He glances at her. "Went over the side in his Benz."

"Wow. I'm so sorry."

Ezra parks the car into a space on the street. "Eh, it was before I was born."

"What happened? He just … drove into the water?"

"Someone cut his brakes."

Olivia's jaw drops. "How could you not tell me this after I told you that I—?"

"Yeah. Weird." He unclips his seatbelt and climbs out of the car. "Honestly, I didn't even think about it until now."

Olivia comes and joins him on the sidewalk. "Did they ever find out who did it?"

"No." Ezra sticks his hands in his pockets. "He was getting slapped with a class action suit for malpractice or something. My dad said rumors were flying that it was a former patient. He was a cardiologist."

"Damn, that's crazy."

"Yeah." He shrugs and stares at the green river churning under the nearby bridge. "Guess my family's not as normal as we seem."

ANGELA

It's not lost on Angela that, mere minutes after she walked in on her son getting groped by their new temporary ward, the two teenagers left in the family car. As she sits in her office, she taps her nails on her desk in a calming rhythm and debates whether she's done the right thing by enforcing an open-door policy in her home. She's an adolescent psychiatrist. She's well aware that, in the end, they'll find a place to have sex if that's what they're determined to do. Maybe she shouldn't have come on so strongly right out of the gate. She just sort of panicked and snapped. She scrolls into her menstruation tracker on her smartwatch—late now by a month. Menopause has started. Next thing she knows, some toddler will be calling her grandma.

"Mom?" Eliza asks in a whisper-shout from the doorway. "Are you on a call?"

Angela smiles. "No, come on in."

Eliza is looking so grown and pretty and soft since she went back to her natural hair color. It reminds Angela of when Eliza was a little girl—that long hair Angela used to brush and braid into two plaits every night while she sang "When You Wish Upon a Star." She misses that little girl with an ache. How long those days seemed, how endless, how exhausting ... and then suddenly those days are over. She was foolish to think parenting would get easier. When her children were younger, she might have been more tired, but it was only because she was direly needed. At least she knew what to do, how to keep them safe and happy. Nowadays it's like fumbling in the dark when she tries to relate to the young adults they're becoming. The thought of letting them go, of them moving out on their own, is terrifying.

"Someone's here to see you," Eliza says.

"Who?" Angela asks.

Eliza shrugs. "Some lady."

Angela waits. "Name?"

"I don't know."

"What does she look like?"

"I don't know, Mom. She had, like ... brown hair, I think?"

Angela breathes in sharply. "Tattoos?"

"Not sure."

Great. Angela shakes her head. All week she's been nauseated, waiting for Jaycee Sandoval's mother to show up on her doorstep. The silence has been almost as worrisome as the string of threatening phone calls.

"Eliza," she says, annoyed, standing up. "In the future, could you please screen any guests that show up to the house uninvited before telling them I'm home? This could be a patient or something."

"I don't think it's a patient, Mom. She's old."

"How old?"

"Like your age."

Angela sucks in, ignoring the blow of Eliza's oblivious comment. She watches her daughter turn to head back up the stairs.

"Oh!" Eliza turns around. "I was going to go over to Izzy's, is that okay?"

"Izzy," Angela says, standing up and using her phone to check her face. "You and Izzy are becoming close, huh?"

"Yeah, I guess."

"And your brother's dating your best friend."

"They're not 'dating,' Mom. People our age don't date. And she's not my best friend."

"She's not?" Angela asks, surprised.

"No."

"What happened?"

"Nothing. Just ... drifted apart."

Drifted apart? Lord, teenage relationships move fast. Not three weeks ago Eliza and Olivia were having sleep-overs. Maybe there's some jealousy here and this has something to do with Ezra. Curious that Eliza and Izzy are getting close. The crisscross is interesting. But no time to delve into it now—Eliza already left the room. And Angela has Jaycee's mother to worry about.

Angela takes a deep breath and opens her top drawer. She unscrews her prescription bottle and taps a pill into her hand, chewing it so it'll work faster, wincing at the bitterness. On second thought, she taps another pill in her hand and chews it too. Her mind races with the horrible scenarios she might run into with that unhinged woman on her doorstep. She puts the pills back and pockets her pepper spray and then, at a steady pace, dread building with every step, she heads upstairs.

When she comes into the foyer and sees the woman there, Angela is relieved it isn't Jaycee Sandoval's mother. The complete stranger wears a pantsuit and a warm smile. Angela's first guess is a Jehovah's Witness. She's never been happier to see a Jehovah's Witness on her doorstep. She lets go of the pepper spray in her pocket, relaxing.

"Hello," Angela says. "Can I help you?"

"Angela Hunter?" the woman asks brightly.

"Yes. And you are ...?"

The woman holds out a manila envelope. "You've been served."

Angela just stares at the woman's extended hand as the meaning registers. "Excuse me? There must be some mistake."

The woman's smile, which seemed friendly just a few seconds ago, now seems to be mocking her. Angela's temperature climbs. The panic returns with a vengeance.

"I'm not taking those papers," Angela says.

"You have been served," the woman repeats.

"I have not," Angela says.

The woman steps back and carefully lays the envelope on the welcome mat. "Have a blessed day!"

She leaves, striding across the lawn in her kitten heels —bitch doesn't even have the decency to walk on the pathway. Angela fumes as she bends down and rips open the envelope. Sure enough, she's being sued. Medical malpractice. Elvira Sandoval is the defendant on behalf of her daughter Jaycee. Angela wants to scream. But instead, she sits on the stoop and starts crying.

For some reason, her first thought is her father. She remembers how pissed he was when he got sued. He was miserable for weeks, for months, that anger around him like a cloud. It made him drink more, and when he drank more, he beat her mother more often. When he beat her mother more often, her mother drank more, too, to numb the pain. The malpractice suit was what started the spiral that ended it all. She hates thinking about it. Usually she can push it from her mind, but this is bringing it all back up again. She looks up at the boundless blue sky and she swears she can hear him laughing at her—that cruel roar of a laugh that always preceded a blow or an insult.

"Ange?" Carson's voice says.

She turns her head. He stoops behind her, a hand on her shoulder.

"You okay?" he asks.

Wiping her eyes, she holds the manila envelope up in the air. "Jaycee Sandoval's mother did file a lawsuit, apparently."

"Damn," he says.

"It's going to be mess."

"Want me to kill her?"

She shoots him a look. "Carson."

"I'm kidding. Sort of." He helps her up with a hand and rubs her back. "Look, we'll get through this. Just call Reggie, ask his advice."

Reggie is a friend of hers from college who moved on to law school after undergrad. He's always her first call when anything legal comes up. Sometimes he and his husband drive out to visit. He has a place in Tahoe he always tells her is open for them to stay at in the summertime, and they have nearly every year since the kids were small.

"I will. Right after I call CPS." Angela stops and looks at Carson, a dull ache coursing through her from head to toe. "It's all crashing down on me at once. I don't know how much more I can take."

"Look, we'll get through this. I was just coming down here to tell you that Chaz called just now." Carson's eyes twinkle. "We can pitch this, I'm sure of it, and soon. There'll be renewed interest since the twenty-five-year anniversary of the last victim is coming up in three years."

"Has it been twenty-two years?" she asks, surprised.

"It has."

"Wow. Feels like a lifetime ago." She swallows. "Well ... good news. I hope—"

"It's *great* news for us, Ange. I can't wait to tell this story. You know how much we need the money."

She nods. Sometimes Carson drives her up the wall. He snores louder than a jet airliner. He's childish and his taste in music is abominable. He has an affection for Hawaiian shirts and puns. But he's a gentle, loving father and the sweetest husband she could have asked for. Passion is a flame that inevitably dies. But loyalty burns forever.

And secrets can sew two hearts together.

CARSON

Carson walks around for the next few days with an extra bounce in his step. The world is sunnier, his coffee tastes fresher, his own house sparkles as if it's new. When a man has a book on submission with major publishers, anything is possible.

Tuesday morning, Chaz emailed to say he sent out a few "feelers" to some editors he thought might be interested in the Ravens Landing Dismemberer story. Chaz's email read, *Don't get your hopes up, just casting a line to gauge initial interest. There may be none.* But Carson chose to rewrite it in his own mind: Chaz is pitching an exclusive submission of his work. Carson also chose to revise Chaz's exasperated call with him this past weekend (*Twenty texts and six voicemails, to talk about this? On a weekend? This couldn't wait until Monday?*) by editing it down to the important details: Chaz thinks this project is important enough that he *did* end up having a phone call about it over a weekend and he agreed there could be something there.

It's hard to get much done at times like these, so Carson spends the week cleaning and reaching out to contractors about the mold problem in the garage. And checking his email about a thousand times a day.

"Kids, there's a guy coming over here at eleven a.m. tomorrow to look at the mold situation in the garage," Carson says on Thursday afternoon, standing in the living room. Ezra and Olivia lie on opposite ends of the couch with their noses in different books. How long has it been since Ezra spent this much time reading? What a positive influence Olivia is on his son!

Ezra sits up, using his finger as a bookmark. "Where in the garage?"

"In the corner, near the freezer," Carson says.

The expression on Ezra's face—you'd think Carson just gave him a cancer diagnosis.

"What's up, buddy?" Carson asks.

"Just—I have things in there I—I don't want them touching," Ezra says.

Carson can't think of anything in the garage that Ezra would be remotely interested in. All they keep in there are Christmas decorations, extra bedding, and gardening tools. "Like what?"

Ezra glances at Olivia, as if she has the answer. Olivia looks as confused as Carson is.

"What?" Olivia asks.

Ezra shakes his head and lies back on the couch. "Never mind."

"Alrighty," Carson says.

Female laughter drifts from upstairs and the three of them point their gazes at the ceiling.

"Eliza and Izzy seem to be having fun up there," Carson says.

"Wish they could have fun a little quieter," Ezra mutters.

When Carson was young, know what he did all summer? Rode his bike around town. Swam to beat the heat. Worked a summer job at the deli, On a Roll. What a cliché he's become, but, man, kids these days. They park their asses on the couch and never leave the house. Although, to be fair, Eliza worked all summer until Tutu Camp was done last week. And Olivia is likely feeling anxious and preoccupied with her dad's disappearance. Still.

"Why don't the four of you go somewhere together?" Carson asks.

"The four of us?" Olivia asks.

"The girls—" Carson points to the ceiling. "—and you two."

Olivia and Ezra just stare at him as if he proposed they get in a cardboard box and fly it to the moon.

"A picnic?" Carson says. "I don't know, go ... shopping? Go see a movie?"

"Dad, we're *reading*," Ezra says, annoyed.

"It's literally the healthiest thing we could be doing for our brains," Olivia says.

"Plus, we don't really hang out together." Ezra points to the ceiling. "Us and them."

"It would be weird," Olivia agrees.

How? Carson shakes his head. Clearly some teenage politics are at play that he isn't privy to. But you know what? Fine, if they want to stay inside a dark house together reading novels, that's their prerogative. He checks his email for the hundredth time this morning. Nothing from Chaz. Sigh. Oh well, think positive, it'll happen in time. It has to. It just has to.

CARSON

Whatever is going on with the Ezra-Eliza-Olivia triangle makes for a very awkward dinnertime. When Carson serves mac and cheese, the lack of conversation is so potent he hears everyone chewing and swallowing, every scrape of every fork against the dinner plates.

"Well, Miss Riverwood's just two days away," he says cheerfully, taking a swig of his beer. "You excited, Eliza?"

She nods but doesn't say a word.

"You guys are planning on going too, right?" Carson asks Ezra. "To support your sister?"

"Do we have to?" he asks, pushing the food around his plate.

"Ez, come on."

"We'll go," Olivia says, nodding. "Sounds fun."

Another excruciating spell of silence. Carson scours his mind for something to talk to them about. He could ask Olivia how the phone call with the police went after the missing person report was filed online yesterday, but that's kind of a bummer. He'd love to regale them with stories of the Raven's Landing Dismemberer, which he's been going over all afternoon, but his family has reminded him several times in the past that severed limbs are considered taboo when it comes to dinner conversation, unfortunately. Speaking of limbs, he's pretty sure there's some footsie going on under the table and Eliza is stealthily scrolling her phone on her lap. Oh, this is pure hell. Carson shoves his dinner down his throat as fast as he can, makes up a plate, and goes to deliver it to Angela downstairs in her office.

"Your supper, m'lady," he says at the entrance. "Homemade mac and cheese. How was your appointment?"

"I'll talk to you about it later," she says, looking exhausted.

"But you're okay?"

"Yes, fine, healthy, all that."

Carson knows Angela's grappling with feelings about going through menopause. Her moods have been up and down. Women don't have it easy, do they? Carson thanks God he was born a man.

"Ange, my love, mi amor." Carson walks over to her desk, gently putting the food behind her open laptop. "I know what'll cheer you up: carbs."

Over her shoulder, he can read the webpage she's on: *Coping with a medical malpractice suit.*

"We might need to take out a loan," she says, her voice a little hoarse. She's been on calls all day. "I don't know how I'm going to keep managing my workload and this lawsuit at the same time."

"Does it even have merit, though? What did Reggie say?"

"He says it's not going to be easy, Carson."

"I don't understand what they could accuse you of. You were trying to help the girl. You prescribed her medication. What did they expect, sending their daughter to a psychiatrist?"

Angela swivels in her chair, taking off her reading glasses. Her eyes are red. "I keep thinking about my dad. About the suit against him. For the first time in a long time, I wish he were around, just so I could ask his advice."

"Come on, you don't wish he was around. Jesus."

"Just for one minute."

"He'd probably yell at you and tell you what an idiot you are."

"I know." She nods. "You're right."

Carson is well aware that people are complex. They aren't all good or bad. Dr. Walter Atkins helped save lives and pushed his kids on swings and bought his wife flowers. But overall, he was an asshole, a tyrant, and Carson knew it from the moment he first met the man.

The day Angela introduced Carson to her father, he stood there with a steely glare and said, "You may think you're cool shit, boy, but if you touch my daughter the wrong way, you'll be a floating corpse in the river." He said this while Carson had his hand extended, a smile on his face. He said this while he stood next to a wife whose nose was crooked from being broken by him so many times. He said this while his daughter still had bruises on her arm and he had a bandage on his forehead from being whacked with a poker. The irony that a human being that heartless was a cardiologist is not lost on Carson.

The world is a better place without Walter Atkins in it. Human beings are complex, indeed, but sometimes it's just simple math. Subtract one person and the world's a better place.

"Maybe this lawsuit's karma," Angela says as Carson massages her shoulders.

"Oh, we're Buddhist now?" He moves her hair so he can dip down and kiss her neck.

She shivers and relaxes under his grip. "I don't know. Payback."

"Your father's ghost is avenging us with lawsuits."

"And house repairs," she jokes.

"Mmm. Maybe that's what those noises are that you keep hearing in the vents. It wasn't rats. It was your father."

"Could be. You never saw a rat, did you?"

"You're becoming superstitious in your middle age."

She smiles. He loves when he can turn Angela's lights back on—a challenge that never gets old.

"Speaking of middle age, I—"

"Mom?" Eliza asks, appearing like a ghost at the bottom of the basement steps.

Carson and Angela gasp. He stops massaging her.

"You snuck up on us, kid," Carson says.

"Are you ... busy?" Eliza comes forward. She's doing that hair-twirling thing that she used to do as a kid.

"What's up?" Angela asks.

Eliza collapses on the couch and clasps her hands. Jesus, what's coming? A confession? She's pregnant, she's gay? Oh, he hopes she's gay. Please be gay and not pregnant.

"Um, I just wanted to—talk about Olivia," Eliza says.

Phew!

"Just wondering," Eliza goes on, "like ... how long is she going to be here?"

"Well," Angela says. "Depends on when her dad returns and whether we find some other better living situation for her. I filed for emergency temporary guardianship, but the court hearing's not until next week."

Eliza keeps twirling her hair and chewing her lip.

"Like, she's going to be okay," Angela says. "I know this situation is scary. I know you're thinking of what happened with Amanda, but this isn't like that at all. Olivia will stay here safe with us."

"What if I don't think she ... should ... stay with us?" Eliza shifts her gaze from her bunny slippers and finally makes eye contact.

Angela and Carson exchange a mirrored look of confusion.

"Sorry, come again?" he asks.

Eliza sits up straighter "Just, I don't know. I don't think it's a good idea having her here."

"Why?" Angela asks.

Carson narrows his eyes, trying desperately to understand. "She has nowhere else to go. Her father is *missing*."

"She'd be in foster care if she didn't stay here," Angela says. "You want a repeat of what happened to Amanda? You were *so* upset about that."

Eliza shakes her head. "This is different."

"Are you jealous of her relationship with Ezra?" Carson tries.

"No." Eliza bats her hand through the air as if this is ridiculous. "Not at all."

"Did something happen between you two?" Angela asks. "A falling out?"

Eliza rolls her eyes. "No."

"Then what?" Carson says, getting exasperated. Jesus, sometimes extracting information from a teenager is harder than a police interrogation.

"I don't think she's a good person," Eliza says.

The statement changes the air like a stink bomb thrown in the center of the room.

Angela crosses her arms. "Please elaborate."

"For one, she shoplifts," Eliza says. "She stole crystals from Izzy's mom's store."

"Not that I approve, but a lot of kids and teens shoplift," Angela says.

"Yeah, remember when you took those M&Ms from the drugstore in third grade?" Carson reminds her.

Eliza's cheeks flush. "That's different."

"Listen, I know it must be hard," Angela says, her tone shifting, oozing sympathy. "Olivia and your brother have grown very close, very fast, and it's natural you feel left behind."

"Don't use your therapy voice on me, Mom."

Angela closes her eyes, collecting herself. "I'm just saying—"

"It's not about Ezra." Eliza's pitch climbs. "This has nothing to do with Ezra."

"She's practically a part of the family." Carson's patience is thinning. "We're not going to throw her out on the streets. Eliza, forgive me, but you have no idea what kind of hardship that kid's been through. You're acting pretty selfish. She's got no one in this world but us right now."

Eliza stands up. "Look, if her dad went missing, *she's* probably got something to do with it."

Angela's jaw drops. "Eliza!"

"She *hates* her dad. Hates him. She told me once she wants to kill him!" Eliza stamps her foot.

Carson heaves a sigh. "Oh, come on. Kids say BS like that all the time."

"*Especially* kids who come from abusive homes." Angela shakes her head. "I am shocked right now at your lack of empathy, Eliza. I don't have the slightest idea what happened in the past few weeks that made you go from best friends to *this*, but you need to put your hurt feelings aside right now and exercise a little compassion."

"Yeah, this is disappointing, kid. Do better."

Eliza's face is so red now she looks like she's about to explode. She utters a small scream, spins on her heel, and stomps upstairs.

"Jesus, what was that about?" Carson asks.

Angela shakes her head, her eyes shining. "She has no idea what it's like."

He knows, from that faraway look, that it isn't Olivia she's thinking about.

Weeks after they started seeing each other, Angela told Carson everything. She never told anyone these things before—not her best friend, not her exes, not her school counselors. Her father appeared to be a wealthy, respectable doctor, but underneath that costume, he was nothing but a sadistic brute whose entire family lived in constant fear of him. He used money to control everyone in his household and threatened to cut people off whenever they disagreed with him. And now he was battling a malpractice class action suit. They had so much, yet the fear of losing it hung over the household like a black cloud.

And then there was Penny Patterson.

When Angela assaulted her father with a fireplace poker, it was because of Penny Patterson—a nurse her dad was apparently having an affair with for months. Over a glazed ham their mother prepared, her dad informed the family he was going to leave his wife. He was going to dissolve his children's trusts. He was going to kick them out of the house. The family—Angela and her brothers and her mother with her far-off stare—sat quietly in shock. After delivering this earth-shattering news, her father went to sit by the fire and drink an old-fashioned the way he did every night. And Angela got up, took the fireplace poker, and whacked him over the head with it.

"Are you sorry you did it?" Carson asked her when she told him the story.

Angela turned to him. He saw a distant fire in her tiger eyes, a danger that made him never want to look away from her again.

"The only thing I'm sorry about," she said, "is that I didn't hit him hard enough to kill him."

Carson was quiet. He reached out and grabbed her hand and squeezed. "You know, I just read the most interesting story."

"What's that?"

"About a guy whose brakes got cut. Ended up in a fatal accident. Was impossible to prove who did it and why." He raised his eyebrows. "Bet you that kind of thing happens a lot more than you'd think."

"Really," she said, her eyes flickering brightly.

"Really." Carson reached out and tucked a stray lock of golden hair behind her ear. "And hypothetically, a man with quite a few enemies—with a class action lawsuit pending against him—they'd never have any idea who did it."

Olivia

Olivia sits on the edge of her bed in a state of shock. Though there's sunlight in the air, slanted in golden rays where dust sparkles, her mood is much closer to midnight. She's beyond angry. Her fury has morphed into something far worse, far more dangerous: despair.

"Traitor," she whispers.

Betrayer. Deceiver. Double-crosser. Judas.

Not a half hour ago, Olivia was looking for Ezra when she passed Eliza's room in the hallway and heard the word "Olivia." She heard it spoken, loud and clear. Can you blame her for walking into Eliza's bedroom to investigate? And when Olivia discovered the name wasn't coming from the room, but was drifting up through the wide vent in Eliza's wall—could Olivia really be blamed for getting on her hands and knees and pressing her ear to the grating to get the whole story? And then once she started listening, how on earth could she stop? Because what she heard was the sound of Eliza stabbing her in the back over and over and over.

Olivia isn't a fool. She can tell Eliza's uncomfortable with her being here. Olivia still has no idea what she did to deserve to be basically ghosted by her former best friend, but she's tried to take it in stride. It isn't the first time someone has suddenly turned on her and it won't be the last, because people are fickle and untrustworthy animals. Eventually, Olivia hoped she might win Eliza over again if she gave her enough space. She truly loved her friend, even though she frustrates the shit out of her.

Loved, past tense.

That's all over now.

Replaying the horrible conversation she overheard, Olivia balls up a fist and squeezes an invisible stress ball. Eliza tried to get Olivia booted from the house. Eliza said Olivia "wasn't a good person," which hurts, because though she knows she's done many questionable things, she still thinks of herself as a good person. Sure, she doesn't mind hurting people, but she doesn't *want* to hurt people. There's a big difference between having the stomach for horrors and having the lust for it. That's the problem with Eliza. No ability to see nuance. It's why she can't appreciate an excellent book. Speaking of which ... Olivia gets up and tiptoes to her dresser, where the books are stacked in a neat tower on top. Her chest hums as she pulls a thick poetry anthology and dives back onto her bed.

When Olivia's mind wanders, when she's lost, she's always sought solace in words written by people who are now long dead. Magic, isn't it? Ghosts speaking to you from beyond this world. Runes inscribed on dead trees that, with concentration, can make you hallucinate. Olivia stops to smell the sweetness of the pages, then flips to the poem she's looking for: "A Poison Tree." She read it many times in the week before her dad went missing and it speaks to her, it resonates with a new special meaning, as if William Blake wrote it just for her.

I was angry with my friend, it begins.

It's a lovely poem. A real hammer to the heart when Olivia reaches that last line with the corpse of the speaker's foe beneath the tree. To Olivia, this is an ode to patient revenge. It's the years she spent making her dad dinners while he yelled at her, the many times she smiled and said hello when she wanted to spit at him and run away. But now the poem reminds her of Eliza, who she's been nothing but kind to, who she never hurt. The intro before the poem says it's about the importance of communication, but Olivia disagrees. This is a poem about the gorgeousness of getting the last word.

She closes the book, pushes it aside on her bed. It pisses Olivia off that her eyeballs sting, that she let herself care enough for Eliza that the betrayal cuts this deep. They were best friends. Found sisters. And now Eliza wants to get rid of her? Because Olivia stole a fucking crystal, a meaningless rock that the shop owners stole from the earth? Because she said she wanted to kill her dad—which was told in complete privacy and which Eliza acted like she never heard?

But the barb that digs the worst, that she can't let go

of, is Eliza trying to say Olivia isn't a good person. Eliza has no idea what hell Olivia has been through. Eliza's a privileged wimp too chicken to even have a conversation with Olivia. Eliza's the kind of girl who breaks up with people over text message, the kind of girl who lies just to avoid conflict. Thank God her brother isn't anything like her. Olivia calms, imagining the warmth of Ezra's arms, the wet pull of his kiss. The one person on earth who's proved he would do anything for her. He would never betray her.

Olivia seethes, breathing deeply. No more tears.

It's time for revenge—*that apple bright.*

She slides to the floor cross-legged in front of the trunk. Unlatching it with a click, she pops it open. Look at what's there inside: six jars. Six black widow spiders. Olivia taps each of them with a fingernail on the glass. The spiders respond to the light and attention, moving their legs. They're probably losing their minds in there. Poor things.

"Good evening, ladies," she whispers. "I believe it's time to set you free."

OLIVIA

Olivia's heartbeat is still racing as she tiptoes downstairs to put her empty jars in the recycling bin. She can hear Angela and Carson talking in low voices in their room in the back of the house. Appreciation swells—she overheard how they defended her when Eliza tried to badmouth her. Olivia lingers at the bottom of the stairs to try to get the gist of what they're saying, but suddenly the rise of a song on the piano cuts through the air. It's Eliza, practicing. Sounds clumsy, lots of pauses. She looks up at Olivia from across the dark room.

"I didn't know you played piano," Olivia says.

"I haven't in years," Eliza says. "I've been thinking about getting back into it."

"Well, cool. Keep up the good work."

Olivia leaves before Eliza can glimpse the jars in her hands and makes her way to the dark garage.

Cracking open the door, Olivia gets a shiver. The garage has one dim light hanging that lends this room an especially creepy vibe. She crosses to the recycling bin and dumps the glass jars in there with loud clinks. When she turns around and sees a shadowy, tall figure right behind her, she opens her mouth to scream—but then recognizes Ezra.

"Holy shit," she says after a good gasp. "You scared me."

He has the strangest look on his face, like he's far away from her, like he isn't seeing her but seeing *through* her. For a split second, she wonders if he knows the sneaky trick she just played on his sister, but no, there's no way he does. This is something else.

"Are you feeling okay?" she asks.

"Do you hear it?" he finally answers, pointing a thumb to the corner of the room behind him.

"What?"

He waits, listening closely to the air. "You don't hear it?"

"Hear *what*, Ezra?"

"The screaming," he says, his eyes wide. Finally, he's looking at her, really looking at her. And he's terrified. Seeing this in him strikes a note of terror in Olivia, too. What the hell is going on?

"Screaming?" she whispers.

"Yeah, I hear it. On and off, on and off. Coming from the ..."

"From the what?"

He looks back in the corner of the room and sniffs his sleeve.

"Ezra, babes, let's go inside."

She doesn't like seeing him this way—sick or something. He's ... not right. He keeps sniffing his sleeve and staring into the corner of the room like he sees a ghost. Finally, he nods and follows her back into the house.

"You were probably just hearing Eliza playing the piano," she says, smiling.

"Yeah, maybe."

As they head up the stairs, Olivia frowns. Something spooky is going on. She can't quite put her finger on it and she isn't sure when it started. But the air in the Hunter household seems to have shifted. Is it just tonight? Has it been there before?

And then, the most shocking thought of all: is *she* the darkness?

Is she the darkness that has descended upon the Hunter household?

As she passes by Eliza's room with its perfectly made bed complete with childhood stuffed animals on it, Olivia can't help the inner twinkle knowing what she did. She's always felt like she's a blazing fire, a bringer of light. If she wreaks havoc, she always has her reasons.

But maybe she is the darkness.

Maybe she is.

Eliza

When Eliza brushes her teeth in the bathroom tonight, she can hear the lively lilt of Olivia's voice through the ceiling and her little bursts of laughter interspersed with Ezra's low voice. She gazes up at the glossy ceiling as the electric toothbrush buzzes in her mouth, wishing she could have x-ray vision and that she could know what it is they talk about up there.

It's so weird, Olivia living in this house now and being in a relationship with Eliza's brother. It makes home feel like a foreign place. It makes her quiet at family dinners and self-conscious of what she does in her own bedroom for fear Olivia could be listening. It makes her feel like the least interesting girl in the Hunter household. It's hard to explain. Eliza's soul is going through some kind of growth spurt and having Olivia around only makes it all worse.

Spitting in the sink, Eliza eyes herself in the mirror, the brown hair she's still getting used to, the way it softens her features and makes her look both younger and older at the same time. A realization blossoms—one tinged with shame. She tried to get Olivia kicked out of her house not because she thinks Olivia's such a bad person. It's more that it makes life awkward. And she has no one to blame for the awkwardness but herself. It's her own stupid fault for ghosting Olivia in the first place. Now the girl she ghosted is haunting her daily.

Upstairs, the voices of Olivia and Ezra hush and she has to wonder what they're doing up there, though *ew*, she really doesn't want to. She puts her toothbrush away in the holder next to Olivia's toothbrush—a child's toothbrush with Oscar the Grouch on it. Guess Eliza should suck it up and get used to it. Olivia's an "honorary Hunter" now. She's her brother's girlfriend. Here to stay.

Fine, she thinks as she flips off the light and goes to her room. Eliza's going to move on, be mature. Hang out with Izzy and her theater crew. Get back into piano. When she crawls under her covers, she closes her eyes and New York's skyline glimmers in her mind. She sees wet, slick city streets and hears the bump of subway cars. She imagines a dorm and friends and laughter and—

What the fuck is that?

Spooked, Eliza jerks and kicks her legs under the covers. Something is crawling on her ankle. Is it? She stills and steadies her breath. No, she's being paranoid. Her brain is doing that thing it does late at night, trying to freak her out. But—*twitch twitch*—there's a creeping movement on her calf and then another on her arm, followed by what feels like a prick of a needle on the back of her thigh. The adrenaline hits her veins like a shot.

She springs out of bed, yelping and shaking her arms. Runs and turns on the light. When she sees the spider on the floor, its body shiny and black as a bead, she gasps.

"Oh my God, oh my God, oh my God," she says, doing a wild dance to brush off her hair and skin.

When she stops, she sees that there are two more of them in her bed, two more *enormous* black spiders, and it's as if a trap door opens under her.

She's falling through the center of the earth.

She can't move.

Frozen in horror, mouth open in a silent scream, she watches the spiders scatter out of her bed toward the wall, the other spider still crawling along her carpet a few feet away from her.

"No, no, no," she says.

The closest thing to Eliza right now are her pointe shoes hanging on the door behind her. She grabs them and whacks the spider on the floor before it can make it under her dresser. Immediately, it curls up and dies next to the pale pink ballet shoes. Okay. A little whiff of relief.

Until she gets a closer look at it.

It lays there, legs curled in, body the size of a dime.

Screaming-red hourglass on its belly.

Panting, the shock sets in. Her teeth chatter. A black widow. A fucking *black widow* is in her room. And there are more. She dry heaves. There are more of them some-where near her bed, they're in her *bed*, poisonous disgusting spiders in her *bed*. The back of her thigh throbs. Did they bite her? That pinprick she felt—did one of them bite her just now?

Eliza flees her room, down the stairs, at the speed of light. She begins screaming at the foot of the stairs like a horror movie scream queen and she doesn't stop until her parents come running out in their pajamas.

Eliza

"Keep the ice pack there, hon." Angela pets Eliza's hair. "Yes, advice nurse, please," Angela says into the phone pressed to her ear.

The living room is so chilly, it might as well be Alaska. Stupid ice pack only makes Eliza's leg ache worse. She bats her mom's hand away and stands up, abandoning the ice pack on the couch.

"Ice isn't helping," Eliza says, squeezing one hand with the other.

She bends back to squint at the bite. It's hard to see that well without a mirror. It's only been twenty minutes, but already the back of her thigh is red and swollen bigger than it would be with a regular spider bite. Her mom already promised her a dozen times she isn't going to die. They even googled it together to prove it. Still, this is the worst thing that has ever happened to Eliza. Multiple poisonous spiders! In her room! In her *bed!* Eliza's positive she will never sleep again.

"Yes, my daughter was just bitten by a black widow spider," Angela says into the phone.

"So fucked up," Ezra says, seated on one of the stuffed chairs in the dark corner with Olivia on his lap.

Eliza doesn't even look at him. She had forgotten he was there, to be honest. Useless. At least her dad's upstairs trying to find the spiders in her room. Ezra and Olivia are watching like this is a movie they're only halfway invested in. Eliza touches the bite on the back of her burning leg, numb and wet from the ice.

"About a half hour ago," Angela says into the phone.

"Miss Riverwood is *Saturday*," Eliza says. "If—"

Angela holds up a *shhh* finger. "She's fine right now. It's red and swollen."

"And achy," Eliza reminds her.

"Yes. Sure. Uh-huh. You're sure? We need—? Okay." Angela ends the call with a touch of a button and shakes her head. "Get your shoes on, Lize, we're going to the ER."

"What did they say?" Eliza asks, panic flashing.

ER. Hospital. Only once in her sixteen years on this planet has Eliza gone to the ER and that was for a sprained ankle. She wants to cry. This is bad. This is so bad. Instead of going to sleep, she's going to the hospital. None of this makes sense, she's stumbling through a nightmare. How the hell did three black widows end up in her room in the first place?

"They have to evaluate you." Angela grabs her purse from the hook where it hangs on the foyer.

She says it like it's such a pain in the ass. Eliza resists

the urge to apologize for getting bitten by poisonous spiders and imposing on her mom's busy schedule.

With a thunder of footsteps, Carson descends the stairs. He wears a face shield and some kind of hazmat suit thing and carries a can of bug spray in one hand and a roll of paper towels in another.

"How are you, kiddo?" he asks, flipping his shield up.

"Apparently I'm going to the hospital," Eliza says.

"Just a precaution," Angela says. "Don't catastrophize."

"Mom, if ever there was a time to catastrophize, being bitten by *poisonous spiders* might be one of them," Eliza says, wishing she could scare a little fear into her mom's calm face.

"Venomous," Ezra says.

Everyone's attention snaps to where he sits, hunched in the shadows. Olivia is finger combing his hair and gazing at him, face wrinkled in concern as if it's him she's worried about and not the girl with the toxic spider bite.

"Huh?" Eliza says.

"Spiders aren't technically poisonous, they're venomous," Ezra says. "'Poisonous' is, like, inhaled or transmitted through the skin. Venom is injected."

If Eliza wasn't experiencing waves of pain in her leg, she would kick him with it. Instead, she focuses on slipping her boots on.

"Not the time, homeboy. Read the room," Carson says.

"Anyway, we'll be back soon." Angela kisses Carson's cheek. "You see anything up there?"

"Yeah ... we're going to need to talk," he says quietly.

"About what?" Angela asks.

Everyone stills, awaiting his answer. Carson pulls the face shield all the way off and holds it in his hands the way a cop would hold his police cap in a movie where he has to deliver the news that someone died.

"You saw them?" Eliza asks, shivering a little—from the shock of the situation, from the poison—sorry, *venom* —in her veins. "You saw the other two, didn't you?"

He blows a breath out. "I saw five."

A chorus of gasps.

"*Five?* In her room?" Angela's blue eyes are on the verge of popping right out of her head.

"I told you!" wails Eliza.

"Fuck," Ezra says, suddenly paranoid, jerking and turning to look over his shoulder. "Are they all over the house?"

"We might need to get this place fumigated or something, I really don't know," Carson says. "I killed every one I saw in there."

It's not often that Eliza's mom is tongue-tied, but now is one of those times. "I ... don't have the capacity to deal with this information right now," Angela finally says. "I'll text you when we get to the hospital."

"That is so scary." Olivia's brow is furrowed. "Maybe we should inspect the rest of the house? See if we find anything?"

"Let me," Carson says. "The coast is clear in here. I'm going to do another sweep of the house." He puts his hazmat head shield back on.

Ezra and Olivia exchange a look, worry shining in their eyes.

"Let's go out the front," Angela says to Eliza. "Trying to avoid inhaling the mold in the garage as much as possible." She turns to Carson, broken-faced like she might cry. Of course this is the time her mom finally seems on the verge of a breakdown … when it's about the fucking *house*. Daughter bitten by a black widow? Cool cool. House might need work? The floodgates open. "Mold, black widows, this place is really a monster these days."

Angela opens the door, the chilly night air rushing in. Before stepping outside to follow her mother, Eliza glances once more at the back of her leg where the rash is spreading, gruesome as a pink bloodstain along her skin. Then Eliza's eyes meet Olivia's. It happens in one split second. And in that second, it's like the whole world disappears and it's just the two of them: Eliza. Olivia. Each at opposite ends.

With a sick twist of her stomach, Eliza understands exactly what happened tonight.

Because Olivia flashes a smug half-smile and a queenly wave—so quickly that no one else catches it.

ANGELA

A ngela might be a doctor, but ER waiting rooms make her squeamish.

ER waiting rooms are the fluorescent prologue to bad news. It's where people head when everything goes wrong. It's anxiety in architectural form. The Riverwood County Hospital, quaint and welcoming as it tries to be with its fresh flowers and tea machine, is no different. As Angela sits in her bucket chair clasping her hands so hard her fingernails dig into her skin, she enters a horrid backward time machine. She's a teenager again with her mother holding an ice pack to her own head, a slow trickle of blood running down her temple, her nose askew.

The waiting room hasn't changed much since Angela was young, the black-and-white picture of the hospital a century earlier still there centered in the middle of the wall. The confetti pattern on the floor that looks like vomit—a convenient choice. Easy to mask the many bodily fluids that dripped there over the years. Surely her mother's DNA is somewhere hiding in the fibers of those carpets. With a pang, Angela misses her mother. But she doesn't really miss her mother, does she? She misses the alternate history version of her, the strong woman she could have been. Her mother, when alive, was an exasperating textbook example of codependency. And alcoholism. Just a year after Angela's dad's funeral, her mother drank one too many self-medicating negronis one night and drowned in the backyard hot tub.

"Mom?" Eliza asks. "Hello? Are you even listening?"

"Yes," Angela says, snapping back to now.

A spasm of guilt—she's supposed to be here for her daughter, yet here she is reliving her own trauma instead. She counts a breath to center herself in the present moment. Fortunately Eliza doesn't look like she's in pain, but she does look incredibly irritated.

"How are you feeling?" Angela asks.

It's a question that she asks clients so many times it isn't even a question anymore. It's a reflex, same as a kick of the lower leg when the anterior knee is tapped.

"Shitty, Mom. I'm feeling shitty," Eliza answers, as if she's talking to someone with brain damage.

"Can you be more specific? What symptoms are you experiencing?"

"It's itchy. And ... hard to explain. Like a Charley horse."

"Remember what we read online—only four to eight

people die of black widow bites each year out of thousands reported. And then there are all those that *aren't* reported."

"Yes, Mom, I remember what our Lord and Savior Google said."

Angela gives Eliza a side hug. She feels for her, of course she does. Her poor daughter is going through something deeply frightening, but it's strange—sometimes with all the clients Angela speaks to, all the worries she battles endlessly like a game of whack-a-mole, she's drained of empathy. She's a talented problem solver. Nurturing comes harder.

A woman carrying a crying toddler rushes through the doors and heads straight to the check-in desk. Angela watches the woman, how she kisses the child's puffy cheeks and pats their curls. Her stomach tightens with mixed feelings. When Eliza was a child, Angela could meet her every need. Give her a snack when she was grumpy, put her down to sleep, bandage up her scrapes and wipe her tears when she fell. But this young woman her daughter is shapeshifting into—Angela can't tell what she needs and no matter what she says, it never feels like it's right.

Imagine going through it all again, at this age. How could she? It's exhausting and eternal and imperfect, raising children.

"But it's not even the bite, you know?" Eliza breaks the silence. "You weren't listening to what I was saying before, were you?"

Angela squeezes her daughter's arm. "I'm sorry. I got distracted. Go on."

Eliza winces and shifts in her chair. Then she leans in closer to Angela and says, "I was saying that I think Olivia did this."

What does that mean? A beat passes. "I'm sorry. Did what?"

"She put the spiders in my room."

"You think," Angela says slowly, "that Olivia put a black widow in your room."

"Black widows," Eliza clarifies. "Dad found five."

"Okay," Angela says slowly, considering this unhinged suggestion, hoping her daughter is kidding.

But no.

Good Lord, she's dead serious.

The look in Eliza's eyes—both fire and ice. Downright spooky. Angela experiences a wave of déjà vu. Last year, Eliza tried to argue that there were ghosts in the house. It was after some scary movie she watched. She didn't sleep well for weeks. For the most part, Eliza has a rational brain. But when nonsense slips in there, it's sticky.

"Lize," Angela says. "Come on. What would make you think she would do something like that?"

"She hates me."

"There's no evidence that's true."

"She loves spiders. She said she's caught black widows before."

Odd. An odd hobby. But there are arachnophiles out

there. Angela had a client once, a boy with Asperger's syndrome whose passion was collecting spiders. He showed them to her on Zoom, big hairy garden spiders he caught in jars and called by their scientific names.

"I'm concerned about your ... preoccupation with Olivia," Angela says, putting a hand on Eliza's jiggling knee. "Can we put that aside for tonight? I hear that you're looking for a reason this happened. I know how scary this has been. But hon, Olivia's not out to get you. Listen to how that sounds. She's not some mastermind collecting venomous spiders and letting them loose in your room." Angela offers a gentle smile, a little poke. "Come on."

"That's what she wants you to think," Eliza whispers.

Her hand is shaking. Maybe it's the effect of the spider's venom, it is a possible side effect along with cold-like symptoms. But more likely, it's nerves. Nerves are something Angela can help with. She takes a pill case out of her purse and offers Eliza a Valium, who takes it immediately as if it's candy and swallows it dry. It isn't the first time Angela's answer for her daughter's stress is Valium.

"Can you please believe me?" Eliza asks, teeth chattering. "About Olivia? About what she did?"

It's a relief when the doctor comes through the door at this moment, not just because Eliza needs medical attention for the bite on her leg—but because Angela is at a complete loss as to how to respond to her daughter.

The ER doctor, as Angela expected, is useless. He says the bite doesn't look too bad and recommends an over-the-counter antihistamine and ice for swelling before sending them home. Eliza will be fine, besides some swelling and aching and chills. She'll be able to compete in the Miss Riverwood competition, as planned. But none of this assuages Angela's concern.

She's more worried about Eliza's paranoia than the bite on her leg.

CARSON

Sometimes Carson feels like he's the lone voice of sanity in the Hunter household.

His wife's strings are pulled so tight he's afraid sometimes she'll snap. In the middle of the night last week, he awoke to her weeping about the mold. Then it was the lawsuit. Before all this it was rats (which he never found, by the way, all that poison gone to waste) and now it's black widows (he found no evidence of a large-scale infestation there either, just those pesky few in Eliza's room). Angela speaks of the house with a venom in her voice, as if it's a trap. The house she once wanted so badly it felt like an answer. The Victorian dream house on the hill, the one their children took their first steps in. She looks him in the eyes after getting home from the ER Thursday night and just says, flatly, "I hate this fucking house." Angela Hunter is not one to use the F-bomb, so Carson's jaw drops.

Then there's Ezra, who's so smitten with Olivia he

walks around in some kind of romantic zombie state, following her from room to room. It's cute, it is, his son's clearly in love. The PDA is nonstop—like they're two parasitic animals that have to be touching at all times. But Ezra is also not quite himself. When Carson is alone in a room with him, his son zones out and stares at the corner with a paralyzed frown.

After Angela has returned from the ER and heads to bed, Carson is putting away the flashlights used for the fruitless search for more black widows. He goes into the garage and the sight of his son standing there, spaced out in his pajamas in the dim-lit room, makes Carson yell, "Hot dog!" and almost drop the flashlights on the floor.

"What are you doing out here, buddy?" Carson asks.

At first, it's like Ezra hasn't heard him. It reminds Carson of when his son went through a sleepwalking phase as a kiddo and peed in the corner of the living room. Thankfully there don't appear to be any urine puddles this time.

"Thought I heard something," Ezra mutters.

Carson cocks his ear, listening for what his son is talking about. But there's nothing but the whine of the deep freezer.

"Probably that piece of junk." Carson points at the freezer with a flashlight. "Might be time to replace it."

The look of horror on Ezra's face—it's like Carson suggested he amputate a leg.

"Are you okay?" Carson asks.

"I'm fine," Ezra says. He smells his sleeve.

"Long day," Carson says. "I don't know how any of us

are going to get any sleep tonight." He does an exaggerated shiver.

Ezra's brow knits. "Why?"

"The ... the spiders?" Carson reminds him. "The black widows in your sister's room—remember those?"

"Oh. Right." Ezra sniffs his sleeve again. "I'll be okay."

He lurches back inside with a Frankenstein's monster walk and Carson is left alone with an armful of flashlights. He shakes his head and shines a beam in the corners of the room to make sure there aren't any more spiders. But all he sees is the mold eating at the walls, which is almost worse. At least spiders don't cause structural damage.

Then it hits him—that dazed look in his son's eyes. Maybe he's stoned! He's never smelled skunk around the house before, but kids these days have access to a cornucopia of edibles in the dispensaries that have popped up all over the state. There's one just over the hill in Raven's Landing.

Carson walks over to the deep freezer and opens it, staring at the fog that rises up. It *is* loud. Might be time to get rid of it. It's a remnant from the pandemic era when they were living like they thought grocery stores might evaporate at any minute. For the most part, they forget it even exists. Carson reaches a hand in and rifles around the surface, hoping to find something that might serve as a reward for the stressful night of spider-hunting. He reaches a hand deeper and feels something large and solid—a roast, probably, one they'd bought and forgotten —and instead grabs a plastic bag next to it.

"Aha!" he says, fist pumping at his prize: fruit popsicles. He plucks out a grape one and tosses the others back in the freezer, slamming the lid shut.

Inside, he walks to his bedroom at the back of the house. In the dim lamplight, Angela is in her satin pajamas with her hair up, sleepy-eyed. Above her hangs a painting that once hung in Angela's childhood home. It's an impressionistic smattering of wildflowers that Dr. Atkins bought for a lot of money and then, like everything else he gave his family, threatened to take away.

They got it in the end, though, didn't they?

"You think Ezra's on the Devil's lettuce?" Carson asks, chomping the popsicle.

"Shhh." Angela points to the middle of the bed, where Eliza lies on her stomach and snores. Angela whispers, "I gave her a sedative."

"I didn't know the doctor prescribed her one," he says, lowering his voice and coming to sit on his side of the bed.

"I'm a doctor." Angela rests her head against the tufted headboard and closes her eyes. "I took one too."

"Sounds like a party," Carson says.

"Can you please not eat popsicles in bed?"

"Sure." He wolfs down the rest and tosses the stick across the room into the mesh garbage can. He slides under the covers. "Ezra's acting weird."

"We're all acting weird. It's been a weird night."

Eliza moans. Angela opens her bleary eyes and rubs her daughter's back. Soon the moaning turns into buzzy little snores again. Suddenly, time slips away like a rug pulled from under their feet. Carson gets a flashback to those long nights when Eliza was a colicky, restless baby whose tummy needed massaging, who lay there between them all night long in fits of rest and unrest. Here they are again. That's what they don't tell you as a parent—you think your babies are grown, they don't need you anymore, then suddenly they're back again. Time's not a straight line, but a path full of switchback turns. There's a comfort to it.

"You think she's going to be okay?" Carson asks.

"Physically? Yes. Emotionally? I really don't know." Angela takes her reading glasses off the top of her head, folds them and puts them on her night table. She glances down at Eliza and then mouths the words, "She thinks Olivia did this."

Carson props himself up on his pillow and mouths back, "Why?"

Angela offers an exaggerated shrug.

"What happened between them?" Carson mouths. "I don't get it."

"Who knows?" Angela points to Eliza. "I'm worried. Delusional."

"Maybe it was the spider bite." Carson makes a crazy sign by rolling his finger near his ear, which makes Angela cringe.

"It wasn't the spider bite, Carson," she hisses in a whisper.

"Jealousy," he whispers back.

"I don't understand her sometimes," Angela says quietly, eyeing the back of Eliza's skull. "I feel like we're so different in so many ways. Sometimes I look at her and wonder if she's even mine."

"Don't say that." Carson picks at his teeth. "Why would you say that?"

"She's so ... anchorless. Emotionally adrift. You know?"

"She's sixteen."

"Yes, but when I was sixteen, I knew what I wanted."

"Oh yeah? What was that?"

"Not any *one* thing, Carson. I wanted many things. I was driven. I couldn't wait to get out and go to college."

Carson closes his eyes, feeling a prickly annoyance at being cornered into the position of defending his own daughter. "She wants to go to NYU, remember?"

"She *says* she wants to go to NYU, then she writes a speech about how she wants to stay home."

"Because she's smart and she's kissing judge-panel ass."

"She makes a sudden turn and goes 'goth' or whatever, dyes her hair black, nails black, black lipstick. Then, on a dime, she's back to brown hair and jeans and T-shirts. She studied piano, gives it up, moves to ballet. Now she's asking if she can put ballet on pause and go back to piano. Then this thing with Olivia—she's her best friend, she's her enemy. I'm dizzy trying to understand her."

Carson is at a loss, trying hard to keep up with his wife, but not fully understanding what the big deal is and why the focus is on this instead of hitting the hay so they can rest up after the Great Black Widow Incident.

"I don't think she knows *what* she wants," Angela says. "Stay, go, be a rebel, run for Miss Riverwood. She doesn't know what she wants. She—" Suddenly, Angela stops speaking and presses her fingertips to her mouth.

"What?" Carson asks.

Angela shakes her head. A long silence fills the room, one long enough that Carson notices Eliza's no longer snoring. His first worry is that she's listening to them— God, wouldn't that be awful? Poor kiddo. But his second worry is much bigger.

He realizes he doesn't hear her breathing.

"Eliza," he says, shooting out a hand and shaking her back as a miniature panic attack explodes within him.

All at once, his absolute nightmare hit like a deluge, a million flashing images he's feared since the day she was born. Murder, overdose, suicide, hit and run, cancer—it all leads to one place, and that's the thought of his child, gone. Nothing he's ever read, watched, or seen leads to anything more terrifying than this, and Carson has read, watched, and seen a lot of shit in his day.

Wouldn't that be the ultimate punishment for his sins? The cruelest karma.

His insides are screaming, adrenaline surging. He tries to pull her hair back from her face. "Eliza!"

"She's *sleeping!*" Angela says. "Stop."

Carson is about to go into cardiac arrest when Eliza makes a small *mmmm* sound and turns her head the other way, her pink face now uncovered by her hair.

Every godawful thriller he's ever read has the line in it where so-and-so "released the breath they didn't know they were holding" and he wonders if he's merely a character in a godawful thriller, because that's exactly what he does right now.

"What's wrong with you?" Angela asks.

"She's sleeping really heavily," Carson says, hand to his chest as his heartbeat recalibrates.

"I told you I gave her a sedative."

"What'd you give her, morphine?"

"Morphine's not a sedative."

Carson looks down at Eliza, whose mouth is open with an ooze of drool. "What'd you give her?"

"Valium to calm her down earlier, at the ER. Ambien when she got into bed."

"Are you supposed to ... mix that stuff? Especially when she's been, you know, bitten by a venomous spider?"

Angela narrows her tired eyes.

"Did you ask the doctor?" he says.

"Carson, I—"

"Fine, yes, I get it." He fluffs his pillow and sinks his head into it. "You're the doctor."

Angela switches her light off and lies down. A cool ray of moonlight hits Eliza's face through the window and Carson watches her, comforted by the rise and fall of her breathing. Angela's eyes are closed. He still feels the same way about her as the first day he saw her up on that stage, whipping the Rubik's cube back into shape. That smile that doesn't get anywhere near her eyes. That bewitching blond woman with a shadow over her and a head he wanted to unlock like a secret box. He wanted to know everything about the woman who stood waving at the crowd with the Miss Riverwood sash over her yellow summer dress that reached her ankles. Not just know her, but have her. To make her completely his. He'd do anything for her. Anything. And he did.

He's so lucky, isn't he? He got everything he ever wanted.

Here's the secret they never tell you about getting everything you want: once you get it, you live in fear you're going to lose it.

CARSON

MISS RIVERWOOD CONTEST, says the hand-painted wooden sign.

The words are framed by careful little strawberries. It hangs off the stage, which is decorated with balloons also shaped like strawberries. Hey, Riverwood has one thing going for it and that's its strawberry crop, and they run with it. Carson and his family (sans Eliza, who's somewhere backstage) sit in the front row waiting for the festivities to start. Ezra and Olivia whisper to each other the whole time—they now live in a bubble together and no one else is invited in. And Angela seems nervous to be here, darting glances in the direction of the far-off field that was once a parking lot.

"Don't think about it," he whispers in her ear.

She swallows and whispers back, "Think about what?"

He squeezes her hand and smiles.

It's not that he doesn't think about Penny Patterson too. It's hard not to think about her at times like these, when he's back in the same place again, haunting these fairgrounds like a ghost. Yes—back there, in the field that was once a parking lot, was the last place Penny was ever seen in one piece. Search parties and media circuses swarmed it. No one found any clues. Now it's unused, pale overgrown grass and nothing else.

Besides, there are other and much prettier memories haunting him here. Carson puts his sunglasses on and studies the stage, where he first saw Angela and a smile spreads on his lips. The Ferris wheel and carousel twirl behind the scene against a backdrop of pine trees. Bubbles from a nearby machine fill the air, carried by a breeze. Carnival games, a clown twisting balloon animals, children with chocolate-smeared mouths, the smell of deep-fried everything in the air ... it's a good day. His daughter's had a rough thirty-six hours, but she's all right and she's going to dance onstage now in the same spot her mother stood twenty-something years ago. What a comforting vertigo it is.

As the high school band marches up the platform, warming up their instruments in an ear-cringing symphony, Carson waves at passersby. Their neighbor up the street with the Scottish terrier she always holds like a baby. Izzy's mother, hair to her knees and the perma-stoned glaze in her eyes. That old crone from the book-shop who refuses to stock his book because of the fabrica-tion rumors, even when he offered to sign copies. Yes, Carson even waves at her. One day soon he'll have his new book out—his redemption book, the first book ever written on the Raven's Landing Dismemberer. She'll be sorry then. Some noob, who must work for the *Gazette,* snaps pictures from the foot of the stage with an ancient camera, press pass dangling from his neck. Lord, Carson hated assignments like this when he was in his journalism days. Finally, after an eternity of baking in the sun, the band begins to play their version of "Dancing Queen" and the black curtains behind them open up.

There she is, his gorgeous sunshine of a daughter, standing in a floral dress right in the middle of a line of ten bright young women. And that's what she is, what a shock—a woman and not a girl. Her hair is upswept and almost blond in the light. She wears coral lipstick and heels she borrowed from her mother. Angela and Carson exchange beaming smiles and applaud. Out pop the phones and *click-click.* Carson's throat tickles with emotion as the ABBA song blares out of trumpets and trombones.

"Wwwwelcome Riverwoodians," Tony Zink booms into the mic as he takes center stage. The man owns the used car dealership on the edge of town, Park Place, that looks like a giant circus tent. Carson went to high school with him and he hasn't changed a bit—same sideburns, same enormous hairstyle that sticks out like he was electrocuted. "Holy macaroni! Look at these living dolls up here, am I right? Is that creepy to say? Is that not PC? You know why we're all here, let's put our hands together for the annual Miss Riverwood contest!"

The crowd stands up and hoots and howls. Sweet,

isn't it? Carson grins, heartened by the cheer of his home-town as he claps. He can never imagine leaving this place. He doesn't understand why Angela has wanted to over the years. For a long time, she held a grudge against Riverwood as if it were the town's fault that her family fell apart. But then they bought the house and took root and all that faded. From the stage, Eliza waves, her posture elegant, a glimmer in her eyes radiant and new. Carson glances at Olivia, on the far end near Ezra, who yawns. Silly teens and their tiffs. They'll be best friends again soon, won't they?

As everyone settles back into their seats, a high-pitched sound knifes Carson's eardrums.

At first he thinks it's feedback from the mic, but no—up there, Tony Zink's expression is equally confused. The Miss Riverwood contenders whip their heads around, too. The high-pitched squeal continues and then another joins it and, in a collective gasp, the crowd begins to realize that people are screaming.

A tension spreads through the air in an instant and folks murmur and speculate, eyebrows furrowed, purses clutched, standing up to find where it's coming from. One child ducks under a chair as if an earthquake is happening. The screaming gets louder, more people joining in, a chorus of unintelligible yelling from some-where nearby but not quite visible, and people start fleeing the funhouse line across the walking path.

"What's happening?" Angela asks, clutching her throat.

"I—I don't know," Carson says.

So many gruesome possibilities play in his mind. A mass shooting. Someone getting decapitated on a fair ride. A mountain lion wandering into the children's area. Carson stands up with a sick feeling, locking eyes with Eliza onstage, who just mouths, "What the hell?" and steps back behind the curtain. The crowd watching the Miss Riverwood competition disperses in confusion, most people exiting to the left, many people pressed against a temporary fence.

"What's going on?" Carson asks the people passing, but all he gets are worried looks. "Stay here," he says to Angela, Ezra, and Olivia.

Carson joins the river of people heading toward the direction of the yelling. A noxious stench fills the air— vomitous rotting meat and compost. As he gets closer to the fencing, the smell gets stronger. People cover their noses with their hands and discuss how awful it is. Peeping over the top of the fencing, Carson locates the source of the sound. It's a woman with one hand over her child's eyes and another pinching her nose closed, paralyzed in fear, mouth open. It's a teenager who looks like she's crying and gagging with a tongue blue from the cotton candy she holds. It's a man filming it with his phone and shouting, "Holy shit! Holy shit!" and an elderly woman turning away, looking sick and yelling, "Someone! Police!"

When his eyes finally focus, Carson sees what it is that parted the crowd, the thing that everyone is surrounding, the thing they're all there to gape at together, suspended in horror.

A raven hops on the ground in the middle of the walking path with a rotting human hand hanging from its black beak.

EZRA

Ezra follows Olivia up the creaky stairs to the attic. When they get to her room, they walk through the doorway and stand still in shock. The sun streaks through the endless windows, the room lit up a cheerful yellow, but all Ezra feels are the goosebumps crawling up his arms. Olivia's eyes widen and stay that way. Ezra opens his mouth to say something but stops himself. It's as if saying something aloud might make it real; he desperately doesn't want this to be real.

Finally, Olivia says, "Okay," and closes the door. "Yeah."

She steps into a hug, nuzzling her head on his shoulder. He rests his chin on top of her skull that smells like his sister's shampoo and stares blankly out the window, circling his arms around her but feeling nothing, like his arms have fallen asleep. Like his whole body isn't his. After this numb embrace, they finally sit on Olivia's bed, fingers laced together. He studies their hands. Hers is so small in his. Then a sick churn of the stomach makes him let it go. All he can see is the raven with the decomposing hand in its beak.

"What the fuck, Ez?" she whispers.

"I—I—I ..." Ezra squeezes his eyes shut. Jesus. Really? He hasn't stuttered in years, not since elementary school. "I didn't—it wasn't—I don't understand."

"You were the one who said that the dumpster in the field was a good idea," she says. "You promised no one would find anything."

It was a horror show back at the Riverwood Strawberry Festival. People screamed as if the grim reaper himself came tearing through the scene. Eventually, someone threw a coat over the raven with the rotting hand and the police showed up and roped the area off. That dumbass car salesman emcee came to the stage where the Miss Riverwood contenders huddled in tears. He announced that the contest would be postponed to a later date because "Someone found a frickin' *body part*, man." A security guard vomited a corn dog near the crime scene and the police announced through a megaphone that everyone had to leave.

As the crowd dispersed, the carnival music piped on, the empty carousel spun round and round, and Ezra glanced back at the police cars parked there with their lights swirling and he thought he might be having an asthma attack even though he doesn't have asthma. The word *checkmate* flashed through his mind with blinking lights. An old woman clutched her purse like she was scared someone might take it and pointed her tiny bleary eyes up at him as the human herd made its way into the parking lot.

"He's back, isn't he?" she asked.

"Who's back?" he asked.

"The Raven's Landing Dismemberer!" she wailed.

There was a chorus of gasps from people fleeing to their cars. He saw his parents exchange a grim look. The whole drive home, no one spoke except Eliza crying about the stupid contest.

"You promised," Olivia reminds him, squeezing his thigh and making him jump back to here, now. Her face is pink and she's fighting tears. Olivia's a warrior, a survivor. She doesn't usually cry. It's a knife through the chest to see it.

"How the fuck was I supposed to know?" he asks, horrified that his eyes are now filling up as well. Clearly this is just a biological reaction to seeing her cry, emotional mimicry, it isn't real. He's not going to cry because of a fucking severed hand ruining a stupid carnival celebrating strawberries and a contest that's nothing but thinly veiled misogyny. Hold it in, Ezra. Hold it in. He balls his fists up and wishes he could implode.

"How could—I don't even understand," she whispers, wiping her eyes before the tears can escape. "Like, we wrapped it all in plastic. We were smart about where we ..."

"I know. I don't know."

"We didn't even go inside the fairgrounds. We put it in the parking lot. I thought—wouldn't garbage have been picked up by someone? Doesn't that happen every week?"

Ezra doesn't answer, examining his own hands, remembering the snap that happened when the butcher knife finally went through the wrist bone.

"Ez!" She shakes him. "Stay with me."

"I don't know," he says, not looking up.

"What do we do?" she asks him.

As if she can read his thoughts, she slips her hand in his and pulls it to her lips. Her eyes quiver with questions and he can tell she wants him to look at her but he can't. He wants to disappear.

Since the night before last when Eliza went to the ER, there's been a gnat of doubt in his head, buzzing around. He hasn't wanted to even ask it. When he tried to bring it up yesterday, Olivia laughed at him and changed the subject. But he's so shaken up right now he has to ask it again.

"Olivia," he says, meeting her eyes, even though doing so feels like staring into a spotlight. "The other night. My sister. The spiders—"

"Ez," she says, sounding exhausted. "Please. Are we really?"

"I have to ask, you know, because—"

"Yes, I know. Because I caught some black widows, you're accusing me of ... you realize how horrible a thing you're accusing me of, right?" She crosses her arms. "It's incredibly insulting."

Ezra keeps watching her, trying to read some sign, but as always, there's nothing but pure, sharp honesty in

Olivia's gaze. Still. He's not an idiot. It's too much of a coincidence.

"Ezra, do you love me?" she asks quietly. "Like really love me? See me for who I really am? *Believe* me?"

"Yes," he says, and it isn't a lie.

"Remember what your dad said when we made the rounds when your sis was in the ER? How he said he looked it up and it was possible, totally possible, to have a property or a room infested with black widows?"

"Yes, but—"

"I mean, hell, that's where I caught them!" she says. "My trailer's practically infested with them. There must be dozens all around our porches and side yard. Maybe it's a Riverwood thing." Softly, she touches his cheek. "Babes, don't get paranoid on me now."

Ezra nods slowly. She's right. There's no way—she wouldn't. After everything they went through together, she would never lie to him.

"Yeah, I'm not. I believe you. You're right." He takes his hand back and studies it again.

"What do we do?" she asks.

"Do?"

"About—about the hand—"

"Nothing. We don't do anything."

Something like silence widens a gap between them.

He recognizes what's happening; Olivia's desperation to keep him here, close to her. His drifting away from her, like a boat being swept away by the tide while she stands on land. In truth, there's never any real silence for Ezra anymore. When things get too quiet, he can hear a muffled screaming. In the dark, at night, sometimes he hears the gurgling sound that came from Olivia's dad's throat while he lay there choking on his own blood. Or the shocking smash of the skull and squish of brain as the cast iron pan met the man's head. The snap of knife to bone. There's no such thing as silence anymore when you've heard such things. And now, in the pause, he can hear something new. Not screaming—it's somehow worse. It's a low laugh, a man's sinister laugh, and he knows just where it's coming from.

"Ez, I'm scared," Olivia says, running a hand through his hair and giving it a gentle tug.

"It's okay," he says automatically, a knee-jerk statement that means nothing.

"Do you still love me?" she asks.

"Yes."

It isn't a lie. He does love her, somewhere. He just doesn't feel it right now. All he feels is cold, shivering cold, like if he puffs out a breath, he'll see fog.

"I'm going to go lie down for a bit," he says as normally as he can.

He pats her knee and doesn't wait for a response, heading back down the stairs. An Arctic breeze blows through him and he smells his sleeve but it doesn't stop the tangy penny smell of blood.

And the distant man in his echoey ears laughs and laughs.

OLIVIA

Olivia is disturbed. She's bothered, agitated, troubled, and vexed. Sickening butterflies in her belly and an ache in the hollow spot where her heart supposedly lives.

A switch flipped in Ezra, right before her eyes. Or maybe it's been slower—maybe it was a gradual slithering that she ignored, and the switch that flipped was her realizing it. But Ezra isn't quite there anymore. Since they did the awful thing, he began to fade. Olivia breathes deeply as she sits in her room, her bougie sunny room, the world getting blurry and hot in her eyes. Finally, she cries. She lets the horrible feelings rain on her lap.

The emotions have finally cornered her. She turns one way and her fear's there, visions of orange jumpsuits and damp, dark prison cells. She turns another way and her father is lying on the kitchen floor in a puddle of blood. She turns a third way and sees Ezra, his perfect face, his brooding brain, his everything eyes, and it hurts so badly to imagine losing him. Finally, there's Eliza, who used to make her feel so loved, like a sister—who rejected her and abandoned her. Who made her do awful things just to show her how much it hurts. Usually Olivia could shut all the doors to her private house of horrors. Usually she could put these things in boxes. But not today. Not anymore.

Here's a new one for the collection: her father's bruise-violet hand dangling from a raven's beak.

Olivia gets up, wipes her face, and paces the floor. She tries to read a book, but her eyes only move over the words. No meaning springs to mind from them. Standing at the window, she gazes down at the yard, where Angela Hunter waters her roses. The spray glimmers in the sunshine and Angela could be a painting in her striped oversized hat and matching green dress. For a brief moment, Olivia lets herself imagine she was born a Hunter. That Angela is her mother. That she isn't just a temporary appendage allowed to sleep in a finished attic, but that she has a home, a real home, a house with a foundation. That she grew up in one place, one town, that she's a part of something.

Her whole life, she's never felt a part of something.

Olivia sniffs and pushes down the yearning. It will always be there. The yearning is so strong—it's the wind that has shaped her into the person she is. The important part is not letting herself get hurt again. The important thing is to keep moving. Sharks, they have the right idea.

Thanks to the years of being on her toes with her father's every emotion and shift in mood, Olivia can read faces as well as she can read novels. Like with Eliza—she knew right away when she had lost her friend. With Ezra, she could tell when he started liking her by the slight melt in his expression, so subtle someone less talented at face-reading would have missed it. And now, today, she can tell she's beginning to lose him. Suspicion flickers in him. The questions. The darting glances. She's had enough flings with boys to detect the moment when the fire dies in their eyes, often coinciding with the moment they zip their pants up again.

With Ezra, it seems real. And the bond they share is one that can never be destroyed. It's like the shadow version of having a baby with someone—they took a life together. Their glue is permanent.

But Olivia has to leave him now.

If she stays, there will only be heartache. She doesn't want to be around when more body parts are found and investigators start putting it all together. She doesn't want to be around when the Hunters find out who she really is. And she really doesn't want to be around when Ezra realizes he isn't in love with her anymore. Let's end it on a good note, shall we? If there's one thing Olivia's good at, it's leaving.

Thanks, Daddy.

She wipes her eyes, stupid defective leaky eyes, and takes her phone out. She researches maps and bus tickets. Idaho catches her eye. They drove through Idaho once and she remembers how majestic it was, snow-capped mountains and tree-dotted plains. A place where nature still reigns supreme. It seems like somewhere she could disappear. There are so many resources online about how to commit pseudocide—a fascinating little word that means to fake your own death. Olivia has visited these sites before. It would be easy for her to cut her hair, get a fake ID, go by a new name. She doesn't even have her driver's license. Her life hasn't even really started yet.

"Matilda Shelley," she whispers.

It comes to her like a light bulb popping: her favorite childhood book and the name of her favorite author, her new identity. She can see it now. She'll have a pixie hair-cut. Get a waitressing job and an apartment of her own. Meet new people, forget Riverwood, forget everything. Discover new books. Write herself a story with a different ending. It'll hurt to leave Ezra. She'll miss the comfort of the Hunter house, the warmest, safest place she's ever called home. But her instincts are telling her she needs to get out of here. Time to go.

She bookmarks a bus trip for Monday morning. She'll pay in cash she grabbed from her dad's bedside table—she only has a few hundred dollars, but she'll figure some-thing out.

"Knock knock knock," she says to Ezra's door a few minutes later.

He doesn't answer.

"Babes," she tries again, hand on the knob—but then she lets it go.

To hell with it. Don't be pushy.

Don't give him any more reason to stop loving you.

Olivia turns, pausing in the hall where the Hunter family photos hang. Look at this perfect family, this catalog family, matching shirts and everything. No matter what Olivia does in life, no matter how far she runs or whether she reinvents herself as Matilda Shelley, no matter how clever she is and what she gets away with, she will never have this. This life will never be accessible to her. She's only a tourist. It hurts to know she's leaving the Hunters, because it means leaving the illusion that, for a brief moment in time, she belonged somewhere.

Downstairs, Eliza is practicing piano again. But up here, her bedroom door is ajar. She hasn't stepped upstairs since she was bitten by the spider. Understandable. As a clumsy version of "Für Elise" meets Olivia's ears and she gazes at the round-faced toddler version of Eliza in a Christmas dress on the wall, Olivia regrets what she did. But only for a split second. What's the point of regret? Nonsense. Serves no purpose. She moves to go back up the attic stairs again when she hears the low voices of Carson and Angela. Pausing at Eliza's door, Olivia pushes it open and tiptoes inside.

Dust sparkles in the air and the room remains a crime scene—the bed pulled from the wall, sheets balled up on the ground in a lump, a lamp knocked over. But the vent is still visible and accessible. And that's where the voices are coming from. Olivia drops to her knees and presses her ear against it to listen. They're speaking so quietly it's hard to make out the words at first, but Olivia gets up and closes the door and shuts her eyes and concentrates, really concentrates, and soon she's able to make out what they're saying.

"There goes the goddamn book." Carson. His voice

moves, as if he's pacing the floor. "There it goes, poof, gone."

"I can't believe that's what you're focusing on right now," Angela says.

"Come on. Get real with me here. Chaz isn't going to be able to pitch a book on a cold case that is now getting reopened because there's another dismemberer on our hands."

"What is this? A copycat?"

"Copycat of a copycat?"

"Stop it."

Olivia's brow wrinkles as she tries to understand what she's hearing. The conversation stops and there's some low murmuring, faint whimpering. Olivia realizes that what she's hearing is Angela crying and Carson comforting her.

"They're never going to come for us," he says.

Come for us? Olivia wonders.

"Why wouldn't they?" Angela scoffs. "You think we're so invincible?"

"Track record's good so far, you can't argue with that."

"It took two decades for my stomach to stop being in knots every time I passed the fairgrounds. I thought it was finally over. Then you started writing this damn book and it's like Pandora's box opened again."

"Do *not* try to blame this on me. I was writing the book that was going to exonerate us. The sheriff is dead, the dead can't defend themselves, and everyone with half a brain knows he killed four of those women. Penny was one more name on the victim list."

What on earth are they talking about? Exonerate them from what? Olivia's so gripped with suspense that she clutches her dress in front of her chest, balling it up as tightly as she can in her fist.

"Even the crime reporters were speculating it was a copycat at the time, Carson. You would have had to include that information and that could have led it back to us."

"Well, I'm not writing the goddamn book anymore. Happy?"

"Yes. I'm so happy. Look at me. Aren't I *happy*?"

The cruelty and pain in Angela's voice is sharp. It makes Olivia wince to hear it. But most of all, her head is spinning. These two did something together. Something bad, something related to Carson's book, the dismemberer, and the fairgrounds. What is it?

"It's all falling apart, don't you feel it?" Angela weeps.

"What's falling apart? We're *fine*."

"This house. Us. Our family. My practice, the lawsuit ... I—I—I feel like I'm trying to pretend we're all okay and I can't *do* it anymore. I can't deal with an investigation opening and cops showing up on our doorstep asking questions."

"Okay, so let's get out of town. Reggie's place in Tahoe. Didn't he just offer that up to you? We'll go out there, clear our heads."

"No."

The silence is so long that Olivia wonders if she lost them.

"What I mean is that I think we need to get out of Riverwood," Angela says. "For good."

"You're not seriously—"

"Start over. Get away. I want to be far, *far* away when this media circus around the Raven's Landing Dismemberer starts up again. My sanity—I can't take it. I pretended to forget it a long time ago. I put it behind me, I focus on right now, I take sleeping pills to get away from the nightmares. I block unpleasant memories from my conscious mind."

"Ange—"

"I'm telling you. I need you to listen to me. Look at me. Really look at me." Her voice cracks as she continues. "I'm falling apart. I can't keep up anymore."

Everything gets so quiet, it's as if a wind has been sucked right out of the house. Olivia feels the fierce electricity of her beating heart beneath her palm. She isn't quite understanding what they're talking about, where this conversation came from, why Angela is breaking down in her office. But what Olivia does understand is how she feels. It's as if Angela's feelings are in harmony with her own. She too wants to run away and never leave. She too feels tired of pretending.

"And I'm pregnant," Angela says, the word cutting through the silence like a sword.

ELIZA

E liza sits on her parents' bed, hugging her legs and
gazing out the window.

Her mom's rose garden is right there, flowers dancing
in the breeze. The late afternoon pours sunshine all over
their yard where, long long ago, Eliza ran through sprinklers and played tag. Once upon a time, there was a
swing set in the corner. Now it's a garden shed. Everything changes all the time. It's impossible to get her
footing on a world that refuses to sit still. Eliza never feels
like she has balance, like she has time to understand
herself. She wipes her eyes, which have been leaking ever
since the Miss Riverwood contest was ruined earlier
today. A decaying human hand. How is this real life?

It took so much nerve to enter the Miss Riverwood
contest. At first, she was tempted by the thousand-dollar
prize. It's more than she made all summer at Tutu Camp.
But after a while, she became more focused on finally
having a shot at her mother's admiration. Maybe if Eliza

follows in her footsteps and becomes the next princess of their small town, her mom won't just love her out of obligation, but *like* her. Nothing she does gets a reaction. When she changed her style, when she painted her walls black, when she danced in *The Nutcracker* last year, when she played piano in recitals in junior high, when she quit and said she hated it. Angela just shrugs through all of it and says, "Do what makes you happy."

But what if nothing makes her happy?

There are creaking footsteps above her head and Eliza's gaze floats up to the ceiling, as if it's made of glass and she might see what's on the other side. She knows Olivia's footsteps now by heart. They pitter-patter quick as a mouse while Ezra's are clunky and slow. She's a little sick every time she thinks about that secret smile Olivia flashed her before the trip to the ER. Something's very wrong with her, but when Eliza's tried to point it out to anyone, *she* looks like the crazy one.

Olivia slowly took over Eliza's life. She ate away at her family like a disease, sucking up to her dad, milking her mother for favors, and turning her brother into a love-struck sleepwalker. And let's not forget she tried to kill Eliza with poisonous—*venomous*—spiders. It wouldn't be a surprise to learn that Olivia had killed her dad, too. Maybe the man's lying somewhere covered in spider bites and no one's discovered him yet.

Eliza feels something like hate passing over her like a shadow.

"Kiddo, you seen your brother lately?" Carson stands in the doorway, phone in hand.

Snapping back to reality, Eliza stretches. "No. Why?"

He holds his phone up in the air. "I'm about to pick up pizza for dinner. Can you find him and let him know?"

She gets up and crosses the room to the doorway. "Sure."

"You doing okay?"

"I mean, no. Been a crappy couple of days."

"We're going to get an exterminator in to examine the house, all right? We'll make sure your room's safe. You'll be all right."

"Sure," she says, though the only thing she's sure of is that she'll never sleep well in that room again. Eliza will spend the rest of her life terrified of what crawls under the covers.

"And the Miss Riverwood thing, I ... I'm sorry. Maybe they'll hold it in August."

"Maybe."

Carson opens his arms to give her a hug. "I love you, little one."

"Love you too, Dad."

"You're everything to me. You know that, right?"

Eliza nods, eyes welling up as she loses herself for just a second in his familiar scent—woody aftershave, minty lip balm. "Yeah. Thanks for saying it, though."

They pull apart and she touches his arm, shooting him a smile even though she hurts. Because what he's willing to give her is something she deeply craves from someone else.

Eliza goes upstairs slowly, eyes checking for spiders

every step of the way. At the landing, she freezes. Her door is ajar, her room dark. Her brother's door is shut. How could anyone stay up here knowing there were half a dozen black widows in her room the other night? A shiver creeps up her spine. She takes a step and knocks on Ezra's door.

"Ez," she says.

When he doesn't answer, she bangs harder.

"Ez!"

The last thing she wants is to walk in on her brother jerking off or something, but she opens the door a crack and peeks in. No Ezra. His bed is unmade, his phone and wallet on the nightstand. Upstairs in the attic, she can hear Olivia walking around back and forth, back and forth. The door to the attic room is open and no one is talking. He doesn't seem to be up there, either. Eliza hurries back downstairs, relieved to be away from the second floor of the house. Black widow PTSD.

Seeing Ezra isn't in the living room, Eliza walks through the kitchen and heads to the garage. She opens the door and steps into the dim room with one buzzing, creepy overhead light bulb and almost jumps when she sees Ezra there. He's hunched over the deep freezer, talking. Mumbling. Smelling his sleeve once, twice. At first Eliza assumes he's on the phone, so she waits to see if he might look up at her and break whatever conversation he's having. But then she remembers that she saw his phone on his nightstand.

He's talking to himself.

Alone. In the dark garage.

"You have to stop," Ezra is saying. "You have to move on now. I can't think, you know? I can't hear anything with you in my fucking head."

He smacks himself on the side of the head and the sound is so loud Eliza winces.

"Ezra," she says, walking over. "Who are you talking to?"

ELIZA

Everything gets still and quiet. Ezra glances at his sister, face blank. He stands taller and walks a step toward her and says, as if everything's normal, "Hey."

Truly at a loss, Eliza manages, "Are you okay?"

"Yeah," he says cheerfully, nodding and smiling.

But ... Ezra doesn't usually nod and smile. And he *never* says things cheerfully. This response makes her belly flop. Her brother isn't himself. She's seen this look in people's eyes—druggies at school, mentally ill people on the street. It's the look of a person who is physically present and mentally absent.

"Are you on something?" Eliza tries.

Ezra glances behind him, then turns around and says, enunciating each word into her ear, "He is in my head."

"Who?" Eliza lays a hand on his shoulder, her heart pounding. "Ezra, are you messing with me right now? I really don't like this."

"It's the trade off," Ezra says. "Right? The punishment. You kill someone, you're the one who's got to live with it. That's what he's laughing about. Crime and punishment."

Ezra's eyes are wide and blazing. He must be on something. He's been acting distant and weird for a while, but this is frightening. What *is* this? His reality shattered, just shattered, like someone hurled a brick through it.

"Okay, okay, I get it now. I understand. I have no feelings, it's fine, I can live with the, uh—" Ezra points to his ear. "In my ear all the time. The question is, why doesn't *she* hear it?"

"Why doesn't who hear what?" Eliza asks, frowning.

Ezra speaks very slowly, as if Eliza is an idiot. "Why doesn't Olivia hear her dad, too?"

What in the ...? The words dry up and Eliza's about to give up on this conversation. She backs up. "I'm ... going to get Mom."

Ezra scratches his head and glances back at the corner where he was talking to himself. "I could handle the screaming, sort of. But the laughing?" Ezra breaks into a strange, snickering laugh of his own. "You know? All the time? Could you imagine?"

"I don't know what you're talking about." Eliza turns toward the door. "Ez, I'll be right back."

"Don't get Mom. I'll be all right."

Eliza turns to behold him there, sad, a forlorn overgrown child with his mussed hair and wrinkled, oversized T-shirt. He reminds her of the Ezra from years ago, the awkward years when he had braces and scared eyes and

hadn't yet mastered the art of the scowl. A sudden pang
of love for him washes over her as if she's losing him. He's
her brother. He's a know-it-all and his room smells gross
and he leaves his towels on the floor, but he's her *brother*.

And apparently he's losing his mind.

Eliza hurries back into the house and bounds down
the stairs to the basement, where her mom is doing her
usual thing of staring lovingly at her computer screen.

"Mom."

She doesn't look up. "Hmmm."

"Mom, something's wrong with Ezra."

Still doesn't look up. She's typing now. "What's
that?"

No alarm in her voice whatsoever. If there's a comfort
somewhere, it's that there's no favoritism when it comes
to her mom's emotional neglect. She and Ezra are equally
ignored.

"Mom, I'm serious, I'm worried. He's—he's—hallu-
cinating."

That word does it. Angela pushes her reading glasses
up on top of her head and looks up at Eliza.
"Excuse me?"

"Come. Come see, in the garage. Ezra's—I don't know
what he is. I don't know what to do."

As if her mom thinks this is a prank, she rises from
her chair slowly. Eliza's heart pounds as she comes
upstairs. Her mom follows with slow, measured steps.
When they get to the garage, Ezra's still where Eliza left
him, mumbling unintelligibly.

"Ezra?" her mom asks, coming into the garage.

"I tried earplugs," he says, turning to her, talking amiably, as if they're mid-conversation. "Didn't do any good."

Eliza and her mother exchange a look, Eliza widening her eyes as if to say, *See? I told you so!*

"Ezra, are you on anything?" her mom tries.

A shake of the head. "No, no."

She puts a hand on his back and rubs it. "What's— what's going on, honey?"

"Mom," he says with a gush of relief, turning to her as if he just noticed she came into the room. And then, twisting his face, welling up, he wails softly, "Mommy."

It's so pitiful Eliza wants to either throw up or cry. He hasn't called her *Mommy* since grade school.

Ezra stumbles into their mom's arms, a lurching giant engulfing her in a hug. She peeks over his shoulder, her eyes almost unfamiliar—glassy and bright and fearful— and says to Eliza, "Give us a few minutes, won't you?"

She steps inside, shuts the door behind her. All she can hear is her brother sobbing. What the fuck is going on? This isn't her brother. She never hears him cry. *She's* the crier. The shock of the situation, the mystery of what's going on behind the closed door, it's giving Eliza the chills. Her ears ring as she walks up the stairs, a magnet pulling her. His words he said—*why doesn't Olivia hear her dad, too?* No idea what their meaning is, but they nauseate her.

Turning right, passing through the hall, she does not think of spiders, does not think of spiders, does not think of spiders. Up the second narrower set of stairs she walks, *creak-creak-creak*, the ones that lead to the attic room. She doesn't bother knocking once she gets there. She pushes the door open without permission. Know why?

Because it's *her* house.

Olivia sits on the window seat with her phone in her hand, cloud gazing. When she notices Eliza, she startles.

"Oh," she says. "Um, hello?"

"What the fuck did you do to my brother?" Eliza asks.

No response. The pause expands. Olivia tilts her head at her quizzically.

"You broke my brother," Eliza says.

Putting her phone down, Olivia shakes her head. "I'm truly confused."

"My brother is downstairs talking to himself in the garage."

Olivia doesn't react. She seems to be thinking hard. Finally, she says, in a thoughtful voice, "Yeah, you know ... he's been doing that lately."

"It's you." Eliza crosses her arms, tightly, hoping it might keep her rage inside her ribcage. "You did this to him. Did you drug him?"

Olivia's taken aback. "What? No."

"Put spiders in his bed?"

"Come on."

"I know that was you. Don't try to bullshit me."

To her credit, Olivia doesn't. She just offers a tight smile.

"You tried to kill me," Eliza says.

"I did *not*. I've seen the statistics. Mortality rate is less than one percent." Olivia tucks her hair behind her ear, and clarifies, "Research for that book I was writing. That's how I know that, by the way. Research."

The very thing she used to love and envy about Olivia—how ever-calm she is, how unafraid—now enrages her.

"Right. That 'book.'" A statement so ridiculous it deserves finger quotes in the air. Eliza shakes her head. "You're insane. And now you've driven Ezra insane with you."

"I didn't do anything to your brother." Olivia's eyes flicker. "What is going *on*?"

"My mom's downstairs with my brother right now. He's basically having a nervous breakdown."

"What do you mean?" Olivia's hand flies to her throat. "Is he okay?"

"I don't know, Olivia, what did you *do* to him?" Eliza stamps a foot, the room rattling with the force.

"I didn't do anything to him!"

Olivia rises and steps for the door, but Eliza blocks her.

"Leave him alone," Eliza says.

Olivia stops, close enough that Eliza can smell the sweet stink of her breath.

"He's talking about your dad," Eliza whispers, trying to find the truth in her once-friend's expression, but it's always a pointless feat. "Why would he be talking about your dad?"

Something subtle flinches in Olivia's placid expression. Her mouth opens but it takes a moment for a response to come.

"I love your brother," is all she says. "I really do."

"That doesn't answer my question," Eliza says.

With a sniff, Olivia's eyes take on a teary shine. It must be a trick, right? Just another manipulation. Crying wouldn't look right on her. "I love him so much."

"Like a flea loves a dog."

Olivia inhales sharply. "Fine. Okay."

It's all twisted up inside Eliza right now—every grievance she holds against Olivia. The push-pull of their relationship. No one in her life has ever made her feel so special and so terrified. It's aggravating to never know what's really inside Olivia. Her presence makes Eliza question her own reality, become a stranger in her own house, unravels her.

"I love him, and I love you, and I'm sorry." Olivia wipes her eyes with careful fingertips. "I'm leaving Monday. I'll be out of Riverwood, out of the state, out of your life. You won't have to worry about me anymore."

Eliza's brow furrows. "Why?"

The pause is agonizing. Eliza wants to push her, get a rise out of her.

"I can't tell you," she says. "But it'll be better this way."

"What, because you did something to your dad?" Eliza says. "Is that why?"

A shadow passes over Olivia's expression. She's not crying, but her eyes are wet.

"You are a curse," Eliza says to her. "My biggest

mistake was inviting you into this house." Her voice thickens, a lump growing in her throat. "I think you're evil. You know that? That's why I didn't want to be friends anymore. Because I started seeing right through you. All your ... your bullshit. Your lies. You're evil. I cannot wait until you're out of this house."

"I'm evil," Olivia repeats with an edge of surprise, as if she just learned a new word and she's saying it aloud to try it out.

"You are."

"*I'm* evil."

"Yep."

"I'm *evil*."

What the hell is this? A mirroring exercise? Eliza rolls her eyes. Pointless. She turns to go back downstairs and check what's going on with her brother, but Olivia grabs her shoulder.

"Let me tell you something," she says in a syrupy-sweet voice. "Today, I overheard a private conversation between your parents. The old crouch-on-the-floor-and-listen-through-the-vent trick—learned that from you, friend. And I've been doing some research on my phone. Ever heard of Penny Patterson?"

The name sounds vaguely familiar, but maybe Eliza is just imagining it.

"She was the Raven's Landing Dismemberer's last victim." Olivia holds her phone in the air. "I've been on forums for the last hour, poring over all these *fascinating* theories."

"About what? I don't get it."

"She was killed four years after the last victim. Big gap of time. And people who've been following the case have long wondered if it was a copycat killer—it was a much messier dismemberment, different tools used, you don't want to know the details, believe me."

"What does this have to do with—"

"Penny was a nurse at the Riverwood County Hospital. She worked in cardiology. Same department as your grandpa?"

Eliza's head is spinning, trying to follow. "And?"

"And she died a few months after your grandpa's mysterious death. Went walking to her car at the fairgrounds and was never seen again."

"So?"

"There are some rumors in some of the forums that they were having an affair and he was going to leave his family. That his family—*your mom*'s family—they stood to lose everything."

"Still not following."

"Eliza, I have some news for you." A bitter smile, dimples and all. "I don't think your family's as good as you think they are."

ANGELA

After Angela's father died, his upside-down car in the river, his soggy body dragged to shore and zipped up in a blue bag, reporters flooded the scene.

It all happened on a Saturday morning. Angela and the rest of the Atkins clan arrived in their gold minivan, her mother emerging from the backseat, looking small and frail among her tall sons and daughter. They stood outside the police tape. Angela held her mother as she quietly wept into her scarf. Her heart beat wildly and she locked eyes with her youngest brother, a shared stony relief. He was gone. No more insults. No more threats. No more bruises. The air felt fresher, the day sunnier, the river calmer just knowing that Dr. Walter Atkins was no longer welcome in the land of the living.

But then she spotted Penny Patterson in her scrubs, face red as if she was experiencing an allergic reaction, scurrying toward the crime scene in her rubber shoes.

She was Angela's age. Curvy, messy ponytail, nails like little pink knives, skin tan as leather.

"My baby!" she was yelling. "My baby!"

The sight of this woman, the gall of her making such a scene, made Angela's skin crawl. Her dad was ready to give it all up for her. To sabotage their lives, to leave them destitute, to take everything away, for *her*. She'd seen her from afar before, but never up close enough for her to be real. And here she was, sniveling and yelling. How dare she?

The ball of rage, of hatred that lit Angela at that moment, was stronger than anything she'd ever felt before. Stronger than the blaze that made her hit her dad with a hot poker. Stronger than every desire she'd ever had. She wanted that woman to go away, forever. It was a shame she hadn't been in the car with him.

"Who did this to him?" Penny dared yell at the crowd, locking eyes with Angela for a second. "Who did this?"

A police officer pulled her back and Angela glanced at her family, who all looked to her as if she had the answer. They often looked at her that way.

"I know who that is," her mother whispered, as if she had no voice left. Her eyes were so puffy they were unrecognizable.

"Forget about her," Angela said, squeezing her.

"She can go to hell," her middle brother said.

"Well," her mom said, looking at the car getting towed from the water with a mechanical groan. "Now she gets nothing."

The investigation determined that Walter Atkins' brake line had failed, but they were unable to pinpoint the cause. The coroner reported that he died of anoxia—brain injury from impact, asphyxiation due to drowning. A boulder went through the windshield after the car pitched over the bridge and into the river. Since Carson was on the crime beat at the *Gazette*, he covered it. Every article mentioned the malpractice suit and soon gossip picked up the storyline. Either it was a freak accident, or someone in the class action suit—which included fifty-three people—had done this. But soon even that rumor fizzled out. Riverwood quickly lost interest in the dead doctor.

Angela believes that soulmates are made, not born. After her dad's death, Carson became not just a lover, but a part of her. A hero who had saved her family. The teller of the story. The keeper of her greatest secret. She knew no matter what, no matter their differences, she would never let him go.

It was supposed to bring peace to her family—slaying the patriarch whose shadow they'd trembled beneath for decades. But unfortunately, from the day he died, Penny Patterson became the new, fresh thorn in her side. The day her father was laid to rest under a phallic monument atop the cemetery hill, Penny Patterson came in a black dress with an obscene amount of cleavage and pulled Angela under a willow tree for a private conversation after the procession.

"We need to talk," she said. Her face was blotchy from crying.

"I can't even believe you had the nerve to show up here," Angela said. "You need professional help."

"And I'm getting it," Penny said. "I have a draft of a will he was working on. You know that? You know he was in the process of—" Her voice broke. "He was going to marry me."

"Well, he's dead now."

Penny sputtered into tears then, her face in her hands. Angela studied the woman and wondered what she was crying for—love, or money?

"Just so you know, I'm meeting with a lawyer next week," Penny said in a quivering voice. "He thinks that the draft of the will makes me entitled to his inheritance. Computer saved drafts can hold up in court these days."

So it was money. Of course it was money. Money was the only language that Walter Atkins ever spoke.

"You realize his estate is still going to have to deal with the malpractice suit," Angela informed her. "It's not going away because he died."

"I'm not finished," Penny said, narrowing her eyes, which were now almost invisible behind her ridiculous false eyelashes. "I'm going to hire a private investigator, too. Because I have a feeling whoever did this isn't part of the lawsuit. They're in the family."

Angela felt her face whiten, as if she might pass out, but did her best to keep a fixed expression.

"Didn't you hit him on the head with a fireplace poker?" Penny asked, with mock innocence.

"Fuck off," Angela whispered.

She hurried out of the graveyard, trying to avoid stepping over the dead. She didn't look back at her father's monument and she didn't look back at his gold digger girl-friend. But the blood-chilling terror that swept her was one of the most intense feelings she ever had in her life—the sudden fear that all she'd done, all she'd sacrificed, was for nothing. That life was inevitably about to become a nightmare.

And the same feeling sweeps over her tonight, when her son, her beloved son, opens the deep freezer and, sobbing and shaking, pulls out a plastic-wrapped human head.

ANGELA

"**W**hat. *Is*. This?" she manages, feeling the bile rise in her throat.

She can see through the plastic, the blood-smeared mess of a man's face, the shapes of teeth in an agape mouth. "My God, Ezra, what—what am I looking at?"

Ezra trembles as if he's in a state of psychological shock. Like a trauma survivor, a victim of a terrible accident. Angela drops the bag in the open freezer and grabs him by the shoulders. This can't be. This can't be what it looks like—there has to be a logical explanation for this, there just has to.

"Ezra, is this a joke?" she asks. "A prank? It's—it's some kind of—of Halloween—"

"Mom, it's real," he says.

Inside the house, behind the door, Carson yells that there's pizza. The cheerful, benign life going on behind that door now seems as if it's an entire world away from them. In there, there's pizza and the tinkling of a piano.

In here, it's frozen severed heads and psychosis. She glances at the severed head in the plastic bag and winces. Breathing deeply, she wills the nausea to pass.

"Ezra, I need you to tell me what the fuck is going on," she finally says.

"I killed a man," Ezra says, his voice breaking.

"Who did you kill?"

"Olivia's dad."

Angela breathes deliberately, in and out, in and out, to slow her blood pressure. Her ears ring—stress-induced tinnitus. She has to remain calm.

"Why ... why?" she finally asks.

He shakes his head for a long time, so long she thinks he's not going to answer. But then he says, softly, "Because she wanted me to."

Because she wanted him to. Rage grips her heart.

"The hand—" He swallows. "Today. The hand?"

Angela nods. Her hands remain on his shoulders, as if she's afraid he might fly away.

"It was his, too," Ezra says.

"You killed him," she says in a slow voice, repeating to make sure this is true. "You dismembered him?"

He closes his eyes. Then he sobs. "I'm so sorry, Mom."

"I don't understand," she says, her eyes welling up. She wants to shake him, she wants to scream at him. This makes no sense. He's her boy. Legally, he's still a *child*. He plays video games and was still trick-or-treating a couple years ago, for God's sake. "How did this happen?

Start at the beginning, Ezra. Start at the beginning. Walk me through it."

In horrid detail, Ezra explains how Olivia planned to poison her father, the rat poison that didn't work, the way she flipped out in the middle of the night and called him for help, the impulse decision to end the man's misery with a cast-iron pan. He doesn't say it that way when he explains it—Ezra is soggy and rotten with guilt—but that's how Angela reframes it in her mind, a clumsy kind of euthanasia. She just can't fathom her son murdering someone in cold blood, and really, the more he tells her, the more the words come tumbling out of him, the more she's sure this isn't his fault. Angela is, at her core, a problem-solver. When a crisis happens, she steps into an emotionless, analytical mode.

She has to figure out a solution to this.

The thought of Ezra in jail is too frightening to bear.

"So he was abusive?" she says.

"Yeah."

"Self-defense?"

"It wasn't self-defense."

"Maybe it was. Maybe he was ... maybe he was getting ready to attack Olivia?"

"She'd been planning this for weeks."

Angela chews her cheek and Ezra stands shivering by the tool rack. She glances at the mold in the corner, a flicker of fear that they might be breathing it in—but could they use that as a defense? Her son isn't in his right mind because of toxic mold, temporary insanity? Oh, that's ridiculous.

"So it was premeditated," Angela says, nodding. "Okay. By Olivia. Olivia did this, Ezra, this wasn't you. She's the one responsible here."

Ezra's tears have dried. He seems to be a little more present, a visible relief coming over him from his confession. "Mom, I smashed his skull."

Angela flinches at the thought. "But—but maybe you were coerced. More of an accessory."

They're interrupted by Carson opening the garage door and peeking his head in.

"*Bon giorno!* We got a-pepperoni, we got a-olive, we got a nice-a garden salad, anyone hungry?"

His atrocious Italian accent, his cheerful energy, it's all so wrong for the scene that Angela flinches.

"Carson, get in here. Close the door."

Carson's smile melts and he comes in slowly, shutting the door.

"Are Eliza and Olivia in there?" Angela asks.

"Eliza's in our room, Olivia's in the attic." He walks to Angela, puts a hand on her arm. "Why? What's going on?"

"Go look in the freezer," she says. "And whatever you do, don't scream."

Carson grimaces. "Why? More mold?"

"Just ... look," Angela says.

"Sorry," Ezra says feebly. "I'm really sorry, Dad."

Walking a few feet to the freezer, which is still open, emitting fog like a machine, Carson peeks inside. The moment his brain registers what he's looking at, his face changes entirely, his jaw dropping.

"Is this for real?" he asks.

"I'm sorry," Ezra says again, giving him his answer.

Carson coughs, gags. Then he straightens up and walks across the garage to where Angela and Ezra stand, near the tool bench.

"There's a human head in our freezer." Then, in a tone as amiable as when he was announcing there was pizza, he turns to them and asks, "Why is there a human head in our freezer?"

CARSON

It's high time for a family meeting.

After the Valium kicks in for Ezra—Angela thought it best to calm his nerves, since his emotions were all over the place—Carson pulls everyone into the living room for a family meeting. Beside him, Ezra slouches in a chair by the window. The poor kid's puffy-faced and exhausted, still and pale as a wax statue. Angela's mouth is hardened in a grim line as she paces the room. Every step she takes, the pills in her pocket rattle. Eliza scrolls her phone as she sits next to Olivia. And then there's Olivia: the calmest person in the room, absolutely unbothered. Incredible.

"All right," says Carson, rubbing his hands together. "So this might come as a shock to you, Eliza, but maybe not so much to you, Olivia. We're going to talk about murder."

Angela stops and stands behind Carson, her hand on

his back. Silence. It lingers a moment and finally Eliza puts her phone down.

"Wait, what did you say?" she asks.

Carson studies Olivia the entire time, the bright nothingness of her face. *Her expression shone like a blank page*, he imagines himself writing. It's fascinating for the context to shift when you learn the darkness people are capable of. Like when you see a picture of a serial killer in the news—suddenly you want to just ogle them all day to understand them. Yes, he realizes his son technically smashed the man to death with a frying pan, but Olivia was the mastermind behind it. He knows his son. He knows true crime even better. He's seen a hundred of these stories over the years where one lover convinces the other to kill someone for them.

"Olivia," he finally says. "You murdered your father. Let's talk about that."

Eliza's mouth drops open and it takes her a second to find the word, "*What?*"

"No, I did not," Olivia says with a subtle indignance.

"I killed him," murmurs Ezra from the chair.

"No, you didn't, Ezra," Angela says at the same time as Carson saying, "No, no."

"He *did* kill him," Olivia says.

"What the fuck is going on?" Eliza shouts, as if everyone has lost their minds.

"Olivia killed her dad and—and now Ezra's implicated," Angela says, pacing the room again. *Rattle, rattle, rattle.*

"I did not kill him," Olivia says, a quiver in her voice. "Don't try to pin this on me."

"Your dad is dead?" Eliza says.

"Her dad is dead, hon, and it's because Olivia here poisoned him and then she made Ezra—" Angela makes a bludgeoning motion, a fist through the air. "—finish him off."

"I didn't make him do anything," Olivia says.

Angela comes and kneels near Olivia now, as if she's about to beg for something. Instead she says, with a voice full of arsenic, "Listen to me, you little monster. I know my son. I know what he's capable of. He catches bugs and puts them outside because he doesn't want to kill them. He cried all afternoon when he kicked a soccer ball and it hit a kid's head in fourth grade and knocked him out. *Cried.*"

"He's not in fourth grade anymore," Olivia replies.

Carson can't believe how unruffled Olivia is right now. When Angela zeroes in on anyone with that gaze, it's like being an ant under a magnifying glass in the sunlight. But Olivia doesn't even twitch.

Angela swallows, visibly collecting herself. "You need to turn yourself in," she tries in a different tone. A therapist tone, the concerned tone of someone giving someone else sound advice. "Look, I know your home life was difficult. He was abusive, wasn't he? The court, the judge, they'll take your situation into account."

"Absolutely," Carson says, getting up and coming closer to the couch. "And you're a minor, Olivia. You'll get that juvenile record sealed and in a few years no one will be able to know this happened."

He doesn't mention that, due to the gruesome nature of the death, it's probable that she'll be tried as an adult.

"Is Ezra turning himself in?" Olivia asks. "Ezra?"

Ezra looks up at Olivia and opens his mouth but no sound comes out.

"We're actually thinking it best if you leave Ezra out of this," Carson says. "This murder was your idea. You planned it. You were the one who poisoned him." As he says it aloud, Carson realizes—holy crap—that book she's writing! It's been non-fiction all this time!

"You made my son a murderer," Angela says. "You cursed him with something he's going to have to live with for the rest of his life. The least you could do is leave him out of this and face the consequences on your own."

"So you want me to say that *I* whacked him on the head with a frying pan," Olivia says, counting this on a finger. Her expression remains deadpan but her eyes shine with tears. "*I* cut him into pieces with a butcher knife." She counts this on another finger. "*I* scattered him all over the county. Somehow. With no car."

"This is fucking nuts!" Eliza exclaims. Everyone ignores her because, yes, they're already aware of how fucking nuts this is.

"Yes. We want you to do that," Angela says.

"I'm not going to do that."

"We're not asking," Carson says. "We are *telling* you —you're going to do this."

Olivia's gaze finally moves to Carson. This whole

time, she hasn't made eye contact with him. Since Angela kneeled in front of her, it's as if the two of them have been each other's sole focus. Olivia's hazel eyes narrow. A smile perks her lips up.

"If I go to the police, *Carson*," she says, carefully, as if she's examining every word before it's spoken. "I'll be telling them about how much you helped me plan it."

Carson feels his face slacken, sucker-punched by an invisible hand.

"Remember all those emails?" she asks. "How you were the one who suggested rat poison?"

"Goddamn it," Carson mutters, putting his hands on his forehead.

"And while I'm at it, I'll—I'll—" Olivia sits up straighter and sucks in a shaky breath. It's the first glimpse of any weakness in her, but it's there. Carson's relieved to see it. She's afraid. She's lashing out, saying ridiculous nonsense. "I'll tell them about how I told Eliza I was going to do this." Olivia turns to Eliza, who's on the end of the sofa as if trying to get as far away from Olivia as possible. "She knew."

"I told you she was evil," Eliza says, without looking up. "You didn't believe me. I told you about the black widows, too, and you didn't believe me. Believe me now?"

"No one was hurt," Olivia blurts.

Carson and Angela gasp.

Suddenly, he gets a flashback to one of his conversations with Olivia when he drove her home one day. The girl asked about black widows, about letting them loose in someone's room. For her "story." For her "book." Why didn't he remember until now? God*damn*. What a villainess! And they invited her into their home and fed her meals and let her stay in their guest room and nearly became her foster family. Carson should have spotted this a mile away—he's usually so good at reading people. How did a snake like Olivia West slip under his radar?

He walks behind the couch and hugs Eliza from behind. "Jesus. I'm so sorry, kiddo."

"You ... did that?" Angela says to Olivia, her pitch rising like a hot teakettle. "You did that to my *child*?"

Olivia doesn't respond, just folds her hands in her lap. A low rumble sounds in the long silence. Everyone seems to notice it at once and they turn to see Ezra has fallen asleep. Angela must have drugged the boy good. Carson shoots her a look but decides against saying anything. If ever there's a time to be sedated, it's now.

Olivia clears her throat. "I'm sorry about all this. I really am. But I'm not going to take the blame for it."

"You certainly are," Angela says.

"I certainly am not," Olivia says.

"Do not test me," Angela says.

"This isn't a test," Olivia says. "If you make me go to the police, I'll tell them all about what you did to Penny Patterson."

Carson inhales sharply in harmony with Angela. They exchange a wide-eyed look. It's as if someone came in and yanked all their clothes off and now they stand here naked, nothing to hide behind. No one in their entire lives has accused them of what Olivia dared accuse them of right now—and in their own living room, in front of their children. No one has ever threatened them like this. It's like the air has thinned and he's not getting enough oxygen.

"Penny Patterson," Eliza repeats, as if the name clicks in her head.

"The woman I tried to tell you about." Olivia stands up, as if the conversation is wrapping up. The anger simmers in Carson's veins. He can feel it, building to a boil. "Your parents had something to do with the last victim that was supposedly the work of the Raven's Landing Dismemberer. Some people online said it had all the signs of a copycat." Olivia turns to Carson with a genuinely curious look on her face. "Or ... were they all your work?"

His face feels hot. He's probably red as a lobster. He can barely contain his temper right now, his fear, his embarrassment. Because on the couch, Eliza looks terrified. And the worst part is, that terrified look is probably for *him*.

"I think we need to move to plan B here, Carson," Angela says, putting her hands in prayer pose for a few seconds, as if she's gathering her strength.

"And what's plan B?" he asks her.

He looks to Angela, her blue stare deep as an ocean. All these years, all these memories, all these secrets, and he still never knows what she's thinking. She nods at him somberly. Then, in a motion quicker than a viper hunting their prey, she shoots an arm out and grabs Olivia. Olivia's eyes barely have time to widen before Angela has her in a chokehold.

"Mom!" Eliza yells, standing up.

"Stand back, Lize," Angela warns.

Olivia kicks and tries to scream, her voice nothing but a hiss.

"Mom, you're going to hurt her!"

"Eliza, your mom knows what she's doing," Carson says. "She's not going to hurt her. She's just restraining her temporarily. She's a doctor."

"Mom!" Eliza says, starting to cry.

Slowly, Olivia's face is purpling. Carson's impressed. This is a side of Angela he's never seen. Her biceps are flexed, sweat breaking on her forehead. "What do you need from me, Ange? Should I do anything?"

"This is insane!" Eliza yells.

When Angela doesn't acknowledge the response, Eliza rushes over to where Ezra sits slumped in his chair. She shakes him.

"Ezra!" she yells.

But he flutters his eyes only for a second before nodding off again.

"Eliza, come here," Carson says, walking over to her with his hands up, as if he wants to prove he won't hurt her. "I know this is insane. You're right, it is insane."

"She's going to kill her, Dad!" Eliza says, the faucet on, tears running down her face.

"She knows what she's doing," he says, wrapping his arms around her.

Eliza bawls into his chest.

"I know, my sweet little soul," he says into her hair. "I know. The world's a scary place. You were right all along, weren't you? You tried to tell us who she really was. We didn't believe you. I'm so sorry, Lize. I'm so sorry for what she did to you." He pets her hair and feels her sobs quiet, but she stays there, locked in his embrace. "She tried to kill you, sweetheart. She tried to murder you in your sleep. She coerced your brother into murdering someone. That is ... that is a truly evil person who does things like that. And then she tried blackmail. Trying to—to pin some murder on us. You realize if she goes to the police with everything she just said, that lands everyone in this house in jail but you."

"Oh God," she says into his sweater, her words muffled.

A few feet away, Olivia slumps onto the floor, passed out. Angela hunches over and catches her breath. "We need to restrain her," she says, standing up, wiping her brow. "She's going to wake up in a matter of minutes. Keep an eye on her—I have an idea."

Carson nods at her and Angela sprints out of the room.

"You understand?" He pulls back and looks at Eliza, wiping the tears from her face. "We're not bad people. It's just that sometimes, in life, you come to a place where it's you or someone else. That's nature. That's survival. It's simple math. You or them. Who do you choose?"

Eliza watches him with quivering eyes, dark as a midnight sky. "You choose you?"

"We choose us," he says, touching her chin. "Always. Because we are the Hunters."

Not long after, Angela comes downstairs, lugging the

empty trunk that belongs to Olivia. She thunks it on the living room floor, panting, saying to Carson, "Help me get her in here."

Eliza says nothing as she witnesses her parents picking up the limp girl by the arms and folding her up like a piece of laundry. She says nothing as they shut the trunk and close the latch. Tears fall, and her hands shake, and she bites her nails to the quick—but she doesn't say anything. Neither do Angela or Carson. They just stand back and eye the trunk, holding each other.

Carson's mind fires away, thinking through how they'll get rid of her, how to rid their house of any trace of Olivia West, cut her out, erase her like toxic mold eating at the walls. Wipe her off the planet the same way they did to that homewrecking con artist Penny Patterson. And suddenly he has an idea.

"Pack a bag for you and another for your brother," he says to Eliza. "We're going on vacation."

"What?" Eliza asks. "Dad, I don't want to go back up in th—"

"Just do it," Carson barks. "We're through the looking glass here, Eliza, grow up quick and do what I say."

Hesitant at first, Eliza finally pulls away and walks up the stairs.

"We're going to Reggie's," Carson says. "Get out of here for a week or so. Distance ourselves from this mess."

"Okay."

"Let's get this trunk in the car," he says softly to Angela. "We'll drop her off the Big Storm Bridge, they'll assume it's suicide. Say she ran away from us, we haven't seen her in days."

"What about the head in the freezer?" Angela asks.

"Get the shovel. Bury it in the yard."

He sees the doubt on Angela's face, the exhaustion. He leans in and kisses her, long and passionately, and it's as if it wakes something up in her. It wakes something up in him, too, and he puts a hand on her stomach.

"We've got to keep going," he says. "We're in deep and there's no way out of it but through it."

"Make it stop. This is horrible, all of it, horrible." Angela gestures toward Ezra, who's blissfully asleep. Oh man. *He's* in for a rude awakening soon. "For all of us."

"It's a hell of a lot worse if she survives."

Another long kiss, one sweet and warm enough to forget everything around them for a second. To remind them that they have a fire that nothing in this world, *nothing*, can put out. Enough to remember who the two of them truly are, together.

"You still hate this fucking house?" he whispers in her ear.

She nods.

He takes her face in his hands and says, "You ever thought about burning it all down?"

August

ELIZA

The screaming starts after midnight, somewhere near Red Bluff.

Eliza thinks the muffled, high-pitched shrieking is in her mind at first. Her mom gave her Valium as her parents hastily packed the car with suitcases, coolers, swimming fins and snorkel masks—and a trunk that contains Olivia West.

"This will help," her mom said, popping two pills in Eliza's mouth and giving her a drink of water. All Eliza could see was that quiet trunk—heartbreakingly, horrifyingly quiet—in the backseat under the baggage. "Now go sit in the car and wait for these to kick in. Don't worry. Your dad and I are taking care of everything."

"But what about—"

"I said we're taking care of everything," her mom repeated, more firmly this time. She put a cold hand to her face. "It's okay. You're going to be just fine."

"Mom, I don't want her to die," Eliza said, the words getting stuck in her throat.

"She put black widows in your bed," her mom said.

Eliza choked on a sob. Finally, her mother believed her.

"She turned your brother into a murderer," her mom went on. "She made your father and I accomplices. And then she tried to blackmail us. We have no choice."

Eliza imagined what was happening right now as a chasm opening in the earth, a personal apocalypse. She saw no way out of this, none, where all of them survived. It was paralyzing. *Wake me up*, she begged the nothing-ness. *Wake me up, please.*

"What if we get arrested?" Eliza asked, unable to help the tremble in her voice.

"We won't. We're all covering for each other. We're in this together. No one can pin anything on us if we stick together, you understand?"

Eliza nodded. She was going to go the rest of her life feeling like she was trapped in a nightmare. She couldn't imagine what came after this, how she could ever recover.

"Is there anything inside this house you can't live without?" Angela asked.

"What?"

"If we needed to—to leave this behind and start over."

"Is that what we're doing?" Eliza said, her pitch rising.

Her mom reached out and pet her arm, delicately, like she was afraid her daughter would bite. "Just get in the car and wait for the Valium to work its magic, everything's fine."

The medicine worked for a little while. Not as well as Ezra's, who is currently unconscious and drooling on himself next to her in the backseat. But for the first hour of their journey, it helped dull the panic, helped her drift off to the white noise of the wheels on the asphalt, the black rush of trees outside the window, and she sort of forgot what was happening for minute-long spurts before her memory jerked her back to the horror of the present.

Then the high-pitched noise started.

"What is that?" she whispers to Ezra, who's out cold next to her.

When she doesn't get an answer, she sticks an index finger under his nose to make sure he's breathing. He is, but he's also somewhere far, far away, and oh how she envies him.

Reality keeps hitting like tidal waves. Here they are, the Hunters, driving in the forest in the middle of the night. The sound—it's so strange. Are her ears ringing from the drugs?

"Do you hear that?" Eliza asks her parents, who sits alert and silent in the front seat.

"Hear what?" Angela asks, turning back to look.

They listen together. It's when Eliza peers into her mom's shiny eyes that it becomes apparent what the sound is.

It's screaming. Olivia is screaming from the trunk in the back of the car.

Trapped in there, squeezed into a ball, unable to move or breathe.

It must be like being buried alive.

"Oh my God," Eliza says, her hand over her mouth.

Her mom turns to the front of the car and says, to Carson, "Music."

"Mmm?" he says, as if he's been lost in his own world.

Snapping her fingers, she says, "Now. Music."

"Oh my God," Eliza repeats, her eyes welling up.

It's as if Eliza, too, is confined in a hellish black box. Her chest is so tight. This car is speeding too fast through the darkness. They're about to careen off the edge at any minute, she's sure of it. Her head spins like she's drunk and the Valium isn't doing her any good, everything is still the worst, the absolute worst, the mind-blowingly, heart-shatteringly worst.

The music comes on, Carson bumping it so loud the speakers thump. It's "Gangsta's Paradise" by Coolio. The dramatic synthesizers and eerie harmonies and the lyrics about walking through the valley of the shadow of death, which ring through her like a funeral bell. Carson raps over it, hitting the steering wheel with the beat. Eliza doesn't even have the strength to cringe. Usually her mom would tell Carson to turn it down, but usually there isn't a girl screaming in a steamer trunk in the car with them.

Wake me up.

Wake me up.

A tear rolls down Eliza's face. She squeezes her hands so tightly her fingernails knife her palms.

The music pumps so loud she can't hear the screaming anymore.

That's somehow much worse than the screaming.

OLIVIA

Panic. Terror. Trepidation. Fear. Hysteria. Alarm. Horror. Fright.

Stuck. Trapped. Cornered. Caught. Confined.

Captured. Kidnapped. Ensnared. Entombed. Imprisoned.

Sweltering. Smothering. Suffocating. Asphyxiating.

Heart pounding, mind pulsing, throat screaming with all the breath she has, one word, only one word left in Olivia's vocabulary in the tight embrace of darkness:

Help

Help

Help

Help

Help

CARSON

A little after two a.m., Carson takes the highway exit for Big Storm. There are no lights on as he takes the exit, nothing but rural darkness and low trees as far as the eyes can reach. He turns right, following the green sign for the Big Storm Bridge, and turns up N.W.A. to drown out Eliza's sobs.

Yes, he's aware the world is pressing in on him from all sides, but it's done so before and he lived through it. It happened after he clipped the old tyrant's brakes and sent his Mercedes straight into the Full Moon River. For weeks, Carson pasted a smile on his face and punched in and out of work like an ordinary man, but inside, he was a writhing mess of fear and self-doubt. Every knock on his door, every ring of his phone, every time he met up with Angela and couldn't read what was in her eyes, he feared it was the end for him. But it wasn't. It never is.

Then there was Penny Patterson. The idea of killing the woman was Angela's and he couldn't tell if she was serious, but he took the idea seriously, and soon they were knee-deep in a plan that, when they talked about it out loud, seemed so easy it was almost surreal. Turned out it was much harder to slit a human throat than he imagined, much harder to dismember a body than he surmised, not a fun experience at all, one-star review, would not recommend. And the fear of being caught was a sickness he and Angela were struck with for an entire year. Honestly, the sickness didn't lift until she got pregnant with Ezra. Then they started a new life. Then they became a family and everything changed.

But now here they are again.

With a grim expression, Carson slows the car onto the last shoulder that appears before the formidable arch bridge with the sign that says *Big Storm Bridge*. Four hundred feet above a rocky canyon, this is one of the state's most popular sites for suicides. Over sixty people a year end their lives here. Deep in the web of true crime conspiracies, people speculate it's also a popular spot for homicides, but none have ever been proven. By the time a body hits the jagged floor below, it's all blood pudding and splintered bone.

What a tragedy, he imagines himself saying when Olivia's body is found later. *What an absolute waste. She was such a brilliant girl. She did go off the deep end after her father disappeared. We tried to help her, but she was ultimately unreachable. Despite the fact she burned our house down—all I feel is sorry for her. May she rest in peace.*

How generous he'll seem in interviews, how merciful his forgiveness.

"Carson," Angela hiss-whispers, wrenching him from his fantasy. She pulls his sleeve. "It's the police."

He glances in his rearview and, in a lightning bolt of anxiety, sees what she's referring to—a CHP officer on a motorcycle snuck up on them after the car pulled onto the shoulder.

"Shit," he whispers.

The blood drains out of him. He becomes, in one instant, a dead man. In his side mirror, the officer dismounts his motorcycle and struts toward the car. Carson is frozen, not sure what to do. N.W.A.'s "Fuck Tha Police" is blasting—an unfortunate choice for a soundtrack at this moment—and he shuts the car off. All he can hear, in the silence, are horny crickets out the window, the blood thumping in his eardrums, and the muffled screaming still coming out of the trunk. Jesus, you'd think she'd have run out of air by now.

"You need to put on music again," Angela whispers.

Eliza whimpers in the backseat. "We're all going to prison."

"Shhh," Angela hisses. "Be like Ezra. Pretend to sleep."

Carson watches Eliza squeeze her eyes shut as she continues to weep. He turns the car back on and Angela presses the radio button. It's Bobby McFerrin's "Don't Worry Be Happy." A knock on the car window. The cop is here in his motorcycle helmet that makes him look like some kind of deep-sea diver. He pantomimes cranking something, the universal gesture telling him to roll down his window.

"We're fine," Angela whispers.

"Yes, everything's fine." Carson presses his button to roll down the window and flashes a giant smile. "Hello, officer. How can I help you?"

"Heyo. Everything all right here, buddy?" the cop asks.

"Yep, right as rain." Carson gives him two thumbs up.

"There a reason you're stopped up here on the bridge at this hour?" the cop asks.

"Oh, I ... got a little tired. Thought I'd pull over for a cat nap, for safety's sake."

The cop pulls the visor up in his helmet. "Turn off the engine and show me your license and registration, please."

"Turn off the engine?" Carson says. "I'm sorry, I— we're—our kids are sleeping and they rely on the music, so—"

It feels just as stupid coming out of his mouth as it sounds.

Unfazed, with the passionless delivery of a robot, the cop repeats, "Turn off the engine and show me your license and registration, please."

Carson's life flashes before his eyes as he cuts the engine. Without Bobby McFerrin's whistling and a cappella overdubs, there's nothing to cover up the disturbing sound of muffled screaming. He clears his throat several times and looks at Angela.

"Registration for me, would you, hon?" he says loudly

as he opens his wallet. "God, I love that song, don't you, hon?"

"I do," Angela answers, picking up on his hint as she pops open the glove compartment. She hums it off-key as she gives him the registration and Carson hands over his license and paperwork.

"Be right back," the cop says.

They breathe a sigh of relief as the officer heads back to his motorcycle, likely looking Carson up. The screaming is godawful. Eliza quietly sobbing over it is even worse.

"We're fine," he says to her in the rearview. "Don't worry, be happy," he sings.

She shakes her head, keeping her eyes shut.

"We're fine," Angela agrees.

They hold hands, gripping so tightly that her wedding ring cuts into his fingers.

"Why the hell do you think he pulled us over?" Carson whispers.

"He didn't pull us over," she whispers back. "We were already here."

"Can you imagine if he'd snuck up on us five minutes from now?"

"I don't even want to picture it."

The cop returns a minute later. "Here you go, buddy," he says, handing over the license and registration. "I understand you're tired, but this isn't a good spot to pull over. There's a rest stop about ten miles up the highway if you need to get some shuteye."

Carson audibly sighs to try to cover up the screaming

coming from the trunk. "Really appreciate that, officer. Sure thing. We'll continue on our way."

"Shhh," the cop says suddenly, finger in the air. "Wait. Hear that?"

Carson gulps and Angela inhales sharply.

"You hear that—that noise?" the cop asks again softly, cocking his ear in the air.

Never in his life have Carson's eyes been wider.

So much floods through Carson's head that it's hard to focus. He imagines gunning the car out of here, transforming this family into fugitives in a matter of nanoseconds. Or attacking the cop right now and throwing him off the bridge. He imagines faking psychosis symptoms now to have a cop able to attest to it as a witness, which might give Carson a better chance at getting this case thrown out of court.

"Coyotes," the officer says finally, slipping his helmet back on. "Distress signal. Gives me the willies every time I hear it out here—sounds just like a woman screaming."

"Indeed," Carson manages.

"Wow," Angela says, as if she learned something fascinating.

The entire family sits still and stiff as mannequins as the cop returns to his bike. Carson wipes a cold sweat from his forehead. Here he is again, a cliché in a thriller novel, releasing the breath he didn't know he was holding. Waving at the cop, he drives the car back onto the road and finds his way to the highway.

"We don't have to kill her," Eliza says from the backseat, her teeth chattering.

"Eliza, enough," Carson says.

"We could just let her go," Eliza says.

"We cannot," Angela says. "Stop it. That girl has enough dirt on us to take our whole family down."

As the car speeds into the darkness again, Carson sinks deep into thought and his head starts aching. He turns on Eminem, whose nasal voice cuts through everything like a switchblade and gives them a break from the screams for a little while.

"Think, think, think," Carson says, massaging his temples. He sniffs his sleeve and offers it to Angela, asking, "Do you smell gas?"

"No. I thought you changed your clothes?"

"I did, I'm just checking." He swallows and grips the steering wheel as tight as he can. "We could dump her body somewhere in the national forest."

"There's a record of us being here now that we were run through the system by CHP," Angela says. "We need to be smart."

"That might actually be a good thing. He saw there was no Olivia in the car—we have a witness seeing the four of us."

His phone buzzes on the dashboard, where it's clipped. It says RIVERWOOD PD.

"Goddamn it, give me a break," he says.

"What?" Eliza asks from the back.

"Where are we?" Ezra says, groggy, confused, his eyes searching the darkness of the car.

"I need to take this," Carson says, his finger shaking

over the phone's screen. "You kids need to stay quiet. Everyone stay quiet. Let me take this."

He pushes the green button. "Hello, Carson Hunter speaking?"

"Carson? This is Adrian down at the Riverwood PD."

"Hi Adrian, what's up?" he asks in a chipper voice which is a complete opposite to his sweaty face cemented with a frown.

"I'm sorry to inform you that there's been a fire at your residence on Bloomview Avenue. Are you with your family?"

"Oh my God," Carson says. "You're kidding. Yes, I'm with my family. We're on vacation in Tahoe."

"There's no one at your residence right now?"

Angela and Carson exchange a look.

"Well, there was ... there's a friend of the family who's been staying with us on and off lately. She, uh ..." Carson wipes his brow. "I hope she's not there?"

"You're in Tahoe right now?"

"Nearby, thereabouts."

"We'd like to take a statement from you. Would you be able to come in?"

"I mean, it'll be a few hours. Is the house okay?"

There's a long silence. "I think it would be best you came in here, Mr. Hunter."

"Sure, okay. Okay. Let me, uh ... we'll hit the road and be there soon."

He hits the red button to end the call.

"Guess we need to turn around and head back to Riverwood," he says gravely.

Angela doesn't respond.

"It's going to look wrong if we don't," he says, putting a hand on her knee.

She nods. She seems so tired. So desperate. The despair in the car is so thick he feels like they're running out of air.

"What is that sound?" Ezra asks, squinting at the air.

Carson doesn't answer him, turning up Eminem's "Lose Yourself," making a U-turn across double yellow lines, burning rubber, flooring the gas.

ELIZA

It's morning by the time they pull up the hill to the Riverwood Police Department station, sunshine rising like a fire over the houses in the valley. After another few pills, Ezra fell back asleep and stopped asking questions. Eliza refuses another dose, showing her mom her dry face. It's puffy and pink but she's no longer crying.

"You can trust me, Mom," Eliza says, her voice breaking. "I won't say anything. I'll play along. I know how important this all is."

Such pride shines in Angela's eyes as she turns and squeezes her daughter's hand—the brightest Eliza has ever seen. Every pirouette, every piano recital, every A-plus she brought home pales in comparison.

Carson shuts off the car and they sit in silence for a few breaths. True silence, because the screaming stopped about an hour ago. Maybe Olivia gave up and died. Eliza isn't sure how long someone can survive being locked up in a trunk like that. If Olivia is dead, at least there would be something resembling peace. At least then Eliza might be able to convince herself that her parents aren't murderers, that this was accidental. Wouldn't that be so much easier to live with?

I don't think your family's as good as you think they are, she hears Olivia's voice echoing in her head.

"Ezra, honey, we need to go inside to talk to the police," Angela says, opening his door and laying a gentle hand on his face, the same way she used to when they were children who fell asleep on a road trip.

Ezra moans and stirs.

"Ez, bud, let's go. This is important," Carson says loudly, hopping out of the front seat.

"He doesn't know anything that's happening," Eliza whispers, almost to herself. Her eyes fill and envy pierces her like an arrow. "He doesn't know anything."

"We could leave him in here," Carson says to Angela. "Hope this is quick."

"And if it isn't?" she responds. "And she wakes up again and starts screaming her head off?"

"Do you think she's still alive?" Eliza asks, suppressing a gag.

They don't answer that. Maybe it's for the best because either answer is horrific. It takes a few minutes of coaxing and shaking to wake Ezra up. Outside in the parking lot, everything is cheerful. They parked in the far corner, near a shed and a garden where someone's stooped down, pulling weeds. The valley is so pretty they stop to stare. Beeping the car locked again, Carson leads the way to the front of the building.

"I do the talking," Carson says.

"Where are we?" Ezra asks.

"You were sleeping the whole time. We're going to the police station."

Ezra stops in his tracks. Carson takes him by the arm.

"Don't worry, this has nothing to do with you, buddy." He pats his son's back. "Our house burned down."

"What?" Ezra says, his jaw dropping.

Carson pulls him forward. "I do the talking," he says again.

And they walk through the automatic doors, into the police station lobby.

It isn't long before the four of them are taken into a room near the back. Everyone in this station knows her dad. They're greeted with hugs and apologies and warm drinks. Someone brings Eliza a hot cocoa in a Styrofoam cup. She doesn't drink it. She doesn't feel worthy.

"I'm so sorry to interrupt your vacation, Carson," the cop says. "After the investigation is over, we'll accompany you all to retrieve anything that might be left. I have to warn you, though, there's not much."

"I can't believe it," Angela keeps saying, shaking her head, eyes wet. "I can't believe this happened. Can we go into the house to see what's left? How long until we can go back into the house again? What are the next steps?"

"Is everything gone in the fire?" Eliza asks.

The police officer looks from Angela to Carson and

back to Angela again. "Ma'am, if you don't mind—can we talk to you without the children present? Our dog found something ... something we need to ask you about."

"Your dog?" Carson asks.

"There were human remains found on the property," the cop says.

Eliza exchanges a terrified look with her parents.

"Human remains?" her dad repeats.

"Human remains," the cop says.

"Oh God. Who?" asks Angela. And it's then that Eliza realizes what a fantastic actor her mother is. That she's been secretly acting all her life.

"We don't know who it is yet," the cop says. "It was a head, Carson. A human head in your rose garden.

"Oh my God," Eliza's mom says.

Eliza feels like she needs to play a role, too, though she doesn't want to. It's dizzying, how this is unfolding. "Does this have something to do with the fire?"

Thankfully, the cop wants to talk to her parents alone after that. Angela purses her lips and hands Eliza her wallet as they leave the room. "If you—if you need to eat, hon, here's some cash for the vending machines."

"Thanks," Eliza says, though eating is the last thing on her mind.

Eliza rises and pulls Ezra up by his hoodie to follow her. They walk into 2B, an identical room as the one they just left. She shuts the door behind her and tosses her mom's wallet with its keychain attached on the table, the loud clanking sound of it making them both wince. She wishes she chucked it against the giant mirror and broke it instead. She wants to break things the way she feels broken.

Eliza doesn't know what's going on, but she has a gut feeling they're all fucked.

Ezra sits in a chair with a screech of metal on the cement floor and puts his head on the table.

"I'm so scared," she says to him.

"I'm going to jail," Ezra says quietly.

"No you're not. Don't say that." Eliza wipes her eyes. "Just play dumb, no one will know anything."

"Where's Olivia?" he asks in a medicated drawl.

Eliza closes her burning eyes, tears running down her cheeks. The aching comes in waves. She had no idea there was this much pain out there with her name on it. How did she get here? How did Eliza Hunter, sixteen years old, who lives in a gorgeous house on a hill, who never hurt anyone intentionally in her life, end up here in a cold interrogation room with her homicidal family?

"I think she's dead, Ez," Eliza whispers.

She waits for his response. She thought he would shoot up, demanding to know more. But no.

Instead, he snores.

Eliza is in the gray-walled room for a miniature eternity. This is a personal purgatory. It's as if she has nothing to do but sit with her own brain as she waits, the sickness inside her growing and growing as this surreal hell of a night replays in her mind again and again. It doesn't matter how this story ends. It doesn't matter if her family gets arrested for murder or gets away with it. Nothing will ever be the same. All her memories—the

Saturday mornings that smelled like coffee and French toast. Her dad's stupid jokes that made her groan and the feel of his rough cheek on hers. Her mom's voice floating through the vent and into her room, a constant mystery and a comfort. Hot summer afternoons where Ezra and Eliza set up the waterslide in the sprinklers. So many Halloweens, so many birthday parties, so many nights when she went running into her parents' room after having bad dreams and they put their arms around her and told her there were no such things as monsters. There were no such things as monsters, the monsters said.

All that is gone now, a mountain of ashes.

The ending doesn't matter anymore. Eliza's life already ended.

Eliza might not know who she is. She's never had a working inner compass. She doesn't know what she wants. She doesn't know if she prefers black hair or brown, ballet or piano, big cities or small towns, bright colors or solid black. But in a revelation here in this blank room, as she clenches her fists and turns to the two-way mirror to exchange a look with herself, Eliza Hunter suddenly sure as hell knows who she isn't.

And maybe that's enough.

Eliza gets up quietly, grabs her mom's wallet, and leaves the room. In the hallway, the door next to hers— where her parents are being questioned—remains closed. She keeps walking. She passes the front office area, where phones ring and the clerk types on a computer.

"Be right back," Eliza says as she hurries through the front doors.

Outside, she bounds down the stairs and turns into the parking lot, where her family's SUV is. The garden it's parked next to is so lush, red star-shaped flowers bending in the breeze. It hurts to see it in contrast to the ugliness that's only ten feet away from it.

Eliza beeps the SUV to unlock it. Her hand on the trunk door, she looks around her. There are no other cars parked here this early. The garden shed is still open, but the person who had been there weeding is nowhere in sight.

"Please be alive," Eliza whispers, popping the car's trunk open.

Silence. A dreadful, thick silence.

With shaking hands, Eliza removes a cooler, three suitcases, pillows and blankets, setting it all on the asphalt. At the bottom of the stack is the trunk, which she unclasps with quivering fingertips. She pulls the lid open. She sees Olivia's hair first, so much of it splayed every-where. Then she hears a long, painful, wheezing gasp.

"Oh my God," Eliza whispers, moving Olivia's hair from her face. "Oh my God, Olivia."

The expression on Olivia's face is something that will haunt Eliza for the rest of her life. The terror is so pure, so unadulterated, that there's a blankness to it. It's the look of a ghost, the look of a dead girl. Her skin has a bluish tint to it. She can't even manage a sound. She sits up, slowly, and gasps.

"You need to get out of here," Eliza says, tears stinging. "You need to run far away from here. You need to get away from my family and never, ever come back."

After a few seconds pass, Olivia's face screws up. It's almost like she's hyperventilating. She still can't say a word.

"I'm so sorry, Olivia," Eliza says. "I don't know why all this happened. I don't understand. I know you—you did some bad things. But no one deserves this."

Olivia makes a small noise, like a baby bird trying to find its voice.

"Let me help you out," Eliza says, holding her hands out. "Quick. Hurry. We're in the police parking lot. You need to get the hell out of here before everything falls apart."

Olivia's color is returning to her face as she nods and swallows. She reaches out her limp arms and Eliza helps her out of the car.

"Go," she says, once Olivia is on her feet. "Get out of here while you can."

This is beyond traumatizing. Olivia shakes like someone in shock—she probably *is* in shock. Eliza nods at her and starts loading all the suitcases and pillows back into the car.

"Go!" she says again to Olivia, who stands shivering like it's seventeen degrees instead of seventy.

Olivia turns and stumbles away, toward the garden.

Eliza shuts the trunk and waves at her one last time. They lock eyes. A little whisper in Eliza says, *there goes my best friend.*

Olivia waves back and then disappears.

The Hunters

At ten past ten, a girl who has clawed her way back from the underworld shudders in shock in the bushes.

She's hiding in a garden behind a police parking lot. She throws up bile all over the front of her wrinkled sundress. She can't even think. Waking up cramped in the fetal position, locked in some kind of dark, horrible tomb, she screamed and screamed into the void until she wasn't sure if she was alive or dead. Then she emerged into the sunshine and now she needs to sit beneath a tree and think. She needs to comb through the events to put together what happened.

The last thing she remembers, she was in a chokehold in the Hunters' living room.

Then she was in hell, in an absolute smothering nightmare world. Bass thumping in her ears, heart in her throat.

And now ...

She looks around her, gets her bearings. She can see the glittering little town of Riverwood below, the long road that snakes down the hill she's on and ends up downtown near the river. From here, so charming. From here, a lie.

The anger begins like an itch deep within her. The scathing betrayal, that woman's arms around her neck, the way the husband watched on approvingly before consciousness was lost. Like scratching a spider bite, the more the girl sits under the tree with that memory repeating, with the horror of the cramped coffin she was trapped in looping and looping and looping, the angrier she becomes. Soon the anger courses through her, throbbing like a heartbeat all its own. Soon her own survival loses its glow. It's not enough.

She whispers the words of a poem she knows by heart: "In the morning glad I see/ My foe outstretched beneath the tree."

Standing on legs shaky as a newborn colt, the girl scans the scenery and spots a garden shed. There is a ray of sunshine on it, as if destiny herself has a spotlight. The girl crawls up the hillside and scans the empty parking lot, except for that horrid SUV. She's alone. She sputters a sound that's half cry, half laugh. She creeps to the shed. There, hanging on a rusty nail, a pair of bolt cutters—the same brand she used to cut her dad's brakes once.

She smiles so big she feels it in her chest.

THE HUNTERS

At ten past noon, a family emerges from the police station. Their posture is slack. Their faces are ashen. They will need a lawyer soon. But no one has been handcuffed. No one has confessed to anything. No one has been officially accused—yet. The man and woman still believe they will escape blame, they can pin it on the girl who they believe is locked in their trunk. The son is still drugged and confused. No one questioned him, and he doesn't understand why, because he's a murderer. The daughter's jaw is set and she feels lighter, better, because she has a secret. She believes she did the right thing.

Didn't she?

The family car begins its descent. It's a long, steep hill that is one hairpin turn after another. The valley is lush and violet with wildflowers, winking with cars and homes, the sparkling river cutting through the greenery.

The man is thinking how lucky he is as his foot hits the brake pedal and reaches the floor.

He presses it again and the car continues gaining speed. He yells a curse word and his wife asks what's happening as he wrenches the steering wheel one way and another, clipping trees, trying desperately to slow the car down. But the odometer only creeps up, up, and in mere moments, everyone in the car begins collectively screaming, understanding that they've lost control, that nothing can be done, and suddenly the valley they were admiring not one minute before becomes a terrifying plunge as the car misses a turn and spins off the side, rolling twenty-six times down a rocky hillside, crunching like a tin can, the sound of metal on metal drowning out the screams, the car skidding down an embankment on its side and finally plunging into the green river below. The vehicle bobs up and down in the rapids.

Twenty-four hours later, a girl wakes up in a hospital bed, brain fuzzy from anesthesia, gaze bleary, confused as to where she is and why she can't move her body, twenty bones broken, leg in a sling, head bandaged, her jaw wired shut.

There are no flowers. The visitors' chairs are empty.

There's been a terrible accident, says the nurse.

When the girl learns she's the sole survivor, she can't even scream.

ONE MORE THING ...

Want to read a bonus epilogue for *They Are the Hunters* to know what comes next for Eliza? Sign up for my newsletter and download it for free!

If you enjoyed *They Are the Hunters,* good news: I have another family drama-fueled suspense novel called **The Second Life of Ava Rivers** I think you'll like, too.

I also have a collection of psychological thrillers all set in the same universe. They're called **The Jolvix Episodes**, and you can **grab the first three books in this discounted box set** or read them one by one.

NOTE: These standalone novels can be read in whatever order you want, but *Eve in Overdrive* is technically a prequel to *The Slaying Game*.

- **THE PREDICTION:** A newlywed woman's smart device begins offering chilling predictions about her husband.

- **VIOLET IS NOWHERE:** A kidnapped woman and a stranger on the end of a phone line have one week to figure out how they're connected or their lives are over.

- **WHAT JANUARY REMEMBERS:** A dysfunctional family and their sentient companion bot gather for the holidays for the first time since their last Christmas together— which ended in attempted murder.

- **PEARL IN DEEP:** The love of one woman's life turns out to be a psychopath with a disturbing talent for deepfake video.

- **EVE IN OVERDRIVE:** An outspoken journalist buys a cutting-edge car only to find herself at the mercy of a vengeful internet troll.

- **THE SLAYING GAME:** A former Jolvix employee ends up at the center of a serial killer's deadly game.

- Or you can grab the first three Jolvix Episodes in this box set.

A NOTE FROM THE AUTHOR

If you got this far, I wanted to take a moment to thank you for reading and supporting my work. As an indie author, I put a ton of effort into each book—not just writing, but editing, marketing, and everything else it takes to guide a book through the whole process from a glimmer in the brain to a real, actual thing you can hold in your hands.

If you enjoyed it, please consider leaving a review. Reviews truly make an author's world go round. If you're interested in keeping up with book news, please join my newsletter or follow me on social media. And I love to hear from readers anytime at faith@faithgardner.com.

As always, I tried my damndest to fix every typo, but alas, I am only human. If you spot an error, please let me know! I appreciate every reader who makes me look smarter.

ACKNOWLEDGMENTS

My mom is my rock. Seriously—without her, I wouldn't be writing these books. I can never thank her enough for all her endless support and advice. Oh, and for giving me life. That's pretty cool, too.

My sister Micaela is the other half of the tag team that edits my work, along with my mom. Thank you so much for always dropping whatever you're doing (during moving week this time!) to read my book and help me make it better. You're the best.

Much love to the whole Gardner crew for cheering me on as I chase my dreams and write these twisted stories ... and for being nothing whatsoever like the Hunters. Jamie, thank you for being my partner and best friend and for believing in me no matter what. Roxie, Zora, I love you two more than words can say. Thank you for always giving me time and space to write.

To my writer buddies Noelle Ihli, Steph Nelson, Anna Gamel—you are such fun, talented, and lovely humans. I so appreciate your feedback, encouragement, and friendship.

A big, heartfelt thank you to readers/reviewers out there who dedicate SO much time and passion to reading and boosting authors, all out of sheer love.

And thank you, dear reader, for spending a little time with me and my book.

Also by Faith Gardner

The Jolvix Episodes

The Prediction

Violet Is Nowhere

What January Remembers

Pearl in Deep

Eve in Overdrive

The Slaying Game

Other Books

They Are the Hunters

The Second Life of Ava Rivers

Perdita

How We Ricochet

Girl on the Line

ABOUT THE AUTHOR

Faith Gardner is the author of some YA novels and many suspense novels for adults. When she's not writing, she's probably playing music, cooking up a storm, or reading books in the bubble bath. She's also a huge fan of true crime, documentaries, and classic movies—with a special place in her dark little heart for melodrama and anything Hitchcock. She lives in the Bay Area with her family and you can find her at faithgardner.com.

Printed in France by Amazon
Brétigny-sur-Orge, FR